Haunted Gold

Connie Shelton

Haunted Gold

The Ghost in the Library Mysteries, Book 1

Connie Shelton

Secret Staircase Books

Haunted Gold
Published by Secret Staircase Books, an imprint of
Columbine Publishing Group, LLC
PO Box 416, Angel Fire, NM 87710

Copyright © 2025 Connie Shelton

Book layout and design by Secret Staircase Books
Cover images © BooksRMe, Stockeeco, Nazrul Islam, Brooke E
Becker
First trade paperback edition: July, 2025
First e-book edition: July, 2025

* * *

Publisher's Cataloging-in-Publication Data

Shelton, Connie
Haunted Gold / by Connie Shelton.
p. cm.
ISBN 978-1649142214 (paperback)
ISBN 978-1649142221 (e-book)

1. Emily Plankhurst (Fictitious character)--Fiction. 2. Taos,
New Mexico—Fiction. 3. Paranormal activity—Fiction. 4. Library
setting—Fiction. 5. Women sleuths—Fiction. I. Title

The Ghost in the Library Mystery Series.
Shelton, Connie, Ghost in the Library mysteries.

BISAC : FICTION / Mystery & Detective.
813/.54

For Dan, always

Chapter 1

Emily Plankhurst slipped on her special gloves, reached into a cardboard carton, and pulled out a handful of yellowed documents, breathing in the scent of the paper. Letters, a map, an old diary—she smoothed a crease here and there, sorting them by topic, and lovingly placing each in an archival quality protective folder.

The carton on the table in front of her was one of, literally, hundreds that had been haphazardly stacked in the various rooms of the library when she'd taken over. It would take years, she realized, to have this place in shape. She marveled at the fact that her grandfather had once been able to locate documents with such ease.

Outside, the muted scrape of a leaf rake attracted her attention. She turned toward the window and spotted Victor Martinez in the tiny parking area out front, clearing

fallen leaves from the huge cottonwood tree at the edge of
the property. The local gardener startled and spun around,
as if he'd seen a ghost (except Emily knew he didn't believe
in ghosts). When he spotted her, his face relaxed and he
gave a friendly wave.

She picked up her tea mug and held it up, a silent offer
of a beverage, but he shook his head and pointed down
at the massive pile of leaves he'd collected. She smiled
and gave a thumbs-up. He knew she always had the kettle
ready, in case he wanted to come in when he was finished,
although he rarely did. Considering what the poor man had
been through earlier this year, she was pleased that he was
back at work.

She set her mug aside and stood, stretching the kinks
out of her shoulders and lower back, before she returned
to the accumulation of leather-bound volumes, stacks of
correspondence, and journals dating back more than a
hundred years. To anyone else, it might seem like chaos,
but to Emily the materials showed history unfolding in real
time. Each page she examined felt like a piece of her family
puzzle. Many of them actually were family-related. Others
told the many stories of Taos County and the surrounding
regions of northern New Mexico.

As always, when Em became engrossed in history,
time got away from her. Noticing a shift in the sunlight,
she glanced up and saw that Victor's truck and the leaf
pile were gone now. She eyed the elegant brass clock on
the wall. It chimed four o'clock. A shaft of deep peachy
autumn light illuminated dust particles floating above the
creaky floorboards.

She got up and walked over to the window on the east
side of the building. "Okay," she murmured to the room,

"I'll finish this box and then I am outta here."

She eyed the purple and yellow chrysanthemums in the neat flower bed next to where her Jeep was parked. A walk down to the plaza, four blocks away, would definitely help the tightness in her lower back. Still, despite the lack of exercise, she savored spending her days here, in this sunlit adobe room surrounded by her legacy, the small library that lived through five generations of the Plankhurst family. The air was filled with the scents of time itself—aged paper, polished oak, leather, ink—and a vivid reminder of the time she'd spent in Taos as a child.

Behind the library, across a cozy flagstone courtyard, stood the adobe home she loved—the place where she'd spent summers with her grandparents. Fond memories lived in the thick walls, the vigas that crossed the ceilings, her grandmother's artwork and needlecraft, and the warm kitchen. The appliances might be outdated, but she wasn't about to change anything. It was her favorite space to make a cup of tea and try out Grandma Valerie's recipes.

Turning back to her worktable, she sorted another pile of brittle papers, glancing at them as she organized them in little piles. Property deeds, ranch accounts, survey maps of areas that were still wilderness. Here was a long, chatty letter to David Plankhurst—her grandfather—from an old-timer with an implausible legend to tell, and here, tucked in beside it, a photograph of three bearded men who could have been trappers, miners, or highway robbers. Emily smiled at the romantic notions her mind conjured when she handled these memories from long-ago people.

Outside, cars passed with a muted whoosh, reminding her she was still in a world of the living. But once she moved deeper into the library, she knew the stacks would be silent and secretive, the way it was in her childhood memories. She treasured the silence, and she loved the unexpected finds she was constantly coming across.

Once, on the second floor where the more obscure collections were housed, she'd spotted a set of apothecary bottles alongside a library of how-to for séances and spirit-channeling books in one dusty corner, their labels blurred by the years. She'd begun to organize them under the heading of Occult. Her friend Riki once asked her if people really believed in ghosts. Emily didn't answer the question directly—she *knew* they existed. She had merely replied that anything was possible.

She let her eyes travel across the library to the arched windows in the thick adobe walls, high against the east wall and flanked by the wooden bookshelves. She admired their sturdy construction. Back to the box, she reminded herself. Peering inside it, she saw there was only one item remaining, a bound notebook.

When she picked it up, an image of Grandpa David's face came to her. She flipped open the first page to see that the notebook was filled with his tiny, perfect penmanship. She would read it tonight at home, her idea of a perfect evening. Taos wasn't exactly the center of the universe for twenty-somethings, but she fit right in with the pace of this little town.

She fingered the corner of the grandfather's notebook again. Lifting it from the table, she leafed through a few of the pages. An entry dated twenty-five years ago: *I believe the legends of the conquistadors are true, and I am very close to proving this in ways that will startle even the most cynical historian. This is a private note for my own files. Must confirm the next time we meet.*

So typical of Grandpa, Emily thought, the way he teased

himself with research and speculation. The conquistadors? Was he hoping for another riddle-solver in his family? And a meeting? She wondered who it might have been. She added the notebook to a stack to carry home with her, and shut off the brass lamp on the table.

She made the rounds of the back rooms, switching off lights. Then she heard the creak of the heavy wooden door at the library's entrance. Uh-oh. Should have locked the front door first.

She hurried forward, ready to send the newcomer away, and came face to face with a woman she'd never met before—silver-threaded dark hair in a firm bun, sturdy twill pants, tan turtleneck, and a supple leather jacket.

The visitor looked around, taking in the height of the ceilings and the layout of the room. Her eyes landed on Emily, traveling upward the way everyone's did when they realized they were greeting a six-foot-tall young woman. She moved forward briskly, wasting no time. "You're Valerie Plankhurst's granddaughter," she said. It was not a question.

Chapter 2

The woman gave Emily a searching look before uttering another declarative sentence. "I'm Dr. Francine Morales, looking for a colleague who probably came by here." Her voice was pleasant but firm, without any hint of doubt or hesitation.

"Um, no one's here right now … You'll need to catch me up." Emily hugged the leatherbound journal closer to her chest.

"Right. Sorry." Dr. Morales held out a hand and reintroduced herself. "I'm with the history department at UNM. A colleague, Dr. Clifford Littleton, seems to have dropped off the radar, and the last anyone heard from him he was headed to Taos in search of some new information on the conquistadors and their search for gold."

Emily tried to keep her expression neutral. Was it a

coincidence that she'd come across a similar reference in her grandfather's notebook within the last hour? In her experience, coincidences usually meant something.

"… the Morton Library, of course. And naturally, I'd met David and Valerie on several occasions. You have to be related." Her eyes again traveled to the top of Emily's head, eliciting a laugh.

"The women in our family do tend to be tall. And yes, I mean, yes, I believe Dr. Littleton was here," Emily told the historian, trying to catch up with her questions. "It was maybe two weeks ago."

"More like three. Well, that's when Cliff left Albuquerque." Dr. Morales's directness took her by surprise, and the name 'Cliff' took a moment to register. "Did he happen to mention where his research might take him next?"

Emily shook her head. "I can pull the materials he was looking at, Dr. Morales—"

"Francine, please."

"Of course. Francine. I can look up the specific materials, but it will take a little time. As you mentioned, he wanted information on the legends, firsthand accounts, if available. The old stories about missing treasure and the likelihood of a curse. My grandfather's notes were really scattered, so Professor Littleton went through some of the letters himself. He was very nice about it."

Francine gave a tight smile, so Emily set aside the journal she'd intended to read at home and turned her attention to one of the piles of folders on the long library table. "There was one story he seemed particularly interested in. It came from a man in the 1940s—someone my grandfather had interviewed about sighting the ghost of a conquistador who was supposedly searching for his gold stash." Emily slid the interview page across the table and then risked a look to gauge Francine's reaction.

"A ghost, was it?" Francine asked, her skepticism apparent.

"Here in Taos, there are loads of legends involving ghosts, you understand. I have to admit, Dr. Littleton was more than a little fascinated with that aspect."

Francine nodded. "He would be. I'm more of a fact-based historian, myself. It's well known that the myth of the seven cities of Cibola was debunked a long time ago."

"Yes. Well, I'm not sure what else to tell you."

"Sorry. I don't mean to come off as judgmental. Cliff and I have a few different ideas about things, but I really do respect his work. We at the university are just a little concerned about him at this point. It isn't like him to take off on a research trip, especially one this close to home, and not check in with anyone for several weeks."

"I assume you've tried calling him?"

"Oh, everyone has. He hasn't picked up, even for the department head—or his daughter." Francine looked down for a moment, picking at a cuticle. "Of course, the man isn't the most tech-savvy person on the planet. And half the time he forgets his phone charger or doesn't plug it in. *Brilliant* in one area doesn't mean *smart* about everything."

A picture began forming in Emily's mind. Francine was as interested in the absent professor as she was in the library. Her intensity, her focus, was undeniable, but something else showed as well. The older woman, although polished and calm, was genuinely worried.

Emily softened her voice. "I'm sure Professor Littleton is fine," she said. "When he was here, he seemed pleased to dig through the material. I think he would have been at it for days if I hadn't needed to close up that night. He planned on being back." She'd barely uttered the words when she remembered that she had allowed Dr. Littleton to check out a rare book and borrow one of their maps, something she almost never did. Only for a person of Dr. Littleton's credentials. Now, what if she never got them back?

Francine was still talking. "He didn't mention my name? Or say he'd be gone this long?" She pulled out a short, handwritten note. "This was on my desk when he left Albuquerque."

Emily gave the paper a quick glance, reading the lines in the missing professor's tight script: *More to report soon. Something big in the works near Taos. Back in touch by next week. Interesting meeting lined up.*

She looked up again, searching Francine's face for the answer she half expected. "This meeting. Is it with someone you're worried about?"

The older woman offered a wry smile. "I really have no idea."

"It sounds like Professor Littleton knew what he was getting into," Emily said after a moment. "Even if he wasn't sure it was going to work."

"Cliff was always stubborn that way. More optimism than caution, at times," Francine said. She leaned against the sturdy table and considered the young woman in front of her, as if gaining a clear sense of how helpful Valerie Plankhurst's granddaughter would be. "Cliff left one other phone message, a very brief one, saying he might head toward Denver, depending on what he learned here."

Emily filled in the blanks: if Cliff hadn't planned on spending his entire time in Taos, he'd been gone even longer than they knew. And Denver was only a half-day's drive from here.

The more Emily thought about it, the more she wondered if Francine was right. Had someone convinced Professor Littleton to go against his instincts, and what could this 'interesting meeting' have been about? Especially if Cliff believed the remote chance that the treasure and the legends attached to it were within reach.

Emily remembered the words of the old man, from her grandfather's interview she'd found earlier today. Again, coincidences often meant something. It was one thing for her grandfather to give up everything for a passion, but Clifford Littleton was an academic, studying his area of expertise. She glanced again at the letter about the ghost and the last line caught her attention: *Still think the Spaniard haunts the place, because the land is too barren and the locals too smart to haunt. Not sure what else would make them leave so quick.* She had no idea what that meant and wasn't sure she should share everything with her visitor.

"What if he's right?" she asked, mostly thinking aloud. "About there being something really important at stake? I mean, even Professor Littleton seemed intrigued."

Francine eyed the document in Emily's hand, then looked directly at the young woman. "Let me guess. That's the ghost story? And there's a curse of some kind?"

"Yes, but I think it's interesting, anyway." She set the paper down, feeling a little foolish and defensive at the same time. "Most of them end like this. Curses. Ghosts. Treasure just waiting to be found. I've even heard gossip about there being some kind of tour operator starting up. My grandfather loved those intriguing parts, and even if he had his doubts about their veracity, he'd never ignore it, not entirely. There's more, and it's scattered, but I think the letters are tied to some of the maps we've stored upstairs. I can track those down for you if you'd like."

"Maybe later," Francine said. "Cliff did, after all, get in touch with you, and you said he made copies of the things he felt were relevant. But there's something I've found more than once. The stories usually *sound* great. Even tantalizing. Until you look closely."

"And?"

"And what makes for a great story," Francine said with some deliberation, "is rarely true."

Her bluntness made Emily even more aware of the differences in the two academics' approach. If there was a bit of academic rivalry going on here, Emily saw how Francine would want to derail this talk about treasure hunts before it got any more traction. The only sure thing was that they hadn't heard from the professor. Even if Cliff had second thoughts about his local research and left for Denver, his silence was worrisome.

Emily pushed her grandfather's journal to the side of the table and looked again at the note Francine had brought. "I just don't know," she said. "But I'll try to find out. Would you like me to make a few calls?"

"That would be helpful, thanks. I'm starting with the hotel he was supposed to check into, but in case he gets in touch or comes back this way, you might let him know we're looking. I will say that Cliff has a penchant for both Mexican food and sweets. Any place he might stop for dessert and think twice about his plans?" Francine stood up. "And I'd be interested to know if that tour operator really is in town. If it's more show than real history, Cliff would have figured that out quickly," Francine replied.

Emily nodded. "I just thought of one other area where we might take a look, if you have a few minutes?"

Francine smiled. "Absolutely. Following Cliff's trail is the reason I'm here."

Chapter 3

Emily led the way to a narrow staircase at the back of the building. "There's a ton of stuff up here." She turned to face Francine when they reached the top. "I carried a lot of heavy boxes up when I first took over, just to clear space downstairs and get better access to the shelves. I'm afraid my grandfather was not very organized. Much bigger on collecting things than putting them in order."

They entered a medium-sized room where stacked boxes lined the walls. A worktable sat in the middle of the open space with two high stools beside it, and some flattened boxes were propped against the wall near the door, ready to go to the recycling center.

"What I want to show you is this." Emily led the way to a closed door with a label, in handwritten block letters, DAVID PLANKHURST COLLECTION—SPECIAL

PROJECTS. "It's where we keep the older materials, especially those dating back to the 1540s when the Spanish entered the territory. Professor Littleton was most interested in this area."

When they stepped inside, Francine automatically reached to zip up her jacket.

"Yes, it's a bit chilly. We keep the temperature at sixty-four degrees and the humidity around forty percent. Unlike many parts of the country, we actually have to add humidity to our air."

"Right. Same in Albuquerque."

Glassed-in cases lined two of the walls, and Francine noted a humidifier that sat near the door. Wide, flat drawers held maps, while books and journals stood upright on the shelves. A fan system circulated air, and the tightly fitted door was designed to keep pests or rodents out.

"The map cases and everything else were packed too tightly to breathe when I first came in, so we redid the configuration of the space." Emily walked to one of the shelves and pulled out a blue folder. They walked back into the main room and Emily set the folder on the table. We use only acid-free, lignin-free, and buffered paper and board for storage and enclosures."

"So," Francine said, settling onto one of the stools. "When Cliff came here, was he working alone?"

Emily flicked a switch and a diffused overhead light came to life. "I think so. I have a grad student, Kevin, who comes in a couple days a week. He was here during one of the professor's visits and thought he might be consulting with someone."

Francine considered that as she slipped on the special gloves Emily handed to her. "He rarely partners with other historians, especially outside our department." Her gaze traveled to a very modern brochure laying at the far edge of the table and she reached out. "A treasure hunt, with tours claiming to take people to where the conquistadors hid their gold. We saw this mentioned on television a few months back, and Cliff thought there might be more to it than a tourist gimmick."

Emily's eyes skimmed the slick page but she didn't recognize it. Kevin must have left it behind.

Francine continued. "For a man normally rooted in pure history, the mention of a treasure always brought a gleam to his eye."

"I noticed," Emily said with a tiny smile. She opened the blue folder and handed a document over to her guest. "I pulled this folder because it was one that interested your friend. He made copies of the pages in it."

"What's that?" Francine pointed to a square of gray paper protruding from an envelope in the folder.

Emily opened the envelope and pulled the gray sheet from it. A single word had been handwritten on it: *Tertulia*.

Francine studied the page, touching the paper and staring at the writing. "It's a Spanish word, more common in Spain and South America than here in America. It means a gathering of people, usually for some kind of literary or artistic purpose. The paper isn't ancient, but it's not new either. Judging by the nice paper and the writing style, I'd guess it's at least a hundred years old, and it looks like it would have been an invitation to an event—except there are no details about the place and time. Did Cliff mention anything about this?"

Emily shook her head as she carefully refolded the sheet and tucked it back in its envelope. "Not to me. I haven't figured it out, and haven't had time to ask anyone. I just remember that he went through this blue folder quite a bit. He spent hours in this room when he was here."

Francine's eyes grew sad. "With his health—" She broke off, glanced at Emily. "He's probably running low on his heart medication." She chewed her lip.

Emily said, "It's surprising that he didn't check in with you. He was here several times, and then one morning he just didn't show up. Do you think he might have gone to a local doctor?"

Francine slowly shook her head, uncertain. She stood and paced the floor, stopping at a case filled with illustrated maps. She scanned their faded script: Rio del Norte, Santa Clara, Tres Piedras. Her eyes narrowed. "I doubt that. Maybe he's holed up somewhere, lost track of time, forgot what day it is. That sounds more like him." She rubbed her neck, skeptical even as she said it.

"Did he know anyone in town?"

"No. I don't think so. It was his daughter who asked me to check up on him, since neither of us had heard anything." Francine took a deep breath. "I'm starting to think he's bitten off more than he should have."

"Is that why you're so anxious?"

"His absentmindedness has become worse in the past year."

Emily's mind darted back to the beginnings of her grandfather's condition.

Francine straightened and turned toward her. "Can I see anything else he was working on?"

Emily stepped back into the Special Collections room and came back carrying a box. "I kept these things together, thinking he would come back for another look." She pulled a leather-bound diary from its depths and placed it on the table. In its margins were hand-drawn figures of Spanish soldiers and simple but colorful depictions of Catholic saints. The ink had faded over centuries, but its significance was clear to both women. "It's a conquistador's diary. I think the professor made a connection to these other things."

While Francine perused the diary and its sketches, Emily began placing journals and boxes on the table, looking for the rare book and map, hoping Cliff might have returned them here without formally checking them back in. So far, no luck. She opened one box to reveal letters, each in a protective sleeve. "These go back nearly five hundred years."

Francine lit up. "He always wanted to trace the treasure stories back to original sources." Her eyes followed Emily's movements, observing her swift but careful handling of each fragile item. Then she spotted the cheaply printed treasure hunt brochure on the table. She picked it up and opened the tri-fold page. On the back, a glossy photo of a man caught her attention. "Vince Hutchins? I'd swear I've seen this guy before."

Emily, perched on a wooden stool, shrugged. "Do you think Professor Littleton came here to make contact with him?"

"I think it's more than just coincidence that Cliff decided to come here at the same time this outfit showed up," Francine said.

Emily regarded Francine closely. "You don't really think he might believe in their claims?"

"Not in any serious way, no. But I think he might have checked it out." The answer came quick, a little defiant.

"And you're determined to find your friend?" Emily was matter-of-fact.

"Of course." Francine didn't hesitate. "The forgetfulness is one thing, but missing his heart medication … that's important."

"Give me a couple of days. I'll try to remember who he talked with, and see if he left any of his own notes behind, maybe something on this tertulia thing," Emily said, glancing at the collection of maps and journals that crowded the table.

"Anything might help," Francine said. "The only thing we have to go by is his abiding interest in the whole period of Spanish exploration in this region." She picked up one of the letters, holding it gently, cautiously optimistic. "I just hope—"

"There is one thing." Emily handed Francine a sheet of fragile parchment in a protective sleeve. She gestured to another map on a nearby wall. "We didn't even know this was in the collection. Kevin found it when he was going through my grandfather's files, the same morning we last saw the Professor. He spent time going over this map with another patron. I didn't think it was that important until just now when we saw the gray slip of paper among the notes."

"It sounds like this tertulia might have been a regular gathering. Maybe Cliff was getting this all blown out of proportion, getting carried away with a miniscule fact. It would be like him," Francine said.

She glanced up at the window, realizing it was dark outside. "I'm sorry—I've overstayed. If you find anything Cliff might have left behind, notes, papers of his … would you let me know?" Francine set the parchment back on the table, retrieved her pen and a small notepad, and pulled a business card from her bag. "You've already given me more of your time than I'd hoped for. This is a huge help." She looked almost embarrassed as she stuffed the notebook back in her bag. "Sorry, I'm going overboard."

"I understand," Emily said. "And it's really no problem." Plus, she hoped to use Francine's help to find those two unreturned items. Why hadn't she insisted the book and map remain here on the premises?

Francine took one last look at the crowded shelves, closed her eyes, opened them again as if she expected an answer to jump out at her. "Let me know if you hear from him. Or if you think of anyone else I can ask."

Emily walked with her toward the door. "I'll be sure to call," she said. "You might try the bakery, Sweet's Sweets, in the morning. If he was a fan of desserts, he probably heard about the place."

Francine paused at the bottom of the stairs. "You said Cliff talked a bit with your assistant, Kevin? Any idea how I could reach him?"

Emily gave a smile. "He'll be in tomorrow afternoon." She took out a card and handed it to Francine as they made their way through two smaller rooms and into the main one. "Here's our number. I'll let him know you're coming back."

"How long have you been at the library?"

"A bit over a year." Emily let out a long breath. "It was my grandpa's. I want to keep it open." Her tone was wistful but also firm, and she pointed toward an antique display cabinet as she went on. "As you've gathered, this thing for rare books and maps goes way back in our family. So, when Grandpa was diagnosed with Alzheimer's, my grandma ran it. She passed last year. Since then, I've been trying to get everything organized."

Francine started toward the front door. "Thanks, Emily. For everything."

She was almost outside, one hand on the knob, when Emily's voice called after her. "I hope you find him. I'd really like to know if he was onto something."

Chapter 4

Jax Rivera stepped out of the dark blue Ferrari, faintly jealous because whenever they went somewhere to impress somebody, Vince drove; errands were done by Jax in the leased, utilitarian passenger van. But this was business, and Vince was in charge.

He pulled his sport coat closer against the chilly October evening and fell in behind his partner, whose suit was more expensive, his haircut just so, and his cologne one rich people would recognize. Jax ran his hand over his own buzz cut, briefly wondering if he should grow it out to something more stylish. But maybe this was better. Vince portrayed the polished businessman and Jax carried the look of a bodyguard. Or an enforcer.

The upscale lobby at El Monte Sagrado enveloped them in warmth, its rich leather chairs and polished floors exuding an elegance that made certain types of people feel at home. A couple, comfortable in their designer clothes, stood across the expansive room, wine glasses in hand as they pretended they were here to appreciate the pricey art on the walls.

Vince approached with easy confidence, arms outstretched and his smile disarming. His charisma radiated as he greeted them, pulling the couple into his orbit. "You must be the Van Dykes," he said, guiding them toward a grouping of plush chairs. He introduced Jax, almost as an afterthought, failing to mention they were partners in this enterprise.

"Thanks for waiting. The drive into town took longer than we expected." His smile widened. "But not as long as it'll take us to find the treasure without you." He laughed, a self-deprecating sound that seemed to charm the couple despite themselves.

They settled into the chairs, Vince leaning forward with an intimacy that suggested deep confidence. Jax hovered, silent, eyes darting over Vince's animated gestures and the couple's curious expressions.

"I know you've got a lot of questions," he said, lowering his voice as if to share a secret, "but that's what I'm here for." The wife glanced toward her husband and raised an eyebrow, while Jax stood to the side, jaw set.

"You are so lucky to get in early on this," Vince said. "We're on the verge of something huge. I've never seen so much excitement from investors. The only thing larger than the legend itself will be the profits. We're talking nearly a million dollars in the late 1500s, and that's well into the billions today." He spread his arms wide, inviting them into a grand adventure.

The Van Dykes exchanged a glance, the husband tapping the brochures with a polished fingernail. "Your pamphlet doesn't guarantee much, makes it sound like a risky deal," he said, voice smooth and cultivated.

Vince nodded, as if the words confirmed his expectations. "Of course it sounds risky. That's because it's the real thing. No risk, no reward, right? What sets you apart is the vision to see what others can't." He leaned closer, lowering his voice again. "This is a completely separate opportunity from the tourist tours. The tourists get to see a few coins, but with your help, we'll find where the bulk of the conquistador's treasure lies."

The wife studied Vince, skepticism mingling with intrigue. Her eyes flicked to Jax, who remained at a distance, arms crossed and tension in his frame. "How many others are involved?" she asked, careful and direct.

"You'll be one of the first," Vince replied without missing a beat. "In fact, we haven't shared this with anyone else in the country yet. This opportunity is *extremely* limited. We're telling only those who understand the magnitude of this deal." He paused, letting his words hang in the air. "We've done the research and know where the ..." He lowered his voice to a mere whisper. "... treasure is. Your investment would help fund the retrieval of this amazing find."

Jax felt a knot tighten in his stomach as he listened. Vince was in full form, painting a picture with words, but the more he promised, the more Jax became nervous.

"Do you have other investors lined up?" the husband asked. "You must know we can't take too much risk here."

Vince sent them his most persuasive smile. "Absolutely. If we let the word out, it would be a stampede. And we *could* do that. But we'd rather keep it exclusive. This is your chance to get into a very select group." He leaned back, relaxing into the chair as if they'd already signed over their millions. "Once we show people what you discovered, they'll be begging to join."

The wife considered this, tapping her chin thoughtfully. "And the money? How safe is it?"

"We've done this before," Vince said, as smoothly as if he'd rehearsed the answer to the question. "In California, Nevada, Arizona … each time, investors walked away with triple what they put in." He paused for dramatic effect, then added, "All totally secure."

The words floated in the warm air, and Jax felt a grudging admiration. Vince was a master at this, making the unbelievable seem inevitable. But Jax knew the fragility behind the façade. He'd been along for the ride before.

Vince continued, a polished showman in his element. "This is a rare chance to be part of history. The most colossal gold discovery in modern times, and you're right at the forefront." He leaned forward again, sincerity in his eyes. "But timing is crucial. Your place in this expedition depends on it. I'm meeting with more people tomorrow."

The husband looked at his wife, then back at Vince. "We'll think about it," he said, cautious but intrigued.

Vince stood, reaching for the man's hand. "Great. You won't want to miss out. I'll hold your spot for twenty-four hours. Call me on my personal phone, anytime."

As the couple entered the elevator, Vince nodded at Jax, a triumphant glint in his eye.

Jax fell in step beside him. Outside, the hotel's warmth faded against the crisp mountain air as they walked away from the huge adobe building, toward their sleek, dark blue car.

"You really think they're in?" Jax asked, keeping his voice low as he took the passenger seat.

Vince shrugged, grinning with confidence. "Probably. But if they back out, we've got plenty of others lined up. This town's got money."

* * *

Vince started the car and whipped out of the parking lot, making the turn onto Kit Carson Road, then right on Paseo Pueblo del Norte, continuing his laughter and speculation as they drove north. Jax remained silent, half wondering if this time there truly would be gold at the end of Vince's self-created rainbow.

The vibrant galleries and boutiques thinned as they passed the edge of town, entering a straight stretch of road bordered by ranches, and then into the natural hilly terrain with its clumps of sage and piñon. Twenty minutes out of town, rock formations loomed. Vince's verbal plans grew bolder, fueled by the solitude and wide-open sky. He pulled onto a wide spot, parked on the flat dirt, and gestured to a hillside, where a dark smudge showed against the moonlit rock.

"This is it, the right spot for the tours. We bring people here at fifty bucks a head, and we spin out the story of how the conquistadors discovered this place. You watch, the rubes will fall for the idea of vast treasure hidden right near this cave."

But Jax, the realist with a military background, knew the gaps in Vince's schemes, and he stepped out of the car with a growing sense of skepticism.

Vince pulled a large flashlight from the back seat and headed up a narrow trail. By the time Jax caught up with him, he was already at the edge of a clearing, arms outstretched as if embracing the wild scenery.

"You know what's great about this place?" he called back to Jax, voice carrying over the rough terrain. "We're miles from anyone. No one to complain about the setup, and nothing to stop us from spinning a hell of a story."

Jax took in the landscape, the uneven ground and sparse brush. "Not much out here," he said, his tone flat and practical.

"Exactly," Vince replied, seeing it all as an empty canvas for his grand design. He shined his light ahead, revealing an opening in the hillside. He walked toward the cave, pointing his light to various spots as he moved. "Lights here. Projectors there. We'll make it look like an ancient site."

Jax followed, more methodical. He stopped at the mouth of the cave, considering the steep slopes and the rocky ground surrounding it. "You think we can get people to believe this?"

Vince turned, his grin wide and full of confidence. "Of course. You think the conquistadors brought their gold to a spot that was easy to access? The roughness adds authenticity. People want to believe. That's the beauty of it. We give them a good enough story, they'll see what they want to see." He motioned for Jax to follow along, shining the powerful flashlight into the cave, revealing a room that might hold three or four cars if it were a parking lot, and another, lesser one that branched off from it.

Vince continued to map out the plan, his voice excited and impatient at the same time. "So, the tale is that we've found this treasure chest somewhere out here. We tell them we've found traces of digging, and some gold Spanish coins, some nuggets, that kind of thing. I've had some coins made up, plated with thin gold, but heavy enough to feel realistic. Right over here, we'll stack another chest or two, make it seem like there's more than just a few coins. And over there," he pointed to the opening to the smaller chamber, "the ghosts will show up, scaring the pants off everyone."

They walked back to the opening, stepping out beneath the starry sky. "And out here," Vince continued, shining his light toward the scrub-dotted hills, "I see ghostly visions of Spanish soldiers on horseback. We'll rig the holograms so we can make it look like they're riding toward the crowd, or away. What do you think?"

"Vince, this isn't like that Lost Dutchman place. It'll be a lot harder to pull off."

Vince waved a dismissive hand. "Harder, but worth it. Tomorrow, in daylight, we'll come out and set up all the props. We'll check everything out, and should be able to start giving tours within a week. Once word spreads, we'll have more business than we can handle. And when the simple rubes come back from the tour, talking about coins all over the ground—and how much they would have gotten if the ghosts hadn't scared them off—our investors will be lining up." He leaned against a rock, imagining the crowds. "The ones with the mega money will get the better story—that we know exactly where in this mountain sit the multiple chests of treasure the Spaniards took. With their money to fund the excavation, we tell 'em we'll have that treasure in no time. You know what the spot price of gold is these days?"

"Think the Van Dykes will bite?" Jax asked, leaning back against a boulder.

"They're already hooked," Vince said, voice echoing with self-assured laughter. "At a half-million per investor, they'll sign up like the others." He gestured broadly again, casting his vision across the open landscape. "Can you picture it? All those people, convinced they're part of a real treasure recovery."

Jax saw the picture clearly, but it was painted in less vibrant colors than Vince's. He'd been with Vince long enough to recognize the gaps, the points where the plan could unravel. But he also knew Vince's knack for turning skeptics into believers. The guy was a true salesman.

A chilly breeze wafted through the piñons, enhancing the sense of isolation. Vince's voice filled the space. Jax kept still.

"You worry too much," Vince said, catching the look. "We've done more with less." He slapped Jax on the back, a gesture meant to reassure. "Tomorrow, we get the rest of this going. I'll pick up more gear, and maybe some other investors."

Right. They headed back toward the parked Ferrari at the bottom of the hill. Jax was always the one left with the heavy work and the heavier uncertainties. But, who knew? Maybe this time would be different.

As they drove back to Taos, he fixed his gaze on the highway, thinking through the steps for tomorrow's work. Tomorrow, as he labored within the silent terrain and the shadowed cave, Jax knew he'd have to make sure this con didn't crumble.

Chapter 5

Francine pulled up in front of the charming little bakery with the purple awning, where Emily thought she might get more information about Cliff's whereabouts. The front window held a display with autumn themed cakes, cookies, and breads. The wedding cake was elaborate yet with a nature theme, exactly what Francine would order for herself—if she ever reached the point of making that kind of commitment. She stepped out of her SUV, straightened her jeans, and tugged the edges of her leather jacket into place.

Bells above the door jingled a welcome, and the dark-haired young woman behind the counter smiled.

"What can I get for you?" Her name badge read: Jen.

Francine studied the display case for a moment. It was mid-morning and she'd had a substantial breakfast, but that amaretto cheesecake was calling out to her. She pointed, and Jen asked whether she wanted it boxed up to go.

"I'd like a chance to talk with you for a minute, if that's okay," Francine said. "Emily at the library suggested I come by."

"You're Francine. She told me you'd probably stop in." Jen scooped the slice of cheesecake onto a plate. "Take a seat at one of the tables and I'll bring this over. Coffee too? Our signature blend is really magical."

Francine felt herself warming immediately. The helpful friendliness of small towns … she couldn't get over it. By the time she'd draped her jacket over the back of a chair and set her bag aside, Jen walked over with her cheesecake on its china plate, a silver fork and cloth napkin to accompany the treat. A mug of the most amazing-smelling coffee followed less than a minute later.

"Now," Jen said, taking a seat across from her, "I think Emily mentioned that you're a professor from Albuquerque and you're in Taos looking for someone?"

Francine smiled as she took a cut from the cheesecake. This was the other thing about towns this size. Everyone knew everything. She nodded, savoring the incredible flavors of amaretto and the chocolate crumb crust.

"This is one of the most incredible desserts I've ever had—*so* good." She followed it with a sip of the coffee, and caught herself before making the same comment about the beverage. "Yes, so, the person I'm looking for is a colleague. Professor Clifford Littleton. He's got a real sweet tooth, so this seemed—"

"The old guy with the gray hair?" Jen interrupted. "Sorry. I shouldn't have said it that way. The distinguished gentleman with a taste for chocolate croissants?"

"Yes, that's Cliff. I think he was a regular in the library until a week or so ago. And, he came in here as well?" To verify, Francine pulled out the photo she'd brought along and Jen nodded when she saw it.

"A chocolate croissant and a cup of tea every afternoon at three o'clock—more or less."

It didn't sound as if Cliff was becoming *completely* absent-minded. His afternoon dessert ritual was deeply ingrained. "We're concerned about him, especially since he left without a supply of his medication. The last thing we heard, he was tracking down leads on a legend about some gold left by the conquistadors, trying to find an ancient map."

A woman with short gray hair, wearing black slacks and a white baker's jacket came into the sales area, carrying a tray of decorated cookies. She slid them into the display case, removing an empty tray with her other hand, then gave Jen an inquiring look.

"Sam, this is Dr. Francine Morales. She's in town looking for the professor."

"Hi, yes. Emily mentioned you. I'm Samantha Sweet." She dusted her hands against her jacket and picked up the coffee carafe to offer a refill.

"Ah—Sweet's Sweets. Everything is making sense." Francine finished the last bite of the amaretto cheesecake and accepted the full mug from Sam. She gave them the condensed version of what she'd told Emily the previous day, how Cliff had come in hopes of finding a real lead on conquistador history, but his not being in touch with family or work for a couple of weeks now had caused some worry back home.

Samantha joined them at the table. "So you think he

was working on something bigger than he should?"

Francine realized that Sam understood the situation already. "Was he ever with someone else when he came in?"

Jen nodded slowly. "Once. There was a dark-haired man, younger, maybe mid-thirties. They were talking about a treasure hunt—not that I listened in." She blushed a little.

"You don't happen to know this other man's name?"

"Vince, I think. Another guy walked in and called him by name, said he was needed for something, then the other one walked back out again."

"Vince Hutchins," Francine said, and there was a hint of victory in her voice.

Sam was more than a little curious. "Is that who you think your friend was working with?"

"Not exactly working together, but I now have reason to think Cliff was checking on Vince's latest venture."

"Isn't he that guy advertising the treasure hunt tours?" Jen was puzzled. "From what I've seen when I pass their office, that tour thing went nowhere."

Samantha filled in more details. "Word out locally is that they haven't really begun. But they're pre-selling tickets like crazy."

"And?"

"One friend stopped in at their office on Paseo, checking for tickets. She said the map was photocopied and that the guide looked more like a rock star than a serious historian." Sam grinned as she spoke.

"Based on the little I've found out about Vince Hutchins on the internet, that's how he does things. Makes a huge production out of things he can't prove." Francine pushed back her chair a bit, stretched out her legs.

"Do you think Cliff got involved in some way? Maybe this tour operator needed someone with great credentials to add weight to their claims." Sam stood and picked up a damp cloth to wipe down the beverage bar.

"That's one option." Francine felt a little more hopeful than when she arrived. "The other," she added, "is that he's lost track of time. He was growing more forgetful the last few months. It's possible dementia is setting in." She spoke with the weariness of someone who had run through these scenarios before, probably more than once. "Or maybe it's just as simple as him going off to a dig without telling anyone."

"We haven't heard anything more from him," Sam said. "You're welcome to call or come by again. The way people talk, something's bound to turn up." She brushed a stray crumb from the table, but when the door opened and three women walked in, her attention was diverted.

"We thought he'd show up again for chocolate croissants," Jen said, standing. "He was pretty predictable." She nodded toward the windows, indicating the town outside and its throng of mid-autumn tourists. "Or we figured he got what he came for and went home, just another visitor."

Francine watched them both. "I wish it were that simple," she said. "I think I should check in with law enforcement, maybe file a missing person report."

"Good idea," Sam offered. "Sheriff Cardwell is excellent. Of course, you have to take into account that I feel that way because he's my husband."

Francine got up, removed a notebook from her bag. She wrote something down and handed it to Samantha. "Emily said Cliff spent time in the library with her assistant, Kevin.

I can check in with him, so I'll do that," Francine said. "Here's my cell number and the hotel where I'm staying. You can reach me there if you think of anything more."

She paused while the newcomers chose a table and settled in, then walked over and handed Jen her credit card. Although she hadn't gained any firm leads here, she felt better about having a direction for the day. She would inquire at the sheriff's office, stop by the library to speak with Kevin, and she might just check out this treasure tour thing.

* * *

Francine stared at the locked door with its mocking "Be back soon!" sign, her eyes scanning the faded tan stucco of the unremarkable square building and the overly exuberant signage above promising "Gold Treasures!" The storefront was nothing special, a plain building on the main drag through town, bypassed by traffic that whizzed by. The faded paint on the windowsills spoke of neglect, the kind of minimal upkeep that cheaply rented spaces often showed. A brilliantly painted sign above the front porch gave the only evidence of something exciting here. The colorful letters seemed to taunt her: "See Where the Conquistadors Hid Their Riches!" Now and then a car slowed, the occupants pausing to read the blatant come-on.

The October sun was warm on her back as she leaned closer, cupping her hands on the glass, peering through the window, and seeing a room that was just big enough to serve as a lobby with a sales desk. Perhaps there were offices or storage rooms beyond what she could see. The building itself was certainly larger than this one small space.

She made out the contours of the desk, a rack of brightly colored red and gold brochures like the one she'd seen last night at the library, chairs that tried a little too hard to look comfortable, and potted plants that probably required no real maintenance. All that was missing was a smooth-talking huckster with dollar signs in his eyes.

Leaning in closer, she scrutinized the art on the walls—pieces that screamed *mass-produced* with their vivid, Southwest inspired designs. Francine rolled her eyes. She changed her angle slightly, trying to see into the corners of the room. But no lights were on, no shadows moved within. The building was as lifeless as a stage without actors, all pretense and no play. Surprising that whoever was running this show hadn't bothered to be here to sell tickets. If it was Vince Hutchins, this neglected little operation didn't seem like his style. She would have thought he would surely be here to hustle people in person, to give the spiel and take their money.

Francine sighed, stood back, trying to piece together what she knew. Everything about the place was suspiciously generic. Other than the brochures and some wall maps, there was not a single personal touch, nothing that couldn't be packed up in an afternoon.

She shook her head. How typical—a promoter trying to lure people in with tales of fortune that would most likely come to nothing. Her frustration rose, knowing how Cliff would have scoffed at the shameless promise on the sign and the gullible customers who would fall for it.

Or would he? Could the professor have actually found evidence that this one was real?

Francine tried the door again, jiggling the handle with

a futile twist, the intense sun beginning to make the back of her neck sting. The memory of Cliff nudged at her thoughts again. They both hated to see history cheapened this way.

The thought of it made her angry. If Vince had conned Cliff into coming here, she hoped her colleague had made sure it was the last time he ever tried that trick. Right now, the important thing was to locate Cliff and find out for herself what he'd learned and do what needed to be done, before he had some kind of health crisis.

Francine stepped back and looked again at the shabby building. The tour office seemed like a dead end for now, but that couldn't stop her. She'd come too far to back down now and would simply have to come back later. With a sigh of exasperation, she headed back across the gravel parking area.

Pausing beside her silver Honda Pilot, she took one final look at the darkened building. Would Cliff be telling her not to waste her time? Maybe Sheriff Cardwell could tell her more about this operation and Vince Hutchins. But one thing was certain: she was not going to be deterred by a locked door.

As she walked away, her resolve hardened. If this was a con, she'd uncover it. And if Cliff had somehow—heaven forbid—become mixed up in it, she'd find him. Francine cast a last, defiant glance at the gaudy sign and the barren lot surrounding it. There was more at stake here than just some alleged treasure, and she intended to check it out.

* * *

She swung by the Morton Library and noticed right

away that Emily's Jeep wasn't in the parking lot. But a Tundra pickup was there and the Open sign was displayed in the glass pane on the front door. Francine parked beside the other vehicle and walked in.

A young man with dark hair pulled back into a *chongo* looked up from the checkout desk. He didn't look older than eighteen, although to be a graduate student he surely must be, and his distinctive bone structure and coloring told her he was likely from Taos Pueblo.

"Kevin, I assume?"

"Yes?" He pushed the computer mouse aside and gave her his full attention. "Oh. You must be Dr. Morales, from Albuquerque?"

She gave a smile and a nod. He stepped from behind the desk and extended his hand. "Kevin Mirabal. Emily told me you'd be coming by."

"Nice to meet you. I understand you helped one of my colleagues recently, Clifford Littleton."

"Right. He was a hoot. So curious about everything. Obviously, my people's history with the Spanish wasn't always the best, but Dr. Littleton made the research interesting and fun."

"Did Emily mention that Dr. Littleton seems to be missing? We're looking for any clues we can find as to where he might have gone. Did he happen to say anything to you, give away any plans he had in mind?"

Kevin shook his head. "I've been thinking about that ever since Em told me about your visit last night. But no, I really don't think he said anything at all. He came in, nearly every day for a week or more, and then suddenly he just didn't come back."

He moved toward the back of the room and Francine

followed. "I kept most of the books and materials he had me pull, just thinking he might want to see them again and it would save us the trouble of going back through the stacks." With a chuckle he gestured around the room at the tall shelves and the boxes stacked in the 'to be researched' areas. "You can imagine how time-consuming that gets to be."

He came to a section of shelving where several file boxes were neatly lined up. One of them had a yellow sticky note attached with 'Littleton' written on it. He pulled the box, which seemed quite heavy, and carried it to one of the reading tables.

"You're welcome to look through all this. I didn't see that he left any of his own notes behind, but he certainly could have." He lifted the lid from the box, setting it aside, and pulled out a chair for Francine.

She thanked him, declined his offer of water or coffee, and pulled a pair of gloves from the box of disposables nearby. With a sigh, she reached into the box and began pulling out books and papers.

* * *

It was mid-afternoon by the time she walked into the Taos sheriff's department, and Francine felt the frustration of a long day spent with no results to show for it. An officer at the front desk greeted her, taking in her leather jacket and sleek bun. When she told him Samantha Sweet had suggested she stop and talk directly with the sheriff, the officer defrosted quickly. He picked up a phone and spoke softly.

"Right this way, ma'am," he said.

She bristled a little at the *ma'am*, but realized she was probably giving off the type of demanding vibes that warranted it. She relaxed her shoulders and offered chit-chat as she passed through a doorway, joined the officer, and was shown down a hallway and into a squad room. Beau Cardwell, a tall man in his late forties, extended a polite hand and introduced himself, his ocean blue eyes unreadable.

"Sheriff. I'm Dr. Francine Morales, from Albuquerque."

"My wife said you might be stopping by. Let's talk in my office."

Francine followed the sheriff to the glassed-in private office in the corner of the squad room, where he motioned her to a seat. The place was unexpectedly warm, almost homey, with western art on the walls and an antique wooden desk.

Beau settled into a chair across from her, leaning back. "Did Samantha tell you why I'm here?"

"Not much, really. She's been awfully busy with the bakery. I gathered that you came to town looking for someone?"

"Yes, that's right." She pulled the photograph of Cliff from her purse and laid it in front of him, watching for any hint of recognition. The sheriff examined it for a long moment, not giving her the reaction she'd hoped for. "This is Dr. Clifford Littleton," she began, keeping her voice steady but urgent. "A colleague from UNM. He's been missing for over three weeks, and he may have come here to investigate this treasure business that's popped up in your town."

Cardwell listened, nodding now and then but offering little else. Francine found it infuriating and admirable all at once. The man was unreadable, and she wondered if he'd developed that skill on the job, a poker face that would work well in an interrogation.

She felt herself talking faster, aware of her impatience, and forced herself to slow down. "We think he may have been drawn here by the claims of this local tour operator, assertions about finding Spanish treasure. Clifford left in such a hurry he didn't pack much of anything, just enough for a few days—and a few of his notes. To go off on an adventure like this without contacting anyone back home, especially at his age, that's just not like him."

Beau set the photo aside, giving Francine a steady look. "You're thinking he's in danger?" he asked, voice as even as his eyes.

The question hung between them for a moment. "I do," she said finally. "He has health issues, a heart condition, a few signs of dementia. He could be lost or hurt. Something isn't right."

The sheriff let her words settle, pulling his computer keyboard toward him and tapping a few keys. Francine chafed at his deliberate movements; she wanted to make him see the urgency that felt so obvious to her. He looked away from his screen. "We don't have a record of him being in town," Beau said, pausing before continuing. "No incident reports or emergency calls involving someone of his description. Is it possible he simply left town, of his own free will?"

It wasn't the first time someone had suggested that Cliff might have moved on. But Francine shook her head. "He would never go this long without contacting the department or his family. His daughter is beside herself with worry. He didn't take his medication with him for a long absence. We need to find him before it's too late."

"You mentioned the tour operator."

"Yes. Vince Hutchins."

"You think he's involved somehow?"

Francine leaned forward, sensing a way to get through to the sheriff. "Cliff was interested in the historical aspect of the conquistadors, yes. But from what I can gather, this Vince is a showman, not a true historian. He might even be a con artist. You must know about him."

Beau leaned back in his chair. "We've checked out the business," he said, carefully choosing his words. "They have the proper licenses, and we haven't had any complaints. Beyond that, I don't know what to tell you."

"Licenses? I imagine that's the least of it," Francine repeated, a note of disbelief in her voice. "I get the impression this Vince person is adept at appearances. I suspect that Cliff came to Taos to check out the claims that the conquistador's gold has been found. Mind you, he would be skeptical, but he's not as tough as he used to be."

Beau considered her plea, and Francine could almost see the gears turning in his head. "You're sure he isn't doing exactly what he wants to be doing? Maybe he's found a treasure, after all."

"He's not interested in treasures that don't have impeccable provenance attached." She realized her tone may have been a bit too sharp. "Sorry. It's just that I've already been around to the hotels in town, and no one remembers him. And the storefront location for this treasure hunt business appears closed."

Beau was quiet for a long moment, studying her with those impossible-to-read eyes. Francine felt the silence pressing on her, demanding a patience she didn't have. "I understand your concern," he said at last. "I'll have my deputies keep an eye out for anything unusual. But with our resources stretched thin, I can't promise an immediate search. An adult person is free to come and go as he wishes, and if he isn't in actual danger—"

"But I'm sure he is," Francine cut in, refusing to back down. "I tell you, this isn't like him. Whenever he traveled, he spoke to his daughter every few days, and he would check in with our department at the university at least once a week."

Beau gave a polite nod, then turned back to his computer. "Okay. Let's file a missing person report, which will go into the system and other law enforcement agencies around the state can access it."

"Thank you." Francine gave the answers, which he typed in. With the simple form completed, he printed a copy and asked her to sign it. When she was finished, she pushed the paper across the desk.

The sheriff looked over the details. "We'll follow up, Dr. Morales," he said, his voice kind, but not building up her hopes. "If he's here, we'll do our best to find him."

Francine nodded, relief and frustration settling like a stone in her stomach. She stood to leave. "Thank you, Sheriff Cardwell," she said, handing him a business card with her cell number written on the back. "I may be at the Morton Library during the days, following up on the research Cliff was doing here. Please stay in touch on this."

He saw her to the door, all business. "We'll call if we hear anything," Beau assured her, already turning back to his work as she left.

The sun was low in the sky as she stepped outside, the air temperature dropping at least ten degrees. She hurried to her SUV, discouraged. Inside, she let the residual warmth in the car caress her skin, but there was no sense of comfort. She couldn't let go of the image of her friend and colleague out there somewhere, perhaps ill, and no one knew where to find him.

If law enforcement couldn't get to the bottom of it, she would have to do it herself.

Chapter 6

Emily locked the back door of the Morton Library, turning the key with a satisfying click. She glanced at the dimming sky as the last bit of dusk highlighted the Sangre de Cristo Mountains. In the chilled air, her breath made foggy puffs, and she held the diary tightly under her arm. It was an intriguing find, one she had set aside after Francine Morales walked through the door.

Now, she was eager to get back to reading her grandfather's words and learning of his life as a much younger man. The supple leather and yellowed pages promised stories that perhaps no one else had ever seen. She made her way through the silent courtyard, past the shadowy outlines of sleeping trees, and into the warmth of the little adobe house she now called home.

Inside, she walked into her grandfather's study and

flipped on a lamp. It cast a pool of yellow light onto her grandfather's sturdy wooden desk, giving the cozy room a sense of intimacy. The walls seemed to close in around her, comfortable and reassuring. Emily placed the diary carefully in the center of the desk, its leather binding soft and worn, as if the years had barely touched them. She settled into a creaky wooden chair, her curiosity too strong to delay any longer, and opened the cover.

The handwriting was instantly familiar, the same elegant script that filled so many of David Plankhurst's letters and notes in the library's archives. But this was personal, revealing an adventurous personality, a side of her grandfather that delighted her. Emily let her eyes travel the careful lines, catching on words that jumped from the pages. Spanish soldiers. Ghostly horses. Lost gold. Her grandfather's fascination with the legend of the seven cities of Cibola was vivid, urgent in its telling. He described the mysterious nights when he'd personally seen spectral figures riding through the streets of Taos, presumably during their quest for treasure.

The lamp's soft glow filled the room as Emily read the aged ink, absorbing the unexpected passion her grandfather had poured into these entries. His words conjured the long-lost stories, his painstaking research that connected their family to the history of Taos.

Dad and I followed the map, as closely as we could. I wished the makers had known of latitude and longitude. Could have made our journey so much simpler. But, onward we press, knowing only that we are somewhere east of Twining, where we left our trusty old truck parked.

It was as if she could hear his voice, narrating the scenes through the written word. She paused, an uncertainty settling in her chest. Should she keep his musings within the family, or reach out to Francine, who would undoubtedly have her own views on the matter? What she'd seen so far was not even close to historical research; these notes were simply the observations of one man, and she was certain Cliff Littleton had not come across this diary.

The thought of involving Francine stirred an unease within her. Though they shared a bond over historical pursuits, this was different—much more personal to the Plankhurst family. Emily's grip on the diary tightened, and the room grew silent except for the subtle hum of the heating system coming on and the rustle of the pages. Outside, the wind whispered against the windows.

She returned to the diary.

Dad joked about how much simpler our task would be if we had the use of a helicopter. I laughed, thinking perhaps it would, but then maybe not. The ravines are steep and the undergrowth dense.

Emily felt her excitement growing with each turn of the page. It did sound as if they could be searching for a treasure, something buried or tucked away in a hidden place. The part about the helicopter made her smile— today, a drone might be of help. She marveled at the details and wondered at his intentions. She wondered about her grandfather's age when he wrote this; a quick ruffle through the pages didn't list a year, only that the particular trek she was reading about had happened in the month of May. The fact that he called the town Twining, rather than the present-day Taos Ski Valley, was another valid clue.

Astonished to find snow, some of it more than knee-deep. Not sure why that would be unexpected. We've climbed to, I would guess, 9,500 feet or more. If we were hiking Wheeler Peak, we would not be surprised at snow, even in June or July.

For a long time, Emily sat lost in thought. Other

than the random page she had found earlier, she had not found any specific mention of conquistadors or Spanish gold, although David's notes certainly made it seem as if they were looking for something. Her eyes traced the careful script, again and again finding more questions than answers. How had her family been so intimately tied to these stories, and what did it mean for her now?

The shadowed corners of the study seemed to inch closer as the night grew darker and she considered what this legacy entailed. What consequences would arise from revealing any of this to Francine? And what if David's musings were merely flights of fancy, nothing rooted in historical fact at all? Would revealing them bring embarrassment or dishonor to the family name?

She closed the diary with a gentle thud, still undecided.

"I'm not thinking clearly, and I probably need food," she declared to the empty room as she stood and stretched her limbs.

Switching on a few more lights as she made her way through the house, she went to the kitchen and pulled a bag of fresh greens from the fridge. A handful went into a bowl, and she chopped cucumber and tomato, sliced some scallions and black olives, and added bits of pre-cooked chicken. With her favorite olive oil and vinegar dressing tossed over the whole thing, she had a tasty salad to carry back to the study.

Emily eyed the diary on the desk, but chose to snuggle into a corner of the leather loveseat opposite it. The wind had picked up, sending a chilly draft around the window frames, and she pulled a handwoven alpaca throw over her legs as she ate her dinner. The room, filled with the rich scents of old paper and hints of adobe, was still and quiet, calming her conflicted thoughts.

Her gaze flicked to the bookcase on the far wall and the section at the end, where she knew the press of a hidden latch would make the shelves swing outward. Behind it, a narrow set of steps led down into the tunnels that connected with others beneath the town. And all at once, an image of a face came to her. Gabriel Graystone, the very realistic ghost who'd found his way into her life almost a year ago. She blinked hard and shut down the memories. Right now she had other things to tend to.

Her fork clinked against the side of her salad bowl and she realized it was empty. "Wow, Gabriel, look what you do to me." She gave a nervous little laugh as she threw off the afghan and carried her utensils to the kitchen.

With a mug of tea in her freshly washed hands, she reached for the diary, but hesitated. The night pressed in, and the glowing lamplight gave the study a haunting quality. A shadow—she swore it was shaped like Gabriel Graystone—moved like a memory on the walls, dancing at the edge of her vision as Emily processed the diary entries and their implications. "Gabe, I'm busy right now," she whispered softly.

Once more, she picked up the diary and—setting her tea on the side table, snuggling up on the leather loveseat—she returned to its fascinating contents. The pages detailing the story of her grandfather's and great-grandfather's hike into the mountains came to an end. With a couple of blank pages as a buffer, he began writing about his beliefs in whether the conquistador gold actually existed. This was the section she had read yesterday. And although David stated that he believed it *could* be true, he also made the point that historians were in complete agreement that no cities made of gold—the stuff of the legends—had ever existed.

Still, he wrote, *even though no cities were built of gold it doesn't mean there was no gold found. Mining operations existed all over this part of the state. My own grandfather came here from the east, in search of riches. And, although it turned out that the history of the region was the far greater legacy than any physical gold, it was a wise move for Morton Plankhurst to come here and begin collecting the treasures of New Mexico's past.*

As the pages turned, they unfolded more layers of her family's amazing legacy. The connections between David Plankhurst's stories and the library's holdings took shape, like pieces of a map she was meant to navigate. She was the fourth generation of Plankhursts to have a hand in gathering and preserving that knowledge.

She turned to another section, where David's details of certain ghostly apparitions were consistent, recorded across many years, suggesting a pattern or cycle. Emily's eyes narrowed in concentration, absorbing every nuance of his careful accounts, knowing firsthand that ghostly encounters in Taos happened, even today.

But how might this be related to the current problem at hand? Could David's ideas about the conquistadors and the legends of their gold treasure be of any help in finding the missing professor?

The questions placed a responsibility on her shoulders. Her role as the keeper of these stories and their connection to the living history of Taos was undeniable. Yet, she wondered if she would be upsetting the delicate balance of her family's past if she were to share the contents of the diary. Emily read into the night, until her eyelids became heavy and her thoughts blurred into dreams of ethereal riders and their endless search for gold.

The diary dropped into her lap, waking her. Somewhere in the house a clock chimed twice. She closed the worn leather cover and let her eyes close for a moment, seeking clarity in the quiet, debating whether to rouse herself and go to bed or simply melt into the comfortable cushions and stay here. A heavy, expectant air filled the study, almost tangible, as if something awaited her decision.

The stillness was complete … until it wasn't. Emily felt it first as a chill, a ripple in the atmosphere that seemed to hold its breath. She opened her eyes and looked up, catching the shimmering form of her grandmother as it slowly took shape near the desk. Valerie stood motionless, her figure wavering slightly in the dim light. Emily smiled fuzzily, as the ghost's familiar features and flowing clothes came into focus. She reached for the turquoise pendant at her throat, a gift for her twelfth birthday.

"Grandma."

"You've been reading, I see." Valerie held her gaze, her expression sweet. The words that followed were gentle, yet probing, as if they came from both the room and within Emily herself. "You have been wondering how much of our family lore should be shared with outsiders."

Emily's hand instinctively tightened around the diary, pulling it closer. "I don't know. There's so much here … so much Grandpa never talked about." Her eyes moved from the ethereal figure to the pages filled with her grandfather's intimate accounts. "What do you think?"

Valerie moved closer, her form wafting in her familiar way. "We all have choices," she said, her voice soft as the shadows, "and the choices define who we become."

Emily's head tilted in thought, and she let out a small,

conflicted sigh. Valerie's concern wasn't just about the diary—it was about loyalty, about trust, about the line between safeguarding the past and connecting with those in the present. About whom she should trust, among those who came into the library for her assistance. She sensed Valerie's patience as she wrestled with her decision.

"What would *you* do, Grandma?" Emily finally asked, hearing the plea in her own voice.

Valerie's expression softened, her smile lifting in a way that was so familiar from Emily's childhood. "It's your call, baby girl."

The room felt alive with her grandmother's form, and Emily suddenly recalled their many lighthearted moments together. She giggled. "Great way to not answer the question, Grandma!"

Valerie returned her laugh. "Welcome to the world of being the adult in the room."

"So … Francine. I think she really needs my help … but will sharing our family memories change everything?"

Valerie's eyes shone with wisdom. "It might. Changes can happen for better or worse," she countered softly. "Consider what you stand to gain, not only what you fear to lose."

Emily thought of the diary she held and also the many boxes and drawers filled with personal memorabilia in the library.

"Trust yourself, my girl. And trust those who have earned it." Valerie's figure reached out, as if to touch the tip of Emily's nose, the way she used to in real life. "I will leave you with this—remember that not everyone who requests information from you deserves to receive whatever they demand. You have the right to keep things to yourself."

Such as the name I came across in here earlier?

Emily watched as the ghost slowly faded, her form dissolving like mist but leaving behind the sense of a touch, a whisper, an embrace. The room settled into the normal sounds, the rustle of the night wind through the trees softening the echo of Valerie's last words.

For a long time, Emily clutched the diary to her chest, alone in the soft light but filled with the echoes of their conversation. The choices before her seemed immense, and the legacy she held now felt fragile. Yet there was a new clarity. Valerie's visit had left a sense of direction, a reassurance that some answers would emerge.

The night pressed close around the adobe walls, and Emily carried the diary with her as she padded to her bedroom, and sleep.

Chapter 7

It was nearly noon when Jax pulled the white van into the parking lot at Taos Hardware, his mind on the few extra supplies he needed for the setup. He'd spent the morning out at the cave site Vince had showed him, running wires and rigging lights. After each evening's tour, they would need to take the more expensive equipment with them—those holographic projectors weren't cheap, and it wasn't worth the risk of having them stolen or damaged out in the weather.

An older man with an armload of bagged potting soil was pushing the door open, and Jax held it for him. A grateful smile reminded him of the way things were in towns like this. For half a second, the thought came to mind that this would be a pleasant place to live. He shook off the notion; when he and Vince were finished here, it was doubtful they'd be welcomed back.

Inside, the store was warm, smelling of raw wood and paint, as Jax stepped inside. A clerk with deep wrinkles and a red plaid shirt greeted him. "Didn't expect to see you back so soon," the shopkeeper said, grinning wide. "You're working with that tour guy, aren't you? The one with all the treasure maps?"

Jax gave a brief nod, scanning the aisles. "Yeah," he said, keeping his tone cautious.

"Sure sounds exciting! Folks in town are buzzing. Haven't had anything like it in years." The shopkeeper leaned in, eyes wide with curiosity. "Think you'll hire locals for the tours? I bet some of the boys around here would take a job like that."

Jax thought of Vince's reluctance to share the spoils and shrugged. "Don't know about that yet," he said, picking up bundles of extension cords and rope. "Vince is still figuring things out."

"Well, you let him know there's plenty who'd jump at the chance," the man said, laughter in his voice. He leaned back as another customer, a middle-aged woman in a thick brown sweater, stepped forward.

Jax moved to the side, scanning the shelves for some zip ties. He could hear them talking about the treasure tours. "I heard it's not just coins," she declared, "but full bars of gold. Can you imagine?"

A young man with a shaggy haircut paused at the end of the aisle and laughed. "Sure, I can. That's how they hook you, telling a story."

"But what if it's true?" Another man joined the woman at the counter. "Gold's been found in these hills before. My great-grandfather talked about the mining operations all the time."

Jax kept his head down as he gathered more supplies, listening to the chatter. The promise of treasure lit up people's imaginations, much as it had the Van Dykes'. He glanced at his phone, calculating how long it would take to rig everything before the first scheduled tour. The speculation concerned him a little. Gold bars? If people expected that, they were sure to be disappointed. Or maybe Vince already had that in mind, along with a way to pull off the illusion.

The shopkeeper returned as Jax moved to the register, arms full and expression thoughtful. "Ain't it something? We've got people rushing in from all over, wanting to see where that treasure's been hidden." He rang up the items quickly and efficiently. "I hope you boys can keep up with the crowds."

Jax nodded, still distant. "We'll see." He pulled out cash, his thoughts elsewhere.

The shopkeeper gave him a curious look. "You don't seem too excited for a guy about to make a haul."

Jax pocketed his change and lifted the bag of supplies. "Just got a lot to do. I'll tell Vince there's interest in helping out."

He turned toward the door, then hesitated as he heard one last exchange behind him.

"Think they'll find anything out there?" the young man asked, his tone a mix of skepticism and hope.

The shopkeeper chuckled. "They'll find a hell of a story, if nothing else. People love that. Probably make more off ticket sales than any gold they dig up."

Jax could see how this was playing out already, the growing buzz and the long lines of gullible tourists. It had all the markings of a perfect con, just like Vince said. But he knew from experience that *perfect* didn't mean lasting. And the inevitable disappointment among the townspeople had him a little nervous.

He loaded the van, climbing into the driver's seat with heavy thoughts. Vince was counting on the setup and the stories to work their magic, and Jax was the one who'd have to make sure it didn't all unravel.

He drove back toward the foothills, Vince's confident words echoing louder than the engine. The equipment rattled softly in the back, a reminder of the tangible effort it would take to bring Vince's intangible dreams to life. As the town faded into the distance, Jax wondered—maybe this time, they were in over their heads.

* * *

Hours later, Jax walked in through the back door, passing the two storage rooms, catching sight of Vince leaving the space he used as an office as he headed toward the front room—the part the customers saw. A peachy glow filled the room as the late afternoon sun reflected off the slopes of Taos Mountain. Tonight was a run-through where the two of them would test the equipment and make sure the show ran perfectly. Tomorrow, the audience would be ticket holders.

Vince caught sight of him. "You get the van gassed up and cleaned?"

"It's all set, complete with a cooler for the drinks. We'll make a good impression when we drive them out there."

"Perfect. Come on." Vince led the way into the back office. "Real gold, real ghosts," he said, flopping into his chair and tossing a small nugget into the air. "Tomorrow night's group is just a bunch of tourists and locals. We impress them, get them spreading the word, and that'll snag the whales."

"Right. I've got our social media pages set up and we'll do some of the interviews at the scene and others after we return to the office."

"Exactly. Plenty of testimonials to feed the hunger of the next bunch."

He set the gold nugget on the desk where it caught the light, like a promise of riches. "Once the investors see this, they'll throw money at us faster than you can blink." Vince crossed the room and stuck another map to the cluttered whiteboard, his voice rising with enthusiasm.

Jax stood in the doorway, glancing down again at the gleaming nugget on the desk. He needed to bring up the subject that was bothering him. He cleared his throat. "We gonna talk about what happened to that professor guy?"

"He got spooked by the curse, that's all," Vince replied without hesitation, as though explaining the obvious to a slow student. "Spooked enough that he paid up and left us everything."

"But he never paid us anything."

"Yet."

Jax clamped his mouth shut. The old guy swore he didn't have money to invest, but that never stopped Vince. He was determined to figure out a way to get both the professor's prestigious endorsement and whatever cash money he could wrangle. But now … it might be too late.

Vince tossed the nugget in the air and grinned at Jax as he caught it. His train of thought was already back on the tour groups. "And with these, we'll have 'em lined up at the door."

"We've had them lined up before," Jax said. "Just sayin'."

Vince set the nugget on his desk, perched himself on the edge, and grinned again, more broadly this time. "That was before the real action started, my friend. Once we have the internet plastered with endorsements for our tour, everyone will be talking like crazy. They're practically throwing their credit cards at us to get in on the next tour. And when we show them this"—he gestured to the whiteboard—"we'll be raking it in!"

The glimmering nugget seemed to have infused Vince with even more energy than usual. Or he was high on something, Jax wondered. Vince sprang from the desk and flipped open a sheet of blue paper to show Jax the latest version of the plan.

"Yeah," Jax said, glancing around the cramped room. "If you say so."

"I say so!" Vince's eyes were gleaming now, nearly as much as the gold. "They won't be able to get enough."

Jax looked around, fully taking in his surroundings. The office was as chaotic as Vince's enthusiasm. A battered filing cabinet and several cardboard boxes took up the corner. The desk had papers piled high enough to tip at any second. The whiteboard held Vince's usual assortment of indecipherable notes. He'd pinned up sketches of cave layouts, trails through the Sangre de Cristos, and hastily scrawled maps. It seemed that the clutter was there to distract anyone who might come looking for real answers.

"See, we give them the full treatment," Vince went on. "A few sightings of Spanish soldiers. Those ghost-horses trotting by. And a hint that every one of them will find some treasure." He winked at Jax, who pictured the heavy metal coins barely plated in gold. Those weren't going to fool anyone in broad daylight.

"Yeah," Jax repeated, watching as Vince stuck another rough sketch to the board. "We'll see."

"Come on, man. Get into it! They love the spooky stuff. And these maps *look* authentic, you have to agree. You saw how much fun they had back in Tucson with the illusions." He clapped Jax on the shoulder. "Let's step it up. C'mon, help me carry this to the lobby."

Jax lifted the laden whiteboard full of maps, plans, and sketches, while Vince picked up the easel. "It's just gonna get harder to explain when people get too curious, try to pin us down with facts."

They placed the easel and board in a corner where people could walk up and look at it, but where the lighting wasn't decent enough that they'd spot the newness of the paper.

"We're making history here." Vince tossed a roll of tape to him and gestured for more of the faded prints. "If someone tries to get too smart, we'll scare them silly."

"And if that doesn't work?" Jax asked, catching the tape and turning it over in his hand as if trying to decide whether to throw it back.

"They leave, just like that professor did." Vince's answer was too quick and too smooth to sound sincere, and Jax wondered again how long it would be before their luck ran out.

"Easy to say," Jax told him, leaning against the front desk and folding his arms.

"Easier to do." Vince was pacing again. "I've got it all worked out. You know that."

"Yeah." Jax's agreement sounded hollow, even to himself.

"We're adding a little extra spice to the act," Vince insisted. "And you know as well as I do that's all it is—an act. No one's getting hurt."

"No one?" Jax gave him a hard look. "You wanna be sure?"

"You don't really believe in ghosts, do you?" Vince laughed, gesturing for another sketch.

Jax reluctantly handed him the paper. "Didn't use to."

"Just wait 'til you see this." Vince was unfolding the sketch, eyes shining. "Holograms of the soldiers. Coins and nuggets on the ground. It'll blow them away."

"And if they figure out it's all fake?" Jax persisted.

Vince laughed again. "They won't. They never do. People want to believe this stuff—it's like at a theme park. We're giving them what they want."

Jax remained skeptical. "Yeah. For now."

Vince's smile was fixed and confident, but Jax thought he detected a tinge of doubt in the eyes. If so, it was gone as soon as it came. Vince waved at the blueprints with one hand, the other holding up the gold nugget like a trophy.

"The more they get worked up about that curse, the better," Vince said. "Some of them already think we've got ghosts in the cave."

"We've got *something*," Jax said.

"It's all right here, Jax." Vince tapped a finger to his temple. "No one can touch us."

Jax shoved his hands in his pockets and stared at the floor. "If you say so."

He could feel Vince watching him, waiting for him to exhibit the same level of enthusiasm. He knew his silence irritated Vince and he had been doing it more just to annoy him lately. But now he realized Vince's words, Vince's absolute certainty, were starting to wear on him.

"Listen, buddy," Vince said, dropping the nugget into Jax's palm. "When we pull this off, you and I are set for life."

Jax certainly hoped so. But he said nothing. He looked at the nugget in his hand. He looked at Vince, who was so wound up he could probably do this all night. He looked at the display board that was meant to convince the rubes.

Finally, he closed his hand around the gold and nodded. When Vince put an arm across his shoulder, when Vince said this was the ultimate payoff, when Vince said it was just around the corner, Jax took a deep breath, put on a smile, and agreed.

Vince gave him a sideways glance. "Hey, man," he said, keeping his voice smooth and pleasant, "I mean it. It's a done deal. No worries."

Easy for him to say.

"You're the best partner I could ever ask for." Vince slapped a hand on his shoulder.

"That's right," Jax said. "I am." And this time Vince was the one who heard it as a veiled threat.

Vince's expression slipped just for a fraction of a second, long enough to let Jax know that Vince knew exactly how thin his patience was running. It was more satisfying than Jax expected it to be.

* * *

Vince's laughter mingled with the wind as it whipped through the open window of the dark Ferrari. "Can't you picture it?" he exclaimed, gesturing at the desolate landscape while the engine purred along the moonlit stretch of road. But in the driver's seat, Jax clenched the wheel. For an hour now, Vince's jittery enthusiasm had not waned—probably high on something. Jax was glad he'd offered to drive.

"They're going to eat it up," Vince said, beaming.

Jax watched for the turnoff. "You hope they do." He kept his voice low and even, but Vince was already waving at another clump of piñon and scrub.

"Just over there! The ghost horses," Vince said. "You saw how well it worked before."

I saw how we almost got caught before. Jax kept his mouth shut.

"The plan is brilliant," Vince said. "I'll lead them into the cave, start with the spooky stories, and sit back while they run around looking for the treasure."

"Can't believe this stuff works on people," Jax said. "Kids and grandpas looking for gold. And they think it's real?"

Vince was as smug as ever. "Happens all the time. That's the best part."

"Sounds like you've been thinking a lot about this."

"I have," Vince said, and his tone made Jax uneasy. "Thinking about that and about the next step, how we cash in even bigger. And this time, we're doing it on a grander scale. Ghost horses, coins, the Spanish army!" He slapped the dashboard in delight.

Jax remained silent, getting a little tired of Vince's fervor as he pulled over into the wide dirt area where they would park the van and begin the tours. But he had to admit, the promise of the money from the important investors still had his attention. It had to. He'd skipped out on too many debts, things he couldn't go back and face until he had serious cash in his pockets.

Vince seemed unperturbed by Jax's lack of response. "Once a few of them see the show, they'll be climbing over each other to book a spot."

Jax gave him a sidelong glance and cut the engine. "Yeah. Sure."

Vince frowned at him. "Come on. I've got it all figured out. We're golden."

But Jax remembered Tucson. He knew about Death Valley before that. "That's what you said last time."

"We've got it nailed this time," Vince insisted. "You saw them all buying the story about how the Lost Dutchman's gold carries a curse. This is gonna be a hundred times better. Think of it, man," he said. "Think of how rich we'll be."

Jax got out of the car, remaining quiet.

"They want it to be true," Vince told him, nearly shouting now. "You saw how they acted in Tucson. A few phony news reports, a few new sightings—"

"And a few cops showing up," Jax interrupted.

"We've never run it this smooth," Vince said. "And you're bothered? We're not going to get caught, man. This little hick town—they got nowhere near enough cops to handle what they've got *and* come after us." He smiled at Jax. "You and me, buddy. This is the big time. We don't even have to run the tours ourselves anymore. You see the suckers that came by today, trying to sign up?"

Jax thought of the guy at the hardware store, saying local guys would like jobs. "Vince, believe me. Hiring anyone to run the tours would be a *bad* idea."

"Okay. Right." Vince waved him off. "Just leaves more

for us. Makes us richer. Think about it. We're miles ahead of everyone. The best in the business. The best at this *ever.*" And now Jax felt certain Vince was high.

"Come on. We need to test everything and make sure it's working." Jax grabbed his laptop from behind the driver's seat and turned onto a narrow dirt trail.

Jax had worked at the site all day, but it looked different in the dark, especially as he imagined leading a group of tourists up here. He just hoped it wasn't a setup for disaster and that Vince's confidence was enough to make it work. He made a mental note to buy a dozen headlamps for the customers to wear. Meanwhile, he switched on the light on his phone to guide the way.

"We always did daylight tours before, but this night tour's gonna be a huge hit," Vince added, turning and admiring the view. "People love being scared out of their wits. People *love* the mystery. You know that."

"Right," Jax said.

Vince laughed. "It's foolproof." He gestured grandly, wide circles with both arms. "Like I said, real gold, real ghosts."

"I hear you," Jax said.

"We'll hide a few extra stashes of coins," Vince said. "And with the new equipment, those holograms will be better than the real thing."

"They'd better be," Jax said. He needed to know he'd set the projectors up correctly.

"They're all believers," Vince told him. "I'm thinking we can run four tours a week. Maybe five."

Jax shined his light ahead, to the dark spot that was the opening to the cave. He'd rigged battery power to run sets of low lights, enough for ambiance, not bright enough to reveal the fact that the treasure chests were modern and the gold coins were chintzy.

"Hang on," he said. "Let me hook up the battery cable."

He stepped around behind a huge boulder where he'd improvised a little command station where he could sit out of sight while he controlled the special effects. His canvas camp stool was there, and he set the laptop on a flat rock. When he sat down, he wasn't visible to anyone standing at the mouth of the cave.

Jax called out. "Ready?"

Vince stepped around behind the boulder.

"What are you doing? Vince, you know when we start the tour, you have to stay out there, talking to the people, showing them around. You can't let anyone know I'm back here."

"Right, right."

"We need to do this like a dress rehearsal, as if it's the real deal. Because tomorrow night it will be."

Jax had created a script, something to give him cues about when to switch on the holographic images of the horses and soldiers, and when to play the scary sounds. Had Vince even given it a glance? He shook his head as Vince walked back to the clearing in front of the cave.

He knew Vince's basic pitch—he'd certainly heard it often enough—so he would have to figure it out as they went along. He just knew that there were a lot of kinks to work out.

Chapter 8

Emily woke up with a hunger for waffles, the ones Grandma Valerie used to make. And the benefit of moving into her grandparents' former home was that she had everything she needed to make that happen. She pulled on a cozy robe and slippers and walked through the quiet house to the kitchen.

The waffle iron was probably older than Emily herself, but it still made great ones. She plugged it in and stirred the batter, according to the wrinkled recipe card in the box she kept on the shelf. While the iron heated, she brewed her first cup of coffee, pulled out blueberries, some chopped pecans, and the tin of Vermont maple syrup, and heated two sausages to make the meal complete.

Ten minutes later, she was at the kitchen table, taking her first bite from the crispy edge of her waffle. With a sigh, she silently thanked Grandma for teaching her this wonderful little comfort routine. She was halfway through the leisurely meal when she heard a car pull into the library's parking area. A glance out the window told her it was Francine Morales.

Emily watched until she saw the professor get out of her car, then stepped out the kitchen door and called out. "I'm still at home. Come over for coffee?"

Francine swiveled, walking through the wooden gate.

"Can I make you a waffle?" Emily made the offer, although she would have to start over, since she'd only mixed enough batter for one.

"Oh, no. I ate at the hotel's breakfast buffet. Finish yours—I didn't mean to interrupt." Francine seemed distracted, and Emily noticed she had pulled some glossy folders from her computer bag. At Emily's questioning glance, she handed them over while she stepped to the counter to pour her own mug of coffee and doctor it the way she liked.

Emily took her seat again, taking another bite of her breakfast while she looked at what Francine had handed her. She'd seen one of these before. The brochures were from the Gold Treasures operation; the place they'd heard about that was promising the excitement of finding real conquistador gold. The front was printed in a rich red and gold scheme, with historic photos superimposed over a scene that showed Taos Mountain in the background. Inside the tri-folded page, photos of excited people holding gold coins blended with text that played up the chances for becoming wealthy by joining one of the tours.

"I am absolutely furious!" Francine declared, setting her coffee mug on the table a little harder than necessary.

Emily startled.

"They've used direct quotes from some of Cliff's work! Where did they get permission to do that?"

Emily opened her mouth but Francine wasn't waiting for an answer.

"From Cliff himself, I'd bet. It means these cheesy operators were actually in touch with him."

"And that would be a good thing, right?" Emily pushed her plate back. "It gives us a lead on finding him."

Francine grumbled, something about catching someone at the tour office and giving them a piece of her mind.

Meanwhile, Emily tidied up the kitchen. "You must have come here for more than sharing the brochures," she said tactfully. "Why don't I let you into the library to get started, and I'll get dressed and join you in a few minutes?"

That suggestion went over well, so Emily grabbed her keys and tightened the belt on her robe. The two of them walked across the courtyard, and Emily unlocked the back door, switching on lights as they moved through the building. Francine settled in at the long table in the main room, her usual spot, and booted up her laptop.

Within thirty minutes, Emily had showered and dressed in her usual outfit of jeans and a comfy button-down shirt. She'd just walked into the library, intending to ask Francine how she could be of help in locating documents, when she spotted a sheriff's department cruiser coasting to a stop in the parking area out front. Sheriff Beau Cardwell stepped out.

Francine heard the car door slam and she rose from her seat. "I hope this is good news ..."

But Emily knew Beau well enough to know this was not his happy face. She met him at the door and ushered him in. He turned down her offer of coffee and got right down to business.

"We found Clifford Littleton's car, about two miles north of Tres Piedras. It appeared to be abandoned on a narrow side road."

"I can't think of any reason why—" Francine began. But she stopped herself when she realized Beau wasn't finished.

He took a deep breath. "There were some bloodstains in the vehicle. Not a lot, but noticeable. Unfortunately, there were no footprints or tire tracks that might help us put together a scenario of what might have happened. There was rain, four or five days ago, and it effectively erased that sort of thing."

Emily looked at Francine's stricken face.

"I've had the vehicle towed to the county impound lot, where forensics will go through it. If there's a family member we could contact, we can run tests to see if the blood is likely to be Dr. Littleton's."

With a specific task, Francine stood straight and reached for her purse. "Here's his daughter's contact information. She is the only next of kin I'm aware of."

Beau wrote down the information. "One other thing. I stopped by that outfit that's running the treasure tours, since you said that was an interest of Dr. Littleton's. The only person in the office was a young woman who was selling tickets for the tours. She barely knew her boss's name—somebody she just called Jax—and she had no clue about any visit from Dr. Littleton."

Emily felt her shoulders droop.

"I got one bit from her, and I'm not sure if this is in any way related … She told me someone had left a credit card behind and wondered if I could get it returned to the owner. The only reason I mention it to you both is that when I did a basic online search, it turns out this man is also a university historian. Coincidences don't sit well with me." He reached into his shirt pocket and pulled out a plastic card, reading from it. "The name is Russell Pinkney. Is that familiar? Someone who might have a tie to our missing professor?"

Francine's expression became a thunderstorm. "Russell Pinkney. That rotten—"

"Who is—?"

Francine stomped over to the front window and back, releasing angry energy. "Pinkney is indeed another historian, from Arizona State. He has nowhere near the impeccable credentials that Cliff has, and he's always wanted to upstage our history department at UNM."

Emily remembered their earlier conversation. "And you think Pinkney would, what, sell or give Cliff's material to these tour operators?"

"He very well might have. They got it from somewhere."

Emily turned to Beau and held up one of the red and gold brochures. "Francine suspects that someone plagiarized Cliff's work to create the historical data they used here."

He gave it a brief glance and pocketed the brochure. "Maybe the internet?"

"Cliff has never published his work online. Everything he has written has been in the most prestigious academic journals. I highly doubt these guys with their tour business would have access to those. But Russell Pinkney most certainly does."

Beau thanked her for the information and assured the

women that his department would be looking for Pinkney. "If you should hear from the man, please let me know." He gave Emily a knowing look before he turned toward the door. "And do not confront him yourselves."

So, okay, Emily admitted to herself, she did have a little bit of a history of becoming involved whenever a mystery presented itself. But a college history professor … surely, he wouldn't be some psychopath. Would he?

She stood near the desk, watching as Beau backed his cruiser out and drove away.

Francine's voice caught her attention. "I'm going to talk to the tour operators myself. Ask them how they got hold of Cliff's material."

"You heard Sheriff Beau, Francine. I don't know if we should—"

"And Cliff's daughter in Albuquerque. I've got to call her. The sheriff wants a blood test, but I'm thinking about Cliff's files. His notes. There's probably something we haven't seen yet. *Something* prompted him to drive up here, but we don't know what happened next. Did he connect with this Vince person, or did he head off on his own, following maps and research?"

Emily had wondered the same things. Perhaps Francine's colleague had enough data to lead him to potential sites where there might actually be hidden gold. The timing seemed a little too coincidental, but maybe he and these tour guys were on the same trail.

Francine set her phone down, frustrated. "Dammit. No answer at the tour office, and his daughter's phone goes straight to voicemail."

She tapped out a text message to the daughter, but when no immediate reply came back, she went into motion, pulling a Moleskin notebook toward her and moving aside a stack of photocopied maps. "Someone must have gotten to Cliff early, and I don't know who to suspect. It's conceivable that he bumped into Vince Hutchins when he got here, but you know ... I really do see Russell Pinkney as more likely to have stolen Cliff's work."

"So, do you think Pinkney gave that research to the treasure tour people? What would be in it for him?"

"Academic superiority, in his twisted way of looking at things. Russell is not above embarrassing a colleague at a symposium—Chicago, 2013—or rushing to publish a paper with shaky research, just to beat one of us to it." Francine let out a short breath and muttered, almost to herself, "We've missed something."

Emily nodded but felt uncertain. She reached for a bundle of archival letters, sifting through them. These were the same letters they'd looked at yesterday, she realized.

"The way all of this points to Cliff's work," Francine continued, "it's got to be related. But how?"

"Do you believe there's really a treasure out there?"

Francine shrugged. "I have no idea."

For a moment, the library seemed to pause with them, suspended in silence. The ticking of a clock, the distant murmur of a heater, and their own quiet breathing filled the room. Emily broke the stillness. "You're right. What are we missing?"

Francine closed the lid of her laptop, pausing to think. "Brainstorming ideas here—do we think Cliff had competition?"

Emily shrugged. "Competition. Collaborators. Maybe even some he didn't know about." The words popped out without much conscious thought. The idea was audacious, even to her, but it seemed to fill the gaps she'd struggled with. "Francine, I think you're right, thinking that his notes might help. The ones from before he arrived here."

Francine gave a thoughtful nod. "I think I'll drive back to Albuquerque, catch up with his daughter. It's only a couple hours down there, a couple more to come back. The way Cliff left, there's no way he had everything with him." Her voice grew firm, more confident as she spoke. "He worked from home a lot. She'll know. She's got to."

Emily watched, glad to see that Francine had purpose, a clear target she felt certain would yield results. She picked up the stacks of letters she'd been sorting. "While you work on that angle, I'll get some of this filed away, and I'll take another look upstairs in the special collections room—in case we missed something helpful up there.

She watched her visitor drive away and was halfway up the stairs when her phone rang, down in her pocket. Riki's number showed on the screen.

"Hey there, Miss Librarian," her British friend teased. "I understand you are hot on the trail of an immense treasure."

Emily laughed as she pushed her way into the upper rooms and set the letters on the worktable there. "Maybe."

"Well, I've something you might fancy. Tickets to that tour, the one where they claim you'll be able to find some old coins, or some such. I don't know exactly. One of my customers bought them for Saturday night and had to cancel so she gave the tickets to me. I thought it might be something fun for the two of us."

Fun—and a great research opportunity. "I can't imagine a better date for my otherwise uneventful Saturday night."

Chapter 9

The library felt somehow emptier all afternoon, with Francine away, although several of Emily's regular patrons came in and out. Two of them returned books they'd borrowed the previous week—what now felt like a long time ago—and another woman dropped off a box of photographs she had recently come across while going through her father's estate.

That was one of the reasons Emily never quite got ahead in her organizing efforts (and she now understood why none of the previous generations had made headway either); people were constantly adding to the collection. Sometimes the donations made amazing additions, filling gaps in the collective knowledge of New Mexico history.

Other times—like this one—they included stacks of unmarked photos or letters, which would require days or weeks of research to find out what historical significance they held. She always laughed at the way people felt they were being helpful, photos marked on the back with something like "Mom, me, and Aunt Jane." No surnames, no full names, no dates. She sighed and placed the box on a shelf marked: To Be Researched. Kevin, her helper this semester, had a remarkable ability with faces and had been invaluable in making family connections and putting names with them.

As she stowed the new items away, she began another search for the rare book and map Cliff had borrowed, hoping for a stroke of luck, and somehow, the afternoon slipped away. She was surprised to realize it was already dark outside when a text came through from Francine: I'm back in town. Dinner?

Emily tamped down her anxiety over the items she so desperately needed to find and happily agreed to Francine's dinner invitation. They went over the details, saying they would meet at Lambert's in thirty minutes. An easy promise for Emily, since she was no more than five minutes away. She tidied her work area and organized materials that had begun to accumulate in piles since Francine's arrival.

She parked her Jeep in the nearby public lot, realizing that Francine's Honda Pilot was pulling in a few cars away. "Perfect timing!" she said as she trotted to catch up.

Inside, their table glowed under the low, warm light of Lambert's side dining room, an intimate island in a sea of softly clinking cutlery and polished wood. Emily watched as Francine retrieved a folder from her shoulder bag, a frown knitting her brow.

"Well, it was an interesting trip. I didn't actually get to meet with Deandra on such short notice, but she left me a key and everything she found in Cliff's home office was there for me. I have *stacks* to go through, but these are some of his more recent notes," Francine said, as she slid the papers across to Emily. "He was specifically angry over people commercializing historical sites, such as these so-called 'treasure tours' destroying places we cannot afford to lose."

Emily thought of the notes in her grandfather's diary, but instinct held her back from sharing this with Francine, at least for now. She leaned forward, her eyes meeting Francine's. "You think Cliff might have confronted the men?"

Francine met her gaze. "It's conceivable. He cares so deeply about preserving history, more than anything else. He has no qualms about speaking up when he feels something important is at risk." She paused, glancing around at the nearby diners, lowering her voice. "I'd almost say he felt personally responsible for protecting those sites. His notes suggest he found their tactics offensive."

"Was he referring specifically to Taos, to this tour operator?" Again, Valerie's ghostly image floated into her memory, a colorful swirl of long skirts and beads. Valerie had always said Emily needed to reread David's diary, especially the parts she hadn't thought important. Emily looked up, keeping her concerns tightly reined. "These operators come and go, in different places. You think they were the reason he came here?"

"It wouldn't be the first time he confronted someone over their misinterpretation of history." Francine's voice wavered slightly, and Emily noticed the weariness in the woman's eyes. "But from what Cliff says here, I wonder—" Francine pressed her lips together before continuing. "I think he considered them more treacherous."

Emily studied Francine's expression, questioning if

part of the professor's anxiety came from the fact that she was tired from the long drive. "I wonder if this is the same situation mentioned in an old family entry," Emily mused, recalling that her grandfather had mentioned 'looters' at a particular historic site, testing Francine's reaction to the idea. "It sounds a little like what you just showed me."

"Could you be at risk too, Em?"

"I don't think so. But what do you make of all this?" Emily deflected the focus back on Cliff, hoping to ease Francine's tension.

Francine took a deep breath and glanced toward the restaurant entrance, then back to Emily. "You may have read the same news reports he saw. About the Graystone gold and all the rumors that stirred up?"

The name instantly brought an imagine of Gabriel Graystone's sweet face to Emily's mind. But she was *not* going to bring that up with Francine.

"Cliff saw how some in the academic community reacted to it, and then he heard what was happening in Taos with Vince Hutchins and his treasure tours. If Cliff thought he could get them to back off, it might be the reason he stayed so long."

Again, Emily could almost hear Valerie's low voice cautioning her: Don't rush in where you might get hurt. "I'm trying to figure it out."

Their food arrived just then, a beautiful salad for Emily and a steak for Francine, and the conversation turned more personal.

"So, Emily, did you grow up here in Taos?" Francine asked, aiming her fork toward the baked potato on her plate.

"No, actually. Albuquerque. My parents are still there, and my grandfather is in a memory care facility now—

Alzheimer's. Running the library has skipped a generation—
my dad is probably the only Plankhurst without the burning
desire to handle books all day. I stayed through college—
yes, a UNM alum. Library Sciences." Emily chuckled at the
idea of her dad, the building contractor, cooped up inside
the historical archives. "How about you?"

"I grew up in Chimayo, not far south of here."

Emily nodded. "I know the place—well, at least the
fabulous restaurant there."

"In places like that, folklore and superstition were just
woven into our everyday lives. My grandmother shared
stories of curses, haunted places, and restless spirits. She
always warned me and my siblings to respect the past and
fear the supernatural. Then the worst happened, and we
lost a close family member to a tragedy that the community
blamed on a curse. Watching people I loved suffer, due to
superstition and guilt, instilled a deep skepticism in me and
a need to separate fact from fiction."

"Oh, wow. I'm so sorry to hear it."

Francine waved off the condolences. "I was only in
middle school at the time, but the tragedy drove me to
understand the real stories behind these legends. I wanted
to make a career in history, so I got my PhD and specialized
in the Spanish colonial period and the Southwest's
indigenous cultures."

"I imagine your rational approach might have gone
against your upbringing, in some ways."

"In *every* way, according to my mother, who is now in
her seventies." She shrugged. "But I don't believe that the
truth should be sacrificed just to create a riveting story. It's
been the guiding principle of my career."

"And I can see how your ideas align with what Professor
Littleton talked about, the attention to detail and adhering

to true history." Pushing her empty plate aside, Emily glanced again at the folder.

Francine's posture softened, and she leaned back. "I know you're careful," she said. "I just don't want anyone else getting involved if these guys are willing to play rough."

Emily absorbed Francine's words. She recalled Valerie's whispers, urging her to think things through before plunging ahead. Was she being as cautious as she should be?

"I haven't told many people about the diary," Emily said slowly, "but if there are connections between those entries and Cliff's notes, I'll have to rethink it all."

"You're talking about your grandfather's entries?" Francine asked.

"Some of his, and some from other generations' records on family matters. It's been a while since I dug through all of them. What you've shared makes me want to get back in and check." Emily tried to mask the apprehension she felt at Francine's knowing nod. Her loyalty to both the library and to Francine was a factor as she deliberated her next steps. She imagined herself telling Valerie what she was about to do.

Francine studied her. "If you can't tell me everything yet, I understand. But be careful."

For a moment, Emily thought of offering Francine her ticket to the treasure tour. The other woman would probably get more out of it. But then a busboy arrived and removed empty plates from their table, and Emily took the moment to collect her thoughts.

A soft guitar melody filtered through the restaurant, and Emily smiled. It reminded her of a similar evening, when she'd traversed the tunnels beneath Taos with Gabriel Graystone by her side. She blinked herself back to the present and watched the other diners, most in animated conversation and laughter.

After a couple minutes, she turned back to Francine. "Could Cliff have thought this was his last great find? That the risk was worth it to see his theory proven?"

Francine hesitated. "Maybe. He has a knack for discovering long-buried things and proving himself right in the end. He also has a way of holding onto things—like grudges—and bringing them back up when he needs to be right about something."

"A bit stubborn?"

"More than a little." Francine's smile was tempered by something more, something that told Emily the two professors had butted heads at times.

"There was another disappearance in town years ago," Emily said. "I've found certain references in our family papers."

"You're not the only one who noticed." Francine laid a hand on the folder with Cliff's findings. "You found something that connects them all?"

"Perhaps. But if that's the case, the disappearances wouldn't be connected to these tour operators—they're newcomers. But this Professor Pinkney … he's definitely been here in the past." There. She had just spilled one secret from Grandpa David's diary.

Emily recalled Valerie's teasing laughter when she thought Emily was taking things too seriously. *Not this time, Grandma*, she said silently to the ghostly image in her mind.

When she looked up again, Francine's gaze was intense. "I can do some checking on Pinkney's background, beyond the parts I'm already aware of. Will you tell me what you know? I sense there's more and it has to do with your family legacy."

"I will," Emily promised, thinking of her grandfather's notes about his own searches for gold treasure nearby. "I just need to think a bit more on it. It could be nothing."

"It could be everything," Francine reminded.

The table next to them emptied, the couple leaving cash for their bill and hurrying out. Emily sensed their isolation in the restaurant, even with other customers still there. It felt as if they had reached the center of something vast and mysterious, a place where she had become a keeper of secrets.

"What are you going to do?" Francine asked.

"Check through more of our family papers. My grandfather kept lots of records, but a lot of it was left to me to figure out." Emily exhaled, her breath warm in the cool of the room. "What about you?"

"Maybe I'll talk to some of Cliff's other friends," Francine said. "He may have confided more of his suspicions to someone else. And I want to know more about Russell Pinkney's involvement in all this."

"We should be careful. Whoever's behind Cliff's disappearance—they can't know what we're doing." Beau's description of the abandoned vehicle with bloodstains in it still bothered her.

Francine gave a wry smile. "They'll never expect you, the quiet librarian, to take them on."

"Maybe not," Emily said, standing and reaching for her jacket. "But it sounds like we have our work cut out."

They walked to the door, leaving the cozy warmth of the restaurant and stepping into the sharp, crisp air of the Taos autumn. Emily wondered how much the sudden chill was the night and how much was the shadow of the task ahead.

"We need more information on the tour operator,"

Francine said as the restaurant door swung shut behind them and they walked toward the parking lot.

Emily zipped her jacket closed. "Did I mention that my friend Riki got tickets for the tour? She's invited me along, so I'll report what I see."

"I'm serious." Francine tried to stifle a yawn. "We don't know enough about him yet. It would be smart to check with the sheriff again, ask him if he has learned more, especially whether Vince Hutchins has a record."

Emily nodded, unlocking her Jeep, noticing Francine's waning energy. Privately, she thought Sheriff Beau would have brought up the subject of Vince Hutchins' criminal record when he came by the library earlier, if that were relevant. But, then again, he had his hands full with the investigation of the abandoned car and the whereabouts of the missing professor.

"It's been a long day and you're tired. Get some rest and come by the library in the morning. I'll talk to the sheriff, and I'll let you know what I learn. Plus, I'm keen to hear more about what Cliff's daughter gave you."

This time, Francine couldn't hide the yawn. "You're right. I need sleep." She reached out and pulled Emily into a hug. "Thank you. Sincerely. You've been such a help, with your contacts and the resources of the library."

Emily felt herself blushing a little. Even though sharing the library resources was just her job, she had to admit that the intrigue of the mystery had grabbed her. She climbed into her Jeep and watched as Francine walked to her own vehicle, got in, and started it. Tomorrow would be an interesting day.

Chapter 10

Emily woke before dawn, her grandmother's voice echoing through her mind, and although she looked around the bedroom, she saw no trace of Valerie's ghostly image. A name stuck in her head—Bettina Garcia. Where had that come from?

She knew where. Grandma Valerie had obviously been whispering to Emily in her sleep. She jotted down the name before she could forget it. If there was one thing she had learned over the years, it was that Grandma never dropped a subject until you acknowledged it. The moment she wrote the note to herself, the persistent sensation went away.

With a smile and headshake, Emily got out of bed and began her morning routine. As she crossed the courtyard, she could hear Victor Martinez, the gardener, humming a familiar Spanish tune to himself. She walked over to say good morning and he pointed out that he was ready to mulch some of the flower beds for the oncoming colder weather.

"I'll be inside, in case you need anything," she assured him.

"*Bueno.* Everything will be fine."

Emily hoped that was true. Exactly at nine a.m., as she was turning over the library's Open sign, Francine drove up.

With her usual tidy bun and her favorite leather jacket over a blue shirt and crisp jeans, she pulled a tote bag and her computer case from her vehicle and walked in. From the top of the tote came a paper bag in the signature purple of Sweet's Sweets.

"I brought treats. These bear claws were practically shouting at me from the bakery case."

Emily laughed. "I know what you mean. They've grabbed my attention more than once. The good news is that I already have coffee made to go with them."

Francine set her bags on the long library table and the two women indulged in the cinnamon and buttery pastries until Francine could hold her news no longer.

"So, I still haven't been able to speak directly with Deandra Littleton, but she texted me that she would be free for a phone call by ten. Until then, I've been online since I woke up—way too early this morning—and began searching for information on these treasure hunters that have recently shown up here in Taos."

"Sounds intriguing."

Francine followed Emily's lead and washed off the sticky residue at the tiny sink beside the coffee maker before walking back to the main room and opening her laptop.

"Taking the brochure we got the other day, I began doing some searches that used the same terminology. Nothing showed up under the exact business name they're using here, but these guys aren't marketing wizards—or maybe they are; the scheme seems to work. There's nearly identical wording for several other operations in the past two years. It all follows along the lines of 'find the hidden treasure.' In Arizona, it was the Lost Dutchman mine in the Superstition Mountains. In Nevada there was another one. Another in Death Valley, California."

"Wow."

"There are others, but these are the ones that I'd guess could be tied together."

Emily nodded. "Get-rich-quick schemers are everywhere, I suppose."

"Yes, and not always the same people." Francine opened a tab for one of the sites and scrolled down to the comments while Emily read over her shoulder.

"Looks like the people really liked the tours they were given."

"Right. Lots of positive comments. At first." She scrolled down. "And then the skeptics arrive. 'Cheesy video,' says one. 'C'mon, anyone could see those weren't real gold coins,' says another."

"Some people are willing to suspend their disbelief and others aren't?"

"True. We see what we want to see."

"And it doesn't necessarily mean it's a scam. When I was a kid and Grandma took me to Disneyland, I really believed the princesses who walked up to me were real."

Francine laughed. "And the pirates in that one cave ride."

"Right? We lapped it up."

"But—we know Cliff wasn't here for any fantasy ride. If he came and talked to these guys, it was because he wanted to know that they were adhering to real history." Francine paused for a moment, opening a new tab on the computer screen. "These are the types of claims where I think my friend might have gotten himself in trouble."

She pointed out that the site had to do with investing in treasure recovery and highlighted a passage. "This is blatantly recruiting people to invest in the prospect that a treasure will be recovered—in this case it's in the region of California where the original Gold Rush took place. It's as if they've taken an existing legend and put a modern spin on it, claiming that not all the original treasure was removed and there's more to be had."

"For the right investment …"

"Yes. None of these sites name a figure. Interested parties are to give their contact information and the firm will reach out to them. As an experiment, this morning I filled out a form with a fake name and an email address I rarely use. Immediately, the push was on. Long, wordy pages, filled with testimonials and claims of success."

"How much do they want you to invest?"

"It's not that simple. For a 'fully refundable' five-hundred dollars I can get the full prospectus and an appointment with a representative."

"Any bets on how many people get their five hundred back?"

"My guess is that the next step is the full-court press. You'll meet with somebody and get a not-so-subtle push to get in now or miss out on the deal of your life … something like that. There may even be levels of investment, to test the prospect's ability to pay, or their gullibility. The richest prospects will be the ones who get the full wine-and-dine treatment."

"So, these guys win, no matter what. Once somebody gives them much money at all, they'll be too embarrassed to ask for it back. No one wants to appear cowardly."

"Or admit they were ripped off."

"So, are these guys *never* caught?" Emily felt her anger rise.

"There have been plenty of allegations, even some lawsuits. But I haven't had time to dig into court records or even news stories to find out how they turned out," Francine admitted.

"And, do you think these are the same guys who've now come here?"

Francine shrugged. "I really don't know. But since you're taking that tour tonight with your friend, I'd suggest keeping your eyes and ears open for anything that sounds like the same b.s. story I've just showed you."

"Definitely."

"And be careful not to give yourself away, to show too much interest. Can you be invisible?"

"I've been known to be quite discreet." Emily thought of all the secrets the library held, the ghosts she knew personally. "Yes, I can do it."

Francine's phone rang, saving Emily from making any further statements.

"Deandra, hi. I'm so sorry I missed you yesterday." Francine looked up at Emily. "Do you mind if I put you on speaker? I think I told you I'm working with the reference librarian in Taos. I'd like to share the conversation with her."

She tapped a button and introduced Emily to Cliff's daughter.

"I'm still going through the folders you left for me. There's a lot of material there."

"I know," came the voice of a woman Emily guessed was about her own age. "I didn't even know where to begin. I talked with the sheriff in Taos, a nice man, but he wasn't able to tell me anything. This was right before you reached out to me."

Francine quickly filled her in on the fact that Cliff's car had been located. Deandra let out a tiny wail.

"It was north and west of here, a bit. Sheriff Cardwell is a friend of Emily's and we've asked him to keep us up to date on any evidence they gather. Hopefully, there will be some clues that lead them to your dad's whereabouts. He may be in contact with you, for a DNA sample."

They heard a sniffle over the line, and Emily could imagine the daughter nodding her head.

"Deandra, there's a different angle we've been looking at," Emily said. "We think there's a ... what would you call it ... a scheme going on here in town, to lure people to invest in supposedly finding the lost treasure of the conquistadors. Do you think that's a reason your father might have come up here?"

"Well, Dad was always interested in that period in New Mexico history, sure. But to invest? I don't see how. My father isn't wealthy, by any stretch. He's nearing retirement age, and I hope I'm not being indiscreet by saying it—he'll probably be one of those who has only his social security to live on. He's never been a saver or an investor. I could barely get him to put a little bit in CDs at the bank."

Francine was nodding, as if she'd already suspected this, but she reiterated the question anyway. "So, you don't think he'd be tempted by someone promising a huge return on an investment?"

"Tempted, maybe. But he really can't afford that kind of thing."

Francine brought up one final subject: whether Deandra had ever heard her father mention someone named Vince Hutchins or if she'd come across that name anywhere. She said no.

They ended the call by wishing each other luck in finding the answers and promising to stay in touch.

Francine set her phone aside. "I think I'm supposed to feel reassured by what she said."

"But you're not."

A nod. "I know Cliff was feeling the financial pressure of his upcoming retirement. I didn't want to worry Deandra."

"But if he has no money to invest ... that means he *can't* get caught up in it, can he?"

Francine gave her a look that let Emily know how naïve that statement was. "Sadly, it's often the people who can least afford it who do these things. Lottery tickets, casinos ... most of those folks are not the high rollers we imagine them to be."

"Maybe we should have asked Deandra about Professor Pinkney, whether her father had recently been in touch with him?"

Francine stared into the middle of the room. "I kind of doubt it, but I can get back to her later, if need be. We may have other questions by then. Meanwhile, I did put out some feelers to see if anyone knows if Pinkney has been here in Taos recently."

Emily took a deep breath and cleared away their coffee mugs. "So, how about a visit to a local woman?"

"Is this the *bruja* someone mentioned?"

"She's more of a *curandera*, a healer, than a witch, but I'm thinking maybe we can tap her knowledge of Taos history today. Unless you're looking for a cure for something."

Francine smiled. "I can definitely use a break from online searches. Let's go."

Emily picked up the bakery bag that still contained two bear claws, then turned out the lights and flipped the sign to the Closed side. Victor had left, so it looked as if their *curandera* friend would be the beneficiary of both pastries.

She led the way out to her Jeep. "It's not far. I'm not sure what we'll learn, but anyone who wants to hear Taos history directly from someone whose family has been here forever will probably have found Bettina Garcia. She claims fifteen generations here in the county."

"Shouldn't we call first?" Francine climbed into the passenger seat and fastened her seatbelt.

It was Emily's turn to give the naïve-question look to her companion. "She's eighty-five if she's a day, and I doubt she's ever even had a telephone. Yes, those old-timers do still exist."

She backed out of the library lot and turned away from the middle of town and her usual haunts. Winding through back streets, heading generally south and west, she came to an adobe home with a tiny dwelling beside it.

"Her son and daughter-in-law live in the main house. The casita is Bettina's."

"Oh my gosh—this could be my mother's place. How is it you know this woman?" Francine asked as the Jeep rolled to a stop in front of the smaller building.

"Through my Grandma Valerie. I gather the two of

them had some pretty fun times back in the day."

The Jeep had no sooner rolled to a stop than the casita door opened. Out rushed a woman who had a few dark streaks in her gray hair and obsidian eyes that sparkled when she saw Emily.

"*Emilita! Como esta, hija!*" She rushed forward, arms extended.

"*Bien, bien, y tu?*" Emily had to bend far forward to hug the tiny woman whose head didn't even come to Emily's shoulders. They exchanged traditional kisses on both cheeks, and then Emily turned to introduce Francine.

Bettina's face lit up and she clasped her hands in a namaste gesture when she saw the bag from Sweet's Sweets.

"For your teatime," Francine told her, handing over the purple sack. "I hope we didn't interrupt something?"

"Ah, this afternoon is the *tertulia*, but come in, come in. I have some wild chamomile I just picked. I'll brew us a tea."

"Tertulia?" Emily asked.

"Oh *si*. I guess in modern terms you would think of it as a book club. This one has been meeting here in Taos for more than a hundred years." Her eyes gleamed as she laughed and led the way to her front door. "Not the same exact group, of course."

Emily laughed along with her friend. And maybe this was the answer, that Cliff had blown a tiny fact out of proportion when he was making his notes at the library.

Inside, the adobe home held the warmth of early morning embers in the tiny kiva fireplace. Bettina ushered them through the kitchen portion of the main room, and they took seats. Emily guessed that the reason there were three chairs at the tiny dining table was because Bettina's son and his wife were normally the only guests.

While the kettle boiled, Emily got right to the reason for the impromptu visit. "Francine has a colleague at the university, a Dr. Clifford Littleton, who came up this direction a few weeks ago and has lost touch with everyone back home."

Francine pulled the photo of Cliff from her purse and handed it over.

Bettina studied the image for a long time, running her fingertips along the contours of his face, as if she might divine something through touch. Emily supposed it might actually work. With Bettina Garcia, many improbable things were imaginable.

"His interest is history, mainly the legends of the conquistador gold. I had this wild thought that he might have gotten your name from someone in town and come out to speak with you about that." Emily reached over and switched off the gas burner when the kettle whistled.

Bettina looked up from the photo, her wise eyes seeming troubled. "I do not know this man's face. But there was someone, a different man who also said he was from a university. In Arizona, maybe?"

Pinkney.

Emily and Francine exchanged a glance.

"This Arizona man also had questions about the conquistador gold. I catch the local rumors. Someone is here in town. They say they will take people to find the gold. Is this the man?"

"No. That's someone else," Francine offered, accepting the photo Bettina handed back to her.

"Good. Those hunters will find no gold."

"You sound certain about that," Emily said, smiling as she watched her friend drop a fresh chamomile flower into each of the cups.

Bettina looked at up her with a mischievous grin. "Other than death itself, I am certain of nothing in this world, *hija*. But my fourth-generation grandfather spent many years of his life looking in these hills for the treasure of the Spanish conquerors. In the end, during his final days, he admitted—and his son wrote this in a journal—that the long-held legend was probably only that, a story."

Emily handed out the steaming mugs.

Francine nodded at Bettina's words. "I am fairly certain that my colleague agreed. The legend has persisted, but he had found no evidence. *Yet*, he said. He hadn't found the evidence yet. When he left Albuquerque to come up here, I could see the gleam in his eye, though, as if he still wanted to believe it could be true."

Bettina smiled over the rim of her mug. "As I said, I am certain of nothing in this world. But I also like to believe there is much beyond our immediate understanding. The magic in things does truly exist."

They spent a pleasant half hour with Bettina, and it was in the Jeep on their way back to the library when Francine brought up the central question again. If Cliff had no money to invest, why would this Treasure Tours outfit be interested in him?

"Maybe it's something else, something Russell Pinkney was onto?" Emily guessed.

"I'm going to call him and ask," Francine declared. But when she found the main number for the history department at Arizona State, she was told that Professor Pinkney was on sabbatical for the semester.

Chapter 11

Jax stood at the top of the trail, following the beam of the van's headlights as it left the highway and turned into the familiar pull-off spot. Dressed completely in black, with only a small flashlight, which he aimed at the ground, no one would see him here. But Vince knew he was in place. They'd exchanged texts with the details, right before Vince left the office with tonight's tour group.

Last night, they'd had a close call. During one of the holographic scenes that made it look like soldiers on horseback might charge through the group, an elderly man began to grip his chest. They determined afterward that it was just a panic attack, but Jax had already decided he would dial it back a little. Vince's text had informed him that tonight's group of ten included a family with young kids, an older couple and two granddaughters, and two women.

Probably not heart-attack material, but still. He planned to keep a closer eye on things, using the hidden remote cameras he'd mounted inside the cave this afternoon.

He watched as the group assembled outside the van. Vince handed out headlamps and showed everyone how to switch them on for the walk up the trail. Once at the cave, he would collect them until it was time to leave, and Jax would operate the lights he'd strung for ambiance. It wouldn't do for someone to shine a bright light around inside there—like stepping onto a movie soundstage and seeing the cables and wires that were supposed to be invisible.

As soon as the bobbing headlamps started up the hill, Jax melted into his hidden spot behind the immense boulder. He dimmed his computer screen so no one would see the glow, then switched on the muted lighting and tiny spy cam inside the cave. The outside cameras picked up the head of the trail and the conversations. That had been Jax's idea, one he didn't share with Vince, his being able to monitor conversation and make sure no one was getting wise to the imagery.

The young couple with two little boys arrived at the top first, the kids bouncing in place as Vince caught up with them. He put on his best fakey smile—Jax knew Vince thought kids were a giant pain. The two women arrived next—a tall blonde, with a smile that would have grabbed Jax's attention if they'd met in a bar somewhere, and a brunette whose British accent immediately got his attention. He wouldn't mind hooking up with either of these two. But they moved almost out of camera range as the gray-haired couple and two lanky pre-teen girls showed up.

"Okay, everybody," Vince called out. "This is it, the spot

where we discovered, during our *exhaustive* research, that some of the fabled treasure of the Spanish conquistadors has been hidden for hundreds of years." He launched into the backstory, most of which came directly from the brochures they'd hired a Fiverr guy to research and write.

"And now … if everyone is ready … please follow me into the Chamber of Gold!"

Jax winced a little. Vince was always one to change up the script. Chamber of gold, seriously? It was a damn cave, and not a very big one at that. Fifty people would practically be within touching distance of each other in the main room, the only one they planned to show them. It was the reason they'd purposely kept their tour groups small.

He switched his viewer to the interior camera and went into his projectionist mode, flicking on the first of the ghostly images.

"Did you see that?" The grandmother's voice trembled as she pointed toward the spectral image of a Spanish soldier.

The eerie sounds of horses and men echoed off rough stone walls, mingling with gasps and squeals. Vince's tall, dark figure stood at the edge of the scene, guiding their attention, with cool eyes and the precision of a maestro. Behind his boulder, Jax adjusted the settings on the remote projector, sending narrow beams of ghostly light into the central chamber. Before his eyes, the tourists clumped closer together, all eyes fixed on the center of the swirling images of soldiers coming out of the smaller, secondary chamber.

"Don't be scared," Vince called out to them with just the right mixture of confidence and concern. "The conquistadors were trying to protect their treasure, not hurt anyone. What you're seeing is a moment from history!"

One of the little boys tugged at his mother's sleeve, caught up in the excitement. His eyes darted nervously around the stone walls. "Are they real, Mommy?" he whispered, drawing nervous laughter from the group.

Vince took a step into the center of the space, ensuring all eyes were on him. He signaled smoothly to Jax, who was crouched over the equipment and watching the tourists closely. "Some people say the ghosts are still searching for their gold," he said, raising his voice above the echoing hoofbeats that seemed to come from outside the cave. "Look carefully, and maybe you'll see the gold before they do!"

All attention turned to where the haunting forms drifted past walls etched by time. Vince let the tension mount.

"Over there! I saw one!"

Another shriek came, this one more excited, and one of the kids rushed forward, pointing to the stone floor where a gold nugget lay winking in the flickering light. This sent the whole group into frantic motion, scrambling to where he stood. Vince was suddenly among them, offering encouragement and guidance as they searched.

"I knew it was real! We found gold!"

Vince smiled warmly at the woman who made the breathless announcement. "I promised you an adventure," he said with a satisfied grin. The tourists seemed more relaxed, more open to the idea that treasure truly was here somewhere.

One of the teen girls clung to her grandfather's arm. She giggled and looked at her sister. "Can you imagine?"

she said. "A ghost tour and a treasure hunt!"

Vince leaned in close enough for only a few to hear, including the excited teenager and the woman who had called out. "I'll let you in on a secret. There might be more if we look a little closer."

This sparked a renewed flurry of speculation and hope as the tourists spread out to search again. Some were caught up in the dream Vince wove; others seemed skeptical but not completely ready to dismiss the lure of a real find. The youngest child watched as his mother brushed a hand over the cave floor, scuffing the packed dirt and pausing as she touched something unexpected. She knelt and held up her prize.

"Oh my gosh!"

"It's really gold, isn't it?"

Vince spoke loudly enough for the group to hear. "That's not just any gold," he said, injecting a dramatic pause into his announcement. "What you're holding, all of you, are pieces of history. Coins and nuggets like those have been found around here ever since the Spanish first passed through, nearly five hundred years ago. You're seeing actual proof that the legends are true!"

Several in the group clapped and cheered, clutching their finds. Vince's dark eyes glinted in the projector's pale light as the tourists hung on his words, glancing from him to the gold in their hands, dazzled by the tale.

"I'm going to be rich!" a young voice shouted. Jax noticed that the two young women exchanged a skeptical look. But Vince knew tourists, knew they would leave with the seeds of his story planted deep, and when those stories grew and spread, new groups would be back, just as ready to be convinced.

"What if it's haunted?" The boy stepped back, wide-eyed, dropping his coin and taking refuge behind his father's leg. The other young people crowded together, thrilled by the idea of real ghosts.

Vince crouched down, his face level with the boy. "You're safe. Nothing to be afraid of. These ghosts are just like you, looking for gold!"

At his side, the father fingered his coin and frowned, muttering just loudly enough to show his doubt. "Are they, now?"

Vince patted him on the shoulder, speaking with genuine warmth. "Just because you haven't seen it before doesn't mean it isn't real, my friend." He straightened, casting an eye over the full crowd, then sent another nod in Jax's direction.

The noises of snorting horses grew more distinct, sounding as if they were approaching from the nearby mountainside, drawing nearer to the cave. Even the skeptics went silent.

"Another!" The excited shriek came from the other young boy, as he pointed toward the dirt floor.

Some of the other tourists fell quiet as Vince led the family toward the nugget.

"Look, Daddy! It's real gold!"

The father's face broke into a wide grin, and others who had given up resumed their own searches with new enthusiasm. The tall blonde woman lingered at the edge of the group, somehow looking unconvinced.

The young dad grabbed his son and laughed uneasily. "Is that what you wanted, Ryan? Real ghosts?"

The kid struggled free and tugged his mom closer to where Vince stood. His small face held both wonder and dread. Jax, watching on camera, shook his head. Sheesh.

"The horses are almost here!" Vince called out. "We'll have to leave soon!"

Jax's hand moved carefully to the controls, twisting dials raising the volume. Spanish voices shouted out. From the secondary chamber, ghostly figures swarmed, the shadows filled with eerie color and light. Vince kept increasing the intensity of the performance, alive with excitement and warnings.

"I want to get out of here!" The youngest little boy began to cry.

The father reached for his kid's hand and they watched Vince closely, trying to gauge whether he had control of the situation or if the ghosts were now calling the shots.

Vince laughed aloud, a booming sound that carried from wall to wall and mingled with the others. "Don't let them get all the good stuff!" He waved the lagging group back into the fray. "That gold belongs to whoever finds it!"

The older brother gave a squeal of joy, ducking beneath Vince's outstretched arm to scoop up a few specks of gravel. "I found one too!" he shouted, tossing it in the air, revealing nothing.

Jax fiddled with a dial and ran a careful hand across his stubbled chin. More holographic figures burst into the cave entrance, seeming solid and convincing. "Drop the coins! Now!" they ordered.

"We're going to die!" One teenage girl flung her coins down to the ground and threw her arms around her grandfather, eyes squeezed shut as projected figures rose and fell in a ghostly pattern.

Several of the tourists drew close together, shielding themselves behind Vince. "Better do as they say!" he shouted over the cacophony. "This has never happened before. Throw down the coins and I'll lead the way out of here."

The sound of Spanish voices rose to a wail, amplified and wild. People began tossing the gold coins back on the floor.

Now the ghosts loomed larger, men mounted on phantom horses, filling the cave from the second chamber and pushing the humans toward the cave's exit.

"It's too spooky! It's too cool!" The youngest boy was fully invested now, clinging tightly to his nugget.

"I want to get out of here!" wailed the older brother.

"Ryan, do as the soldiers said and drop that nugget." The kids' mother seemed genuinely spooked. She pried the nugget from his little hand and tossed it on the ground.

Vince waved an arm toward the back of the cave, calm in the center of commotion. It was Jax's signal to dim the projector and let the phantom images began to fade, slowly dissipating like smoke.

He looked down at Vince, who was absorbed in the unfolding show, gesturing in the air and watching as the tourists edged toward the exit. At their feet, the gold nuggets that seemed so important a few minutes ago were forgotten.

As the tension reached a fever pitch, Vince announced that he would see that everyone got safely outside, sounding as though he was saving them from something far worse than a ruined vacation. The light thinned, and the echoes fell away. With one hand on a small shoulder and another directing the rest, he coaxed the tourists toward the opening and the freedom of the night.

"Stick close to me and the ghosts won't stand a chance!"

He looked over his shoulder at Jax, who waited at the edge of darkness, hard-eyed and silent.

Jax had one final effect to share, the shapes of ghostly men and horses, racing away into the night. One soldier stood guard at the mouth of the cave, making certain no one had second thoughts about coming back and raking up the coins they'd dropped.

"All right, folks, we're safe," Vince announced, handing out their headlamps. "We've got sodas and water in the van, so let's head back that way. What did you all think?"

Out in the night air most of them laughed and chattered. They'd survived and were excited to get home and tell others about the ghostly apparitions. Jax watched the satisfied group as they put their headlamps back on and hiked back to the van.

Jax slipped from behind the boulder and approached his partner. Vince spun on him, his voice a rasping whisper. "We almost lost them when you cut the bit where the one soldier pulls a sword and acts like he's going to decapitate someone. That was a bad call, buddy."

Jax scowled, keeping his voice low. "Yeah? Only you and I even knew that was supposed to happen. There were little kids in tonight's group." He thought of the elderly man the night before.

"I'm just sayin' don't let it happen again." Vince headed down the trail to meet the group and laugh it up with them on the ride back to town.

Jax shook his head, went back to retrieve his laptop, and waited until he saw the van pull away before he headed down the mountain. When he climbed into Vince's car, he slammed the door a little harder than he intended. How much longer could he pretend to play along?

Chapter 12

Thoughts of the visit to the cave, the special effects, and the pure showmanship of the tour had filled Emily's head and intruded into her bedtime. She couldn't wait to show Francine the gold coin she'd pocketed when the others in the group were tossing theirs on the ground to make the scary horsemen go away.

Practically the minute she got home, she'd scraped an edge of the coin against a brick to see how thick the plating was. Answer: not very thick at all. But the coin was heavy; she was curious what type of base metal they'd used to create them.

She was warming a Sweet's Sweets cranberry muffin for her breakfast when Francine called to say she was following a lead on the whereabouts of Russell Pinkney, Cliff's rival and the man who quite likely convinced Cliff to go off on a wild goose chase without telling anyone. Emily felt a little disappointed that she wouldn't be seeing Francine this morning but countered by offering to make dinner.

"Grandma Valerie had a wonderful marinara sauce recipe. I'll make it." She reached for the butter for her muffin. "And how about if I invite a couple of friends? One is Riki, who took me as her guest on the treasure tour. She might remember some things I didn't catch, and we can fill you in on the adventure."

Francine readily agreed.

By the time Emily opened the library, she actually felt somewhat comforted to have the place to herself for the day. Her task of organizing the collection had fallen somewhat by the wayside, so she pulled a couple of boxes from the shelves and began sorting.

When she went back home for a quick lunch, she decided to start the marinara sauce early. Grandma's method of simmering it for several hours always developed the flavors in an amazing way. She found the recipe and assembled the ingredients. But where was her packet of dried, home-grown oregano?

Emily opened the cluttered kitchen drawer. It had to be there somewhere, jumbled among rubber bands and paper clips and leaky pens she should have thrown out ages ago. A deep breath in, then out. The sauce, heavy on garlic, needed just a little more spice. She opened a second drawer, and a pair of scissors—orange handled—flung itself out of the drawer, landing near her feet.

She muttered a low "what the heck," and bent to pick them up, returning them to the tangle of who-knows-what and spotting the oregano underneath. "Gotcha." Her blonde hair swung forward as she grabbed the little jar and popped open its lid, giving the sauce a fragrant sprinkle. She was so absorbed in her culinary efforts that the voice caught her off guard.

"Don't go *too* heavy with that." She spun around, nearly spilling the jar's contents, and saw a slight shimmer in the doorway, a vague outline that came in and out of focus before it fully materialized. Valerie's ghostly form floated toward her, moving with an airy grace that left trails of wavering color in its wake. Emily set the spoon on the counter.

The air felt cooler. She crossed her arms, pulling the sleeves of her sweater down over her hands. "You startled me, Grandma. I thought you'd let yourself out of the house for a while." Valerie's ghost paused near the table, the delicate colors and forms of her clothing drifting together.

"I was at the library all morning, watching you at work. It's fun, seeing you embrace your grandpa's legacy. You know, that library means so much to our family," the ghost said, in a voice that had become solemn.

"I know." Emily felt a chill along her skin that wasn't entirely due to the temperature drop. She pressed her lips together, a pensive line crossing her forehead. "Something's bothering you, Grandma."

The sauce let out a loud gurgle, and Emily gave it a quick stir and adjusted the burner heat.

"Only what we talked about before," Valerie said, with tender emphasis. "It's important to remember."

Emily hesitated, unsure how to respond. The message was clear, about not giving away too much of the family's personal legacy. She rubbed her hand over her arm, noticing the rise of goosebumps, then moved back to the stove and gave the sauce another stir. Finding a balance between the living world and the legacy of the dead was proving more challenging than she'd ever imagined.

Emily turned, touched her turquoise pendant, and gave her grandmother a tender smile. "I'll find a way to make everything fit, and I won't give away any deep, dark family secrets. You know that." Her words hung in the air with a hint of defiance, and she really hadn't meant it that way.

Valerie's ghost began to fade, colors growing less distinct until they merged with the kitchen light. With a quick shake of her head and a sigh, Emily's thoughts returned once more to the ordinary.

She spent the rest of the afternoon sorting papers at her kitchen table and monitoring the sauce. A bottle of wine was open, breathing on the countertop. Jen said she would bring dessert from the bakery, and Riki hinted that she had a surprise of some kind. Emily wondered if it was one of the gold nuggets from their cave adventure.

The tinkle of wind chimes caught on a breeze through the open window, and Emily rose to see Francine's car pulling to a stop beyond the courtyard gate.

Francine walked in through the kitchen door, setting a fragrant loaf of garlic bread on the counter. "I can't wait to hear your impressions of the tour last night." She gave Emily a puzzled look. "Is that what the sour expression is all about?"

Emily let out a laugh. "I actually hadn't thought much about it today. Between sorting through that box…" She pointed toward the window seat across the room. "…and having my grandmother's voice in my head, I guess that accounts for it."

"Thank goodness it's just her voice." Francine pulled

off her leather jacket and gave her a quick hug.

Emily gave a half-hearted chuckle. Valerie's presence was definitely one of those family secrets to be kept to herself. "Right. Well, we can talk while I work." She went to the sink to fill a pot with water for the pasta and pointed Francine toward the drawer for silverware and the cupboard where the plates were kept. "Anyway, I'm really glad you're here and can't wait to hear what you learned about that Pinkney guy."

She gestured toward a chair, offering Francine the chance to settle in for the telling of the saga. She turned on the burner under the water, then gave the sauce another stir, turning the stove's heat down to its lowest setting to keep it simmering.

"So, Russell Pinkney. Disappointing day. I almost think he's deliberately trying to avoid me and my questions about Cliff. It wouldn't surprise me to learn that he'd sent Cliff off on some wild goose chase, maybe even out of state."

"Do you think someone in his department warned him that we called and asked about him?"

Francine shrugged. "No clue. But I won't give up." She pinched a piece off the garlic loaf as Emily spread the slices on a baking sheet to warm them. "And your grandmother's voice? Giving advice or bringing up memories?"

How was Emily to answer that question—admit that Valerie sounded a bit disappointed in her? And so sure. She pushed up the sleeves of her soft gray sweater, full of frustrated energy. "There's just so much to handle."

"Now there's a surprise. You've only been going at a hundred miles an hour since, what, birth? Okay, at least since I've met you." Francine's tone was kind but straightforward. "You'll sort it out. It's probably what you always do."

Emily gave a rueful laugh, knowing she wasn't about to slow down. "You make it sound so easy." Emily was starting to feel better. "Maybe I should just follow your lead. You've got this thing down."

The banter lightened Emily's mood further. The laughter between them was a kind of relief, an antidote to Valerie's recent and unusual seriousness. She moved toward the wine bottle and the glasses she'd set out. Her questioning glance brought a nod from her guest.

"I'm thinking about sneaking off to someplace with a beach, where I can dig in the sand instead of through archives." Emily poured two glasses and then crossed back to the stove and gave the thick sauce a taste. Perfect.

"See, this is why I show up when I do." Francine grinned as they clinked their glasses together. "So, tell me about the tour?"

"Let's wait until Riki and Jen get here," Emily said, savoring the mild exasperation on Francine's face. "Riki might remember things a little differently than I do, or she may have seen different details."

"Pleasure before business. And that sauce smells fantastic."

Emily's phone pinged with a text. "They're on the way. Five minutes, tops." She stuck the phone in her pocket and felt a metallic little clink. "Ooh, I nearly forgot. I nabbed something from the show last night." She dropped the gold coin onto Francine's palm.

"Impressive." Francine weighed the piece gingerly. "It can't be real, of course."

"No way." Emily showed her the spot where she'd rubbed off the plating. "But it would be interesting to know what the base metal is, and if we could find out where they had these manufactured."

"Can I take it? Do a little further research? I know someone who's in the emblem business. They might be able to tell us something."

"I'd like to hear what you learn."

Headlights swept across the courtyard as two vehicles parked out front. Emily slid the sheet of garlic bread into the oven and dropped the pasta in the pot of boiling water. Jen carried a purple bakery box, which contained one of Samantha's famous amaretto cheesecakes. Riki had brought the salad and a second bottle of wine. The room filled with lighthearted chatter.

As Riki poured more wine, she proceeded with a dramatic version of the tour to the cave, highlighting the blatant way the host had encouraged people to discover the gold coins, then conjured a scary moment designed to make them throw down their finds, in the name of not bringing bad luck.

"Didn't stop our Em, now did it?" Riki raised an eyebrow and directed her stare toward the coin Francine had left on the table.

"Yeah, busted. We're going to have it tested or appraised, or something."

Emily checked the pasta and the toast, enjoying the warmth of the stove beside her. She was glad to have friends who could help her see the funny side, and happy to share it all without too much seriousness.

While they filled their plates and took seats at the kitchen table, the banter brought a welcome lightness to the room, and the aroma of dinner filled the space as the four women joked about treasures, both historical and fake.

"I'll tell you what," Emily said, pretending to consider a brilliant scheme. "I'll get the next round of tickets and you can all catch the Hutchins ghost tour next time."

In the back of her mind were Grandma Valerie's words, but what were a few more things to juggle?

Her laugh mingled with the others as she took another sip of her wine. She felt more in control, more sure of her own pace. Valerie's warning was still there, lingering like the soft notes of distant music, but Francine's visit had shifted her back toward the living world.

When the plates were cleared and the cheesecake sliced and served, Riki stood and tapped her glass with a spoon. "As the evening winds down, I wanted to, first, thank our lovely hostess." Polite applause. "And secondly, to let you know I've a gift for you, Em."

Emily's expression grew puzzled, especially when Riki walked outside into the cool evening air and went to her car. She came back in less than a minute, carrying a vented crate.

"Don't worry. The evening is cool and I left windows cracked open. This little beauty was wandering outside my shop, properly freaked out by all the dogs. But somehow, it seemed to know I would rescue it." From the crate came a plaintive *mrrwowww*.

"A cat? You've brought me a cat?"

Riki handed the crate over, and Emily saw a sleek black body and vivid golden eyes peering out at her. She also caught sight of a swish of translucent skirts just beyond the doorway to the living room. There was more to this story than a stray cat.

Chapter 13

Jax's stomach churned as he walked into the office, fairly certain Vince was out but wanting to make sure. For days now, ever since the tours began, he'd been suspicious of the way Vince reported the money. Peering into each of the storage rooms, Vince's office, and the lobby where the tourists gathered, he satisfied himself that he was alone.

This might be his only chance to learn what he needed to know. Vince was notoriously cautious with his records, especially the ledger. He'd never leave it in his hotel room, and if he really had gone to a spa for a massage right after tonight's tour, he surely wouldn't trust enough to put it in a locker there. It must be here, among the clutter of his office.

Jax leaned over Vince's chaotic desk. Papers littered the surface, haphazardly piled and mixed with empty coffee cups and an abandoned briefcase. He had once admired Vince's flair for disarray, mistaking it for creative brilliance. Now it seemed to point to something far less innocent.

The miscellaneous papers were all for show. Somewhere in this place was the "ledger" a notebook that fit into a coat pocket. He'd seen Vince writing in it once, and when he teased his partner about the old-fashioned bookkeeping method, Vince gave him one of those deadly looks. Computers were there for hacking, he explained. Text messages could be traced. With paper, all you needed was a match, and you could be rid of the evidence in minutes. Right. And if the IRS or somebody came bursting in here, what would Vince do—light a fire? Or start ripping up papers and sticking them in his mouth?

Anyway, that wasn't his purpose here right now. He wanted to know how much Vince had really brought in. It was easy enough to calculate the income from the nightly tours; fifty bucks a head, ten people riding in the van. Although when it came time to divvy up the cash, Vince always shorted him, with the reasoning that he charged less for kids. And sometimes he gave away tickets to someone he thought might be an important investor.

That was the question in Jax's mind right now. Where were these whales, the investors Vince bought drinks for in the fancy hotels, the ones he dazzled with his PowerPoint presentations? The irony was not lost on him: computers were useful for some things.

He came to a locked drawer and his heart beat a little quicker. It didn't take an ex-military man long to jimmy the lock with the tool he kept on his keychain. He pulled out the notebook, keeping ears tuned to both the back and front doors.

He rifled through the pages, quickly flipping and studying the lines of handwritten notes. A deep-set frown creased his forehead as he studied the rows of numbers. The totals didn't match; figures were rounded up or down without any pattern that made sense. Jax began to wonder how he'd been so blind.

Vince was always the charmer, so confident in his schemes. "People want to be fooled, Jax," he remembered Vince saying, that knowing smile tugging at his lips. He'd once admired Vince's persuasive draw, but the slick talk did nothing to quell his unease now. He felt like the one who'd been fooled.

As he flipped to the next page, a stray paper fell loose and landed by his foot. It looked like a receipt, and it came from a place Jax had never heard of, another sign of deceit. Jax crouched to retrieve it, his gaze flicking around the room, a soldier aware he might be ambushed.

He wondered just how deep Vince's plans ran, if the whole treasure investment scheme was really worth anything at all. His thoughts darted back to when Vince had suggested they bring a few others on board, just until the gold came in. Was he talking about the high-roller investors? Or someone else? Were those others part of this, or was Jax the only fool left? He glanced back at the scrawled numbers, knowing he should confront Vince and ask more questions, but he had to admit he was nervous about it.

He knew he needed more information to force Vince's hand if it came to that. Vince never responded well to pressure, not unless he was the one applying it. And he would simply laugh it off if Jax brought up the subject without proof.

Deeper in the drawer, he discovered what must be Vince's business ledger, a somewhat larger notebook he'd never seen before. Names, numbers, addresses, and dollar amounts. Outlines of plans that had not yet materialized. They revealed much more than a simple con; they showed an escape route, carefully plotted and ready to implement. Jax took in every scribbled number with a sense of disbelief, half expecting Vince to jump from the shadows and call it a test of his loyalty.

Jax held the book open to a page with recent entries, pulled out his phone, and opened the camera app. A sound, from the direction of the front door, grabbed his attention. He peered around the doorframe. It was the Ferrari. Shit!

Jax switched off the overhead light, slammed the book shut, and jammed the two notebooks back into the drawer, fumbling by the light of his phone in his attempt to relock it. Vince was at the front door now, fiddling with his keyring. There would be no innocent explanation for the unlocked drawer.

Jax felt his blood run cold. And then the drawer lock clicked into place. He gave a quick scan over the surrounding mess, making certain every scrap of paper, every cup, every pen were exactly as he'd found them. Slipping his phone into his pocket, Jax slipped out the back door, relocked it, and speed-walked to the van.

Lights went on inside the building, but at this point he could just laugh it off—hey, man, I didn't know you were stopping by. But the back door remained closed. Vince must have discovered that you can't just pop up at a nice spa, hoping to get a massage late in the evening without an appointment.

He'd opened the van door when movement caught

his attention. A man in a dark suit peeled away from the shadows and closed in. Jax felt the hairs rise on his neck.

"Your treasure hunt scheme is under investigation," he said, tapping a badge at his waist and flicking a business card into Jax's hand. "You'll be in less trouble if you help us collect evidence against Vince Hutchins."

Jax stared at the man, his presence unexpected, sharp, and utterly composed. The agent—if that's what he really was—wore a look of utter confidence. The words left no room for doubt or negotiation. His sudden presence made Jax feel off-balance, especially since Vince was inside the office now. There were no windows on this side of the building, but Vince could walk out that door at any moment.

Jax's jaw tightened, his instincts flaring, but he steadied himself and met the man's steady gaze. He wanted to run, wanted to argue, or simply to punch the guy out. But this was a time when silence would be the better weapon.

"You can come with me now, help us out here, or you can sweat for a while. But you can't run. We're watching everything the two of you are doing."

Jax looked at the card: Steve Price, FBI. He wondered if the man's statement could be true. How many agents could the government spare, just to watch what had to be a small-time con.

The agent's gaze was confident. "I'll be in touch," he added, his voice like a low electrical current. He turned without another word and walked away, vanishing around the corner of the building, heading toward the street.

Jax stood motionless, the business card pinched between his thumb and forefinger, the whole exchange leaving a strange, metallic taste in his mouth. He read the card again, the implications unfurling in his mind. It was one thing to suspect Vince might be trying to cheat him out of his share, but this was different. This was real, a threat he could not ignore.

He looked around, half expecting another agent—or worse, for Vince to walk out the back door—but there were only the clouds moving across the sky to cover the moon, the normal swish of traffic on the street, as he stood there, trying to collect his thoughts.

The meeting had been brief, efficient, and threatening. He debated what to do: Tell Vince about this and risk Vince bolting, leaving Jax to take the fall. He imagined how Vince would initially react, the smug dismissal, the dangerous charm. But the idea of Vince abandoning Jax to take the heat—that could happen.

Helping the FBI meant turning against Vince, giving up all hope of getting his payout. Not helping meant something much worse. Jax had seen enough to know the repercussions of either choice. He let out a breath he hadn't realized he was holding. The certainty he'd felt earlier began to erode, the ground shifting beneath his feet in the wake of the encounter. Every option felt like a trap.

He flicked the card with his finger, a fidget of nerves that contradicted his usually steady demeanor. Why had the feds chosen to approach him? Because they saw him as the weak link in the chain. For a moment, the basic instinct, the one that had kept him alive through military campaigns and Vince's games, told him to run. But the new instinct, the one forged from doubts and shifting alliances, told him to think. Hard.

Jax knew the agent would be back. He knew Vince's con was unraveling more rapidly than any of them had imagined. And he knew one more thing, as sure as he knew his own name: the choice he made in the coming days would set the path for everything. Jax slipped the card into the deepest pocket in his jacket and climbed into the van, his thoughts echoing the agent's chilling promise. His time was running out, and he still needed to figure out what to do about the situation with that old professor dude.

Chapter 14

"So, kitty cat, what now?" Emily let the newcomer out of its crate as her dinner guests left. Well, the evening had been winding down anyway. "How did Riki know I'd been thinking about a cat recently?"

"And how did your friend know about this particular one?" Valerie appeared, with a swish of skirts, a clatter of beads, and the attendant cloud of chill air.

If Emily felt unsure about how the new cat would react to the presence of a ghost, she was in for a surprise. The sleek black cat blinked its gold eyes once, then stood and sauntered over, rubbing against Valerie's legs.

"How—? What? How did this animal actually touch you? You're ..."

"Ephemeral?"

"Yeah, I guess that's it. I mean, I can't touch you, so

how does it—"

"She. Moonbeam is a she."

"You know this cat?" Emily felt like she'd better sit down. "Grandma, please tell me what's going on."

Valerie drifted into the living room, with Moonbeam right behind. Emily trailed along, picking up her tea mug on the way. She settled into a corner of the sofa. The cat jumped up beside her.

"Emily, meet Moonbeam. Moonbeam, meet Emily—you knew her when she was a little girl, but now I'm guessing she doesn't remember that."

Emily shook her head, bewildered. "Give me the condensed version. I feel like my head's going to explode."

"Very well. Your grandfather and I got this black kitten a number of years ago. As I said, you must have just been a little thing at the time. I wanted to name her Moonshadow—I was a huge Cat Stevens fan—but David laughed. A *Cat* Stevens lyric for a real cat … he wouldn't have it. So, she became Moon*beam*." Valerie's shape had perched on the arm of an overstuffed chair. She gave a one-shoulder shrug. "In marriage, they say to choose your battles wisely."

"Grandma, that cannot be all there is. The cat would have to be more than twenty-five years old now."

"Hmm, I suppose that's true." Valerie met the cat's gaze and spoke to her again. "Moonbeam, I'm guessing you've gone through a few of your nine lives since we last spent time together?"

Mrroww.

"How many?"

The cat stretched forward and kneaded the sofa cushion—left paw, right paw, left, right.

"Four? So, you only have five lives left?"

Mrroww.

"That explains it." Valerie rose from the chair and drifted toward the door.

"Wait! There has to be more."

"Well, of course there is. You'll need to get her a litter box and some food. She likes tuna best. And she's a great mouser. Your grandfather wasn't a cat person, but he quickly realized the benefit of having a cat in the library. All that old paper, you know. Mice chew on it. Moonbeam will take care of them, won't you, darling?"

Mrroww.

"Oh. She also seems to have quite an ability to connect with ghosts." And with that, Valerie's image vanished.

"Ghosts. And mice. What else am I going to learn about you?" Emily took a sip of her tea, which had gone tepid.

Moonbeam walked over to her lap, settled down, and began to purr.

By the next morning the cat had become her shadow. Twice, Emily nearly tripped over her when she turned quickly and headed in a new direction. "Look, you can't follow my every step. If I say I'll be right back, trust me, I will." She reached down and stroked the silky spine and tail, Moonbeam arching her back and purring even louder. "Okay, the routine is that I always work in the library right after breakfast. You coming?"

She didn't need to offer the invitation twice.

Within an hour, Moonbeam had cleared a spot for herself on the reference desk, pushing away papers she deemed unworthy of the space. Emily shuffled everything and laid a towel down as a little nest. The high perch allowed the cat to monitor the room as she twitched her ears and raised an eyelid now and then.

"Okay, I have work to do. You know where your bowls are and your litterbox, back there in the bathroom."

Emily realized she shouldn't have been quite so astounded when Grandma told her about the cat having been here before. Once she started poking around, she'd found all the supplies she would need, tucked away at the back of the bathroom vanity. At some point during the day, she would duck out to get food so she didn't have to share her own tuna with her new companion.

She started up the narrow back stairs, planning to organize the books she and Francine had looked through the other day. Before Emily climbed half the distance, Moonbeam was waiting at the top.

"Smarty." She opened the door and the black cat immediately ran to the table and jumped up.

A bright rectangle of light crept across the floor, where dust motes fluttered like glitter in the angled autumn sun, illuminating some tiny dots in the corner of the floor. Mouse droppings. Why had she never spotted these before? And now, just when Grandma had cautioned her about damage to the books?

"Moonbeam, look at these. Taking care of this problem is your job now."

The cat looked up, stretched her neck, and blinked lazily.

"I mean it." Emily grabbed the broom and dustpan. "I'm sweeping these up and I don't want to find any more."

Mrroww.

"Okay then."

Task completed, Emily turned back to the table and reached for the slender tome with the stories of the

Spanish conquerors who'd traveled northward from Mexico. She would take that one home with her tonight; if memory served, there was a chapter in it that Francine was interested in.

The hush around her deepened, disturbed only by the occasional creak of the old wood and the rustle of autumn leaves against the window. Even in the middle of the day, the quiet of the library gave the building a timeless feel, and she almost expected to see her grandfather stride around a corner, nodding in approval at her efforts. She stacked more books and folders on a nearby cart, making a mental note to double-check the borrower records, and lifted a heavy tome on the Spanish Inquisition.

She moved with familiarity, sidestepping a short ladder and sliding a few books into place on the shelves. And then she caught movement from the corner of her eye. Moonbeam was batting at the slim book Emily had left on the table, pushing it toward the edge.

"No, no, no, no, no!" But the book fell anyway. Emily dashed for it, and barely caught it before it would have hit the floor. "I guess I'm lucky this is still in one piece," she murmured, giving it a new, more secure spot. As she shifted it from one hand to the other, a sheet of paper fell to the floor, its ancient parchment almost transparent in the light.

It was torn and fragile, with ragged edges and delicate, uneven lines across its almost translucent surface. Emily's breath caught. She slipped on a pair of gloves then knelt to pick it up. Smoothing the paper against the polished surface of the table, she stared at the ink's faded outlines. Rivers, valleys, peaks of mountains emerged as she studied it. A hint of something wonderful coursed through her veins, and she looked more closely at the date. 1549.

Moonbeam approached and carefully laid a paw on a particular spot, just inches from the edge of the map fragment.

Emily's eyes darted over the familiar names. Sangre de Cristo. Valle de Oro. Arroyo Seco. They were blurred, smeared by the passage of time, but unmistakable in meaning. This was the region where she'd been for the tour, the place where the cave with the fake treasures was. But had this place once contained real treasure?

"Moonbeam, how did you know?"

The golden eyes blinked once.

Her hand trembled slightly as she lifted the fragment, holding it up to the light to see what else it might reveal. This map itself was a treasure, and Emily knew exactly who she needed to share it with. She pulled her phone from her pocket.

"Francine? I've found something—" She caught Moonbeam's steady stare. "So, actually, the cat and I found something, just now. It's an old map, really incredible."

She could hear papers rustling in the background.

"Your hotel? Sure. I'll head right over." She ended the call to find the cat watching her. "I'll be right back. You take care of those mice."

She carefully slipped the fragile parchment into a protective sleeve, then moved quickly down the stairs.

Chapter 15

Ten minutes later, Emily rushed down the hotel's narrow corridor, clutching the historic map fragment in its wrapper, growing more excited to share the find. She paused in front of Francine's door and tugged down her sleeves, which carried the crisp scents of autumn. In the moments before she knocked, Emily thought she heard voices inside the room and hesitated. But the professor was expecting her; she raised her hand to knock.

The door opened just as her knuckles touched the wood. Francine stood on the other side, taking in Emily's breathless state and beaming. She gave Emily a quick hug as she entered the room. "You said you found something?"

Emily held up the envelope containing the map. "It slipped out of a book," she said, savoring the chance to share the incredible find.

Francine's eyes widened. "Come in, come in" she said, pulling Emily deeper into the modest room and switching off the TV.

Emily glanced at the piles of papers and books that filled the space. The hotel room was small, with only one bed and a dresser in addition to the chair and table where Francine had spread out her materials. Emily laughed at the transformation of the petite quarters into a busy command center. She set the map on the crowded table, careful of the fragile edges within the protective sleeve.

Francine glanced from Emily to the map and back. "This looks like only part of the map, the way it's torn here, with some of the words cut off."

"Yes, I noticed that."

Francine gestured toward a stack of paper on her desk. "These are Cliff's papers that his daughter left for me. Everything he worked on in the months before he left. Tons of notes he wrote in his own brand of shorthand."

Emily took in the oddball scratchings on some of the pages.

"I've been going through them, and I'm fairly sure some of the materials are on loan from the university archives. Luckily, he didn't mark those up."

Her face glowed, and Emily grinned in response. "Looks like you've made progress."

"Cliff had said something about a map, before he left Albuquerque. He wanted to investigate. I had my suspicions then, but wasn't certain what might be involved. Now that we know about Vince Hutchins, I'm sure Cliff is on the trail."

Francine opened a long, flat envelope and slipped out two sheets, laying them alongside Emily's discovery. "Here's the thing I wanted you to see."

Emily stared. One of the sheets was a torn fragment of a map. "This is a find," she said, holding it carefully and studying it in the light.

"I've seen a lot of these maps and not many this old. From Cliff's papers, it looks like he'd never seen anything like it either."

Emily sat at the table and lifted another, larger map. "You're right," she said. She spread the second map and positioned it with the one she'd brought, aligning the rough edges and trying to make them fit. "It doesn't match completely. It's close, but there's still a section missing." She traced lines with her fingertip.

Francine stood next to her, nodding, her dark bun coming loose. She stared at the two fragments, the gears of her mind visibly turning. She looked like someone on the edge of a breakthrough and nodded. "I bet he had yet another piece," she said. "This part—the one you found—was probably overlooked."

Emily felt as if a rock had settled in her stomach. "Or not. I just realized that the book this map was stashed in … it was one Cliff had borrowed from the library and returned. I'm sure of it."

"What—"

"It would be the perfect way to keep a competitor from getting hold of both pieces of the map, wouldn't it?"

"Competitor? Such as Russell Pinkney?"

"Or these commercial tour operators. Vince Hutchins is turning the treasure hunt into a show. He could be planning to take it really bigtime, maybe something for cable, with lots of explosions and very little history."

"Oh, God, no. You can imagine how that would make Cliff feel." Her voice was tense.

Emily nodded, knowing how both professors' passion for accuracy collided with Vince's flair for exaggeration.

"That's why Vince went public with this so quickly," Francine said. "To get all the attention and make it sound like there's a pot of gold around every corner."

Emily thought about it and lifted her eyes from the papers, tucking a strand of hair behind her ear. "There's still one detail that bothers me," she said. "With all this publicity, I'd think that Vince would be bringing forward his academic contacts—Cliff, or even Pinkney. He would relish having someone with authentic credentials to give credence to his claims, right?"

Francine's gaze was intense. "And yet, we still haven't heard a word. Cliff's not one to let people stand in his way. If he got on the scent, he might have left Taos to chase it down before anyone else could." Her expression changed, and Emily saw fear beneath the surface. "I suppose the same could be said about Russell Pinkney, though."

Emily took a deep breath and studied the jumble of papers again. Her attention shifted to a set of documents with blurred reproductions of another map. "Look at these," she said. "This image is different, but it's still old. And the layout seems to be the same as the one we've got. I'll bet Cliff knew what he was looking for. It makes sense as his reason for coming up here to look around."

As Emily watched, Francine pulled more papers into a rough order, thinking how each piece of information brought them closer to their goal. And, although she didn't really expect to find them among Cliff's Albuquerque paperwork, she kept her eyes trained on the materials, hoping her missing book and the old map in its storage tube, would be here somewhere.

"If we're careful, maybe we'll see something everyone else missed." Francine placed documents in neat stacks.

"And you're positive the other map fragment didn't show up anywhere else?" Emily asked, indicating the documents on the table.

Francine shook her head. "Nothing so far," she replied. "If Cliff found it, he didn't make it known. And I'm sure he would have, even if only to outfox Pinkney."

"Or maybe he's staying quiet because of Vince. Do we know for a fact that Cliff and Vince ever made contact? He did leave town about the time the Treasure Tours outfit arrived—I think. I don't mean it's good that he's not around, but he could have something important and doesn't want Vince to know. You're sure this was everything he was working on?" She gestured to the documents on the table.

"I'm not at all sure. His daughter said this was all she found at his home. But Cliff was also careful enough not to take chances with some of his stronger leads. That missing fragment—" She nodded toward the pieced-together map. "—he could be holding it back. Maybe in his office at the university."

She returned her attention to the documents, hands on hips, staring at the map. "I still suspect a showdown with Vince is unavoidable. If Vince—or Pinkney—has another piece of this, I need to stop him before he begins spinning Cliff's work into more treasure-hunting nonsense. We should divide the search," Francine said.

Emily took a flash-free picture of the pieces. "I can look for more fragments back at the library."

Francine nodded. "Then I'll keep working on this. I don't want to tip our hand, but if we haven't found him in a day or two, I'll go talk to Vince. Maybe he'll let something slip. With any luck, we won't need to confront him."

Emily gathered her things, trying not to lose track of the delicate find amid Francine's mass of information. She felt more energized than ever, eager to get back to the library to see what more she could learn.

Francine moved quickly, too, seeing Emily to the door. "Thank you. You've been a great help with everything."

Emily paused at the doorway and smiled back at her friend. "Wouldn't miss this for the world," she said, one hand on the doorknob and the other on the fresh treasure they'd uncovered. "I'll find something at the library. And if I don't, at least we'll know what to do next."

* * *

Emily's thoughts buzzed as she left the supermarket, where she'd remembered to stock up on cat food. She guided her Jeep through the winding streets, past the plaza, and back toward the library. She knew next to nothing about this other professor, Pinkney, who seemed to be in some sort of academic competition for, what, bragging rights? If she found the extra time, she might try an online search. Otherwise, she would leave it up to Francine to make the connections, whatever those might be.

But Vince Hutchins was at least a little bit familiar to her. After the tour she'd taken with Riki, she'd seen the pure showmanship in his act. Turning history into a sideshow grated against her, against everything her family had stood for.

So, how had Vince known where to locate the tours? It couldn't be pure coincidence that this cave was so close to the place marked on the old map. Had Vince seen the map? Had he somehow threatened Cliff, and that was why the professor stuck the map into the book and returned it to the library?

The thought bothered her. If this Vince guy was trying to hook major investors, he might figure it out and come back for the map, knowing that those people would want something authentic, not just a slick brochure with copies of made-up information.

She parked in her usual spot, on the east side of the library, and let herself into the courtyard, intending to make a sandwich before heading back to the work at hand. In the kitchen, she set aside the grocery bag with the cat food, washed up, and assembled a quick lunch for herself.

Grabbing what she needed, she locked up the house. "I'm being jittery," she teased herself, knowing that locking doors in Taos was something she'd rarely done before. She crossed the courtyard and let herself into the library.

"Moonbeam, I've got something for you." She rattled the sack with the cat food in it and the black feline came running. "Okay, you have your lunch and I'll have mine."

Emily settled at the reference desk, checking phone messages and emails while she nibbled at her sandwich. One of her regular patrons wanted to stop by on Tuesday, so she called him back and set an appointment time. She could pull the books he wanted and have everything ready for him.

Her eyes traveled to the antique desk in the corner; one normally used as a place to stack items she was ready to shelve. The top of the desk was clear but for one item, an old diary lying open. Had she left it that way? She would have sworn she hadn't. She glanced up at the front door, but could tell the deadbolt was secure.

Had someone been in here? She glanced at the cat, who was now sitting on a chair near the window, licking a paw and washing her face.

Okay, this cat was talented. She could knock a book off a table. But could she pick one up, place it on a desk and open it to a particular page? Surely not. *Really, Em, surely not!*

Emily crossed to the desk and picked up the book. The diary's pages held descriptions done in words and sketches of men—soldiers, perhaps—with inked armor and worn lines.

"This looks familiar," she murmured, sitting down. She leaned in, absorbing the contents with an intense focus, reading aloud selected passages in a low, deliberate voice. "The ghosts of those who came before us ..." she read, trailing off into a moment of reflection. There was something here, something that reached beyond the pages and ink. It was a whisper from the past, calling her to pay attention.

She paged to the beginning of the book, hoping to discover who had written it. The name on the flyleaf had faded to near-invisibility.

An abrupt chill in the room announced the appearance of Valerie. Moonbeam alerted to the ghostly presence and scampered over to greet her former human.

"Grandma, what do you make of this?" Emily asked, her voice catching slightly. The diary lay open between them, revealing the faded lines, the words that demanded preservation. Emily turned to one of the pages filled with sketches of soldiers and depictions of heavy chests filled to the brim.

"Hmm, I'm intrigued." Valerie looked up, meeting

Emily's eyes. "I think it's real," she said finally, her words thoughtful. "Or at least, real to the person who wrote it."

Emily nodded. "It sounds like the same kind of legend that drives the Treasure Tours stories," she said, her expression somewhat skeptical. "But this is much older, much more personal." Her eyes returned to the diary, reviewing the lines with renewed interest. "And I trust this writer more than I trust Vince Hutchins."

"Accurate or not, the book is definitely old, and it's compelling," Valerie said, breaking the silence. "And if your great-great-grandfather believed it, there may be more to it than legend."

"So, you think Morton Plankhurst was the author?"

But Valerie had done her disappearing act, once again.

Chapter 16

The white van sat at an angle in front of the Treasure Tours office. It was only a little after nine p.m., but Jax was totally on edge as the last of the customers got into their own vehicles and drove away. He'd felt sure they would have to bring an ambulance out to the site tonight when that dude freaked out and grabbed his chest.

Vince had handled it smoothly, driving the couple to the hospital in his own car, leaving Jax to deliver the others back here and send them off with reassurances and a smile. Two of them had demanded their money back; Jax had no choice but to agree to it.

He strode into the messy back room and paused, irritated by the sight of a carton filled with discarded flyers, their corners dog-eared, their promises unfulfilled. They might as well say "cursed."

The storage room looked like a junk shop. Not even yesterday had it been this bad. Vince must have been in here, looking for something. Piles of treasure maps, stacks of full-color pamphlets and forms, all lay scattered. It wasn't as if the room was ever neat to start with. Jax tossed the flyer down. The more he got the runaround from his partner, the more apprehensive he became about getting stuck with nothing, about Vince heading out and leaving him with a giant box of "Sorry, we're closed."

Jax stared at the clutter and rubbed a hand over his bristled head. Vince kept wanting the special effects to be scarier. Tonight wasn't the first time some of the tourists felt they'd barely escaped with their lives. This was really getting stupid. The whole thing could implode if someone decided to start looking too hard, like that old dude, the professor, had. He glanced down again, read the promises of "Gold!" and "Legendary Treasures!" and gave the tattered box a kick.

He heard Vince call his name from the front of the building.

Jax followed the hall toward the front, his steps growing heavy as he drew near. It was one thing to know that he was getting played, another to sit back and do nothing. He clenched his fists, and then relaxed them. Be calm. The thought of bailing out, himself, came up again, this time stronger than ever.

But he'd never been that close to money like this before. Maybe just a little longer. Vince's luck had to come through sometime.

Jax was almost to the open office door when Vince came out, whistling as he balanced a stack of glossy maps under one arm and struggled to open a long plastic tube of posters with his free hand. When he spotted Jax, the glossy pages fell to the floor. "Scare you too?" he said, smirking.

Jax scowled. "How'd it go at the hospital? The man going to be okay?"

"I guess. Didn't hang around to find out. I just walked 'em in, saw to it that the medical staff knew they were there, and slipped out."

"This kind of thing is going to come back to bite you, you know."

Vince brushed him off. "It's running like clockwork, running like clockwork."

Jax knew better. The nosy questions weren't as easy to shrug off as Vince thought, and neither was the scared tour group. Jax didn't see how Vince thought he could continue to pull it off, with half of Taos talking about it, the Treasure Tours office taking calls from cops and news people, the constant rumors about "hauntings" and gold, and how Vince promised the investors they would make huge profits.

Jax grabbed one of the fallen maps from the floor. The Treasure Tours name shouted back at him, red on gold. "Come to the land of El Dorado," they read. He crumpled it up, tossed it aside.

"What?" Vince said, laughing like they were in on the same joke. "You think that professor's woman is catching up with us? She got you as spooked as the tourists last night?"

"Tonight, that group was a mess. You might want to get a story straight before it all hits the fan." He stacked a handful of glossy treasure maps on the desk, but they scattered in a dozen directions. "The hospital staff might report it; the news people will be around asking questions.

Got too close on that one, man."

"They love it, Jax. All that crazy haunted treasure crap? People can't get enough. This bunch is spreading the word even faster." Vince shook his head and started laughing again, low and sure of himself. He pulled a fresh poster from his plastic tube. "If you're scared of ghosts, take a night off."

Jax fixed him with a hard stare. "What about the big money, these investors you're talking to?"

"What about 'em?"

"When are they coming through for us? Like, when are we actually going to see all this money?"

Vince couldn't quite meet his eyes. "Yeah, well. That California couple backed out, but I'm meeting with some venture capitalists. Actually—" He made a point of looking at his watch. "—I gotta get going for a meeting real soon."

Vince handed over the posters and brochures. "Here, get these put up. Replace those ratty ones."

Jax let Vince see that he wasn't laughing, that he wasn't going to be strung along for much longer. He shifted his stance and kept his face firm.

Vince had a look of someone ready to play their favorite trick. And Jax was starting to feel more than ever like a sucker. He moved into the back office. Vince followed, trying to tease his way out of admitting that anything wasn't working as it should, all smiles and stupid jokes. All acting like Jax had to be as blind and clueless as the tourists. Jax went to the small refrigerator against the wall and took a beer from it.

"We've been here before, Jax," Vince said. "Old pros like us? Come on. Not our first ghost story. Remember Arizona and the Lost Dutchman? We made it work there.

Here too." He flopped into his chair, leaned back, put his feet on the desk. "Don't let one scared group of whiners get to you."

Jax twisted the cap from the bottle. He leaned against the wall, deciding how far he could go. Vince looked too calm, like he had it all wrapped up. That was the worst part, when Vince thought he was ahead of everyone else. Didn't matter what the story was. Things always got so he thought the rules didn't apply. A crazy risk this time, though.

"What about Cliff?" Jax said. "What if that lady colleague of his goes to the cops? There's only so much explaining you can do before—"

Vince shot him a warning look. He dropped his feet from the desk and sat up. "You worry too much, my man. You've got no faith in your partner."

Jax gave him a tight-lipped grin. "One of us has to." He decided to keep pushing, see if Vince would show any sign of knowing what kind of peril they were really in.

All it would take was Dr. Morales going to the law, taking her story public, asking too many questions. Somebody in this town would have seen them together, him and the old guy. Jax took a sip of the beer, swallowed hard, didn't let his expression change.

"You've been careless with partners before," he said. "Don't expect this one to sit around and watch it fall apart."

"Was that a threat, Jax?"

Jax took a step back and held up both hands. "No, man. I'm just thinkin' we need an exit strategy and the exit oughta be happening soon."

Vince nodded, gave Jax a condescending look, like a kid would give a slow parent. "Everything's under control," Vince said. "Don't I always make it work?"

Jax remained quiet, fixing him with a steady stare.

Vince laughed, but this time it was louder, more forced. "Get a little faith, will you?" He stood up from his chair, slapped Jax on the shoulder as he walked past. "Got to keep a secret or two, or it won't be a surprise. Remember when—"

"I remember." Jax cut him off, set his bottle on the desk, and wiped his mouth with the back of his hand. "I remember all of it."

Vince waved him off. No matter how bad it looked, Vince had to play it cool. That's what Jax hated.

"I'm just saying. I'm thinking we don't want to be here when it hits the news," Jax said, growing more serious, talking quieter, despite the fact that his fists were clenched.

"Noted. Something else you need to say?"

"I've said it," Jax said, nodding. "No point sticking around once they catch on. Looks like it's getting too close."

"I see." Vince turned his back. His shoulders stiffened a little. "You want out now?"

"What if we did—quit now?"

But Vince just shook his head, dismissive, confident, still in charge. "We'll give it another week with the tours. By then I should have the investors lined up. Don't be so nervous." He laughed over his shoulder as he walked out of the office, leaving Jax alone to brood over what to do.

But Jax had seen something, a hint of strain. That could mean only one thing: a chance to figure it out before Vince left him in the dust. He finished the beer and set the bottle down.

He watched Vince's car roar away, then he went into action. He slipped behind Vince's desk, careful and quiet, and went straight for the locked drawer. This was probably his last chance.

He fumbled a moment with the tool on his belt, forcing himself to be patient, to be steady. In an instant he had the drawer open, the ledger book in hand. If he was going to bail, he needed plenty of real evidence, and he had to move fast.

The small notebook wasn't there, but he laid the ledger open on the desk, carefully smoothing the pages to display the handwritten columns, numbers and dates, people's names. With his eyes locked on the page, Jax slipped his phone from his pocket. He knew if Vince caught him, he was a dead man. But Jax didn't let it shake him. It couldn't wait any longer. Now or never.

The click of the phone's camera shutter sounded too loud in the quiet office. Jax gritted his teeth, slowed his pulse, and kept going. Get the pictures, get them now, he thought. One after the other, he held his breath, moving deliberately, despite the rapid thump of his heartbeat. His mind zipped ahead, planning the next steps.

The feds wanted evidence. The pictures would be vital. They had to be. He slipped through the next few pages, eyes darting from ledger to phone, making sure he had enough. More dates, more money, more names, just like the promises made during the presentations. Only now, Jax could see them for what they were. Empty. He kept clicking, kept his focus, realizing now how much he didn't know. How much Vince had been keeping him in the dark.

He finished going through the book and set it back in the drawer, arranging other items around it. Everything had to look exactly as he'd found it. That meant nothing out of place. If Vince suspected anything, Jax's shot was blown. Now he needed to get out of here without tipping Vince off. He snapped a few pictures, showing the inside of the drawer, just in case.

The second it was on his phone, Jax's breath came rushing back. He hadn't realized he was holding it. One last check of the drawer. One last chance to see if there was anything he'd missed. There wasn't.

And then he heard the back door creak open.

The sound froze him in place.

Pulse pounding, he fumbled to work the lock. It had to look right.

He moved away from the desk, fluidly retrieved his beer bottle and headed out of the office. Footsteps came closer, Vince mumbling to himself. Jax straightened up and tried to calm himself, knowing his best chance was playing it cool, acting like nothing happened.

Vince was closer now. He sounded annoyed. That was better than suspicious, Jax thought. Jax let himself breathe again, his pulse thumping in his ears, but slower now, more under control. He was almost to the front of the office when he heard Vince louder than ever. "Where did I leave it?" Vince was saying, muttering. "Has to be here somewhere."

By the time Vince spotted him, Jax was in the front office, pretending to take a sip from the empty bottle while he clutched a stack of brochures in the other hand.

"Jax," Vince said, sounding put out. "You still here?"

Jax held up the brochures. "Just restocking everything. Like you told me. What about your meeting?"

He dreaded the answer. The money guys had probably cancelled.

"They moved the time. Plus, I forgot the power cord

for the laptop. Can't make the best presentation without the show, right?" He disappeared into his office while Jax held his breath, praying he'd gotten that damn drawer properly locked.

Vince came back, giving Jax a puzzled look for a second. "Found it. Okay, I'm outta here now."

As Vince stepped into the hall, leaving him there, Jax thought again of the FBI agent who approached him, of the life-and-death way he said Jax could still make it right. The agent was right. The clock was ticking, but now Jax knew how to play it.

Chapter 17

Outside the library's weathered adobe façade, Emily watered the plants, the sound of gentle splashes mixing with the earthy aroma of damp soil and sage. She moved between clusters of native flora and autumn-blooming flowers, plucking a dead bloom here and there. Francine's arrival interrupted her focus.

Wiping her brow with the back of her hand, Emily glanced up as Francine got out of her Honda and walked up the gravel path, her jeans neat and a jaunty scarf at her neck. Today, she wore her hair down. "You caught me trying to keep these plants alive a little longer before winter," Emily called, setting the garden hose aside.

"Your garden is almost as impressive as your library," Francine said, coming to a halt, a stack of file folders clutched tightly under her arm.

"Anything impressive is due to Victor Martinez, the best gardener in town. For my part, I can give them regular water, plus a lot of trial and error. They're mostly desert survivors," Emily said with a laugh. She leaned down to study a clump of penstemon that had put forth a few last blossoms in defiance of the season. "Sometimes I wonder if anything will actually make it through the winter."

"Ready for a break?" Francine asked, holding up the documents in her hand. "I have more notes than I can keep track of, but you won't believe how they're starting to align." Her voice brimmed with energy.

Emily turned off the spigot, dried her hands on the legs of her jeans and suggested they move inside.

Once she had settled on the stool behind the desk, Emily accepted the stack, studying the neatly typed columns of dates and places and hand-drawn symbols. "Let me guess," she said. "More of Cliff's mysterious markings. Did you ever make sense of his shorthand style?"

Francine laughed. "I'm beginning to. Maybe." She paused, letting Emily take in the extent of her work. "I saw similar marks on that silly 'treasure map,' but much of it is completely different."

Emily set the papers on the desk, pointing at a spot on one of the maps. "This location is well above 9,000 feet altitude. Maybe this is why Vince's tours seem fully booked. In a few more weeks we could have snow up in the higher elevations."

"These annotations of Cliff's—the ones we talked about last time—go back years. I created this chart, to cross-reference the various facts and figures. I think they tie in with something more than just Vince's treasure hunt."

Emily touched a line of script, noting where it matched a typed date in Francine's columns. Her lips parted as she began to see a pattern. "If Cliff had these historical documents and maps …" she said slowly, "why would he take Vince's version of the story seriously?"

"Pure curiosity? It's one thing to hear a legend, another to see whether it's still in play." Francine adjusted her scarf and took the top page from the pile. "And there are some huge gaps in Cliff's files. Maybe he hoped Vince would fill them in."

Emily frowned, considering this. "What if he did? What if Cliff spoke with him, and they decided to work together?"

"And that's why we haven't heard from him?" Francine shook her head, skeptical but not dismissive. "But then why the secrecy? I think Cliff would have told me, and he would have kept in touch."

True, Emily thought.

Francine rifled through her stack, pulling a sheet covered in pencil sketches. "Look at these," she said, thrusting the page toward Emily. "We keep seeing the same ones. Especially this cross shape, and the eight-pointed star. The Treasure Tours brochure claims that the symbols mean treasure, and everyone laps it up, but we need to figure out what they really point to."

Emily nodded, staring at the symbols with deepening interest. "What did Cliff think they were?"

"Markers, probably. That's how he annotated most of them." Francine sounded a little unsure. "Some kind of a trail?"

Emily's eyes narrowed. "But no mention of actual gold. Just the story and its connections."

"That's the part I'm wondering about. For a tale this old, something would have shown up in real records. Unless … "

"Unless Vince Hutchins knows something nobody else does," Emily finished for her. "Which sounds less likely every time we go over it."

"Would you like to make copies of these pages? Something in your other records might match up, tell us what the symbols mean."

"Sure—great idea." Emily carried the stack to the copier and started the machine. Within a couple of minutes she had copies of Cliff's notes and Francine's chart. The historic documents couldn't be subjected to the light of a copy machine, but she could get decent copies of those with a camera, and Francine agreed to leave them.

Francine gathered her pages into a neat stack, hugging them to her chest as they walked outside once again. A crow called from a nearby branch, its sharp caw splitting the air. Emily listened, her thoughts turning again to Cliff's disappearance. "I still believe Cliff must have talked to Vince. Supposing he did, how would that have gone?"

Francine's voice turned thoughtful. "He'd confront them, whether he thought they were holding out on some real historical facts, or if he believed they were presenting fake history as the real thing."

"That probably wouldn't go well for him, would it?" Again, worry nagged at her.

Francine raised an eyebrow, admiring the young woman's insights. "What are you thinking?"

Emily toyed with the leaves of an autumn sage, their ridged texture collecting drops of moisture. "I'm thinking we don't know enough about Vince and whether he has important connections here in town," she said. "Maybe he's in touch with more people than just tourists."

"I'll start checking," Francine said. "If his outfit has any real connections in Taos, we should find out. I'll see what surfaces."

"I'll ask around, as well, and I'll get photos of those other documents you're leaving with me," Emily said as Francine opened the Pilot's door. "I'll let you know if anything new turns up."

Francine gave a thumbs-up and Emily watched her back out of the lot and drive away. The vehicle was no more than half a block away when another familiar car pulled into the driveway. Kelly Sweet Porter and her six-year-old daughter got out.

"Hey, you two. My gosh, it's been a long time! Ana, I believe you've grown two inches!"

"One and three-quarters."

Kelly met Emily's gaze and rolled her eyes. The precocious little girl was known for details. "Well, we'd better watch out or you'll soon be taller than me," Emily teased.

Kelly held up two books. "Scott apologizes for being late with these. His latest novel is taking longer than he thought it would."

"No problem. You know we don't have deadlines here. It would be impossible to get my type of patrons to work on precise schedules."

Actually, Emily had created a spreadsheet to replace her grandfather's system of index cards in a metal box, and she usually knew exactly whose books were due. Scott was a friend and a regular here, so it never bothered her when he kept materials a bit longer. His children's books were international bestsellers because of his attention to the fascinating facts he included for his kid super-sleuth character.

"Hey, Ana, I've got someone inside for you to meet,"

Emily said.

The three of them walked into the library, Emily taking a moment to wipe her wet boots on the mat. Immediately, Moonbeam pranced forward, leaving her perch on the desk.

"You have a kitty now!" Ana ran up and embraced the cat, without a thought as to whether this would be welcome. It appeared that it was.

"Her name is Moonbeam. Riki found her wandering and it seems she belonged here all along."

Ana let the cat rub against her face as she stroked the sleek fur. "We have a cat too. Her name's Eliza and she's a calico."

"Honey, Em has been to our house. She knows Eliza."

"Moonbeam is on her fifth life," Ana stated. "She says she is really glad to be back in the library. She missed David and Valerie."

A chill passed over Emily's arms. "Did she? Wow, that's amazing."

Kelly noticed the strange look on Emily's face. "It's okay, really. She makes up conversations with our cat all the time too."

Except this conversation wasn't made up. "It's such a beautiful day out, why don't we have tea out in the courtyard?" She wasn't going to get any library work done at this point, anyway.

She ushered everyone through the back, taking care to lock the front door first. "I'll put the kettle on, if you want to take a minute and shake the dust off those cushions on the chairs," she told Kelly.

By the time she walked into the house to gather the tea things, Ana and Moonbeam were down on the flagstone patio, the cat apparently getting some type of a math lesson from the scribbles and lines Ana was drawing in the dust.

Emily took a deep breath. That was a *really* strange thing just now.

She prepared a tray with a teapot, mugs, honey, and milk and then added a packet of cookies she'd found at the health food store.

"This is such a relaxing spot," Kelly commented, walking into the kitchen. "I love the dappled shade from that tree beside the fence.

"It truly is, and I really don't get out here nearly often enough. I'm glad you stopped by."

"Well, returning the books … And I have to admit I'm curious about that treasure tour you went on with Riki. She mentioned it but I guess she wasn't too impressed. I was thinking it might be fun for Ana."

Emily poured boiling water over the tea leaves in the pot and waggled her head back and forth. "There were some kids in our group, but …"

"But …?"

"I think Ana's too sharp for it. She would immediately catch on that all the ghostly images are fake. So is the gold. I actually nabbed one of the coins that we were supposed to throw back 'for luck'. Francine had it tested at a lab and it was lead. Can you believe they would let people take a chance with lead?"

"And pass it off as gold?"

"It was very thinly plated to look like gold. I guess the lead was meant to add weight and make it seem real, but, well, nah. It wasn't a very convincing show."

"Thanks. And that answers the question for me." Kelly held the kitchen door open and they walked back out to the courtyard.

"Hey, maybe Scott could use our experience as the plot for one of his mystery stories. I'd be glad to give him the details."

Kelly laughed. "I will pass along the offer."

* * *

An hour after her guests left, Emily was back at work. It didn't seem to matter how often she promised herself a day off, an afternoon to simply do nothing, the work called out to her. Now, especially, with Cliff still incommunicado, each passing day added to the likelihood that something bad had happened.

Plus, she thought, as she photographed several pages, Francine would be back for the university's original documents, and Emily really wanted these copies for her Spanish Colonial collection. She might as well get the photographs now.

The printer whirred through its start-up process and then Emily sent the first few pictures to the print queue. While those printed, she went back to the desk and gathered Cliff's files that Francine had left with her, several of which she'd barely glimpsed when she'd visited Francine's hotel.

Emily picked up the first manila folder in the stack, ancient, time-yellowed, and packed with material related to mining ventures and lost treasure in northern New Mexico. Several hundred years' worth of history—or myth, depending on who you asked. It seemed Cliff had been as meticulous as Francine in recording his observations. Emily marveled at the handwriting, Cliff's erratic script and quirky shorthand notes that conveyed his passion for a story that spanned centuries.

And now that story spanned generations of Plankhursts, as well. Once all of Cliff's material was copied, Emily would add more papers to the mix, printouts of her own findings on the gold and its twisty legend.

Folder by folder, she sorted documents into stacks: those that could safely be copied, and others that would need to be photographed.

When she had the first folder's contents organized, she placed a stack on the auto-feeder and watched the sheets move through and the copies come out. She found herself staring at everything on the desk, wondering how she'd find time to make sense of the volumes in front of her, not to mention everything still waiting in the shelves and cabinets. It was more daunting than she'd first imagined, a year ago, though no less exhilarating.

She picked up a set of her own notes, about to return it to a box labeled "Family," when a soft creak made her pause. The sound didn't belong to any of the building's natural groans and shifts. Emily stopped to listen more closely.

Another creak came, more insistent, and she saw Moonbeam slinking toward the library's entrance. She held her breath until the knock came at the door and Francine appeared behind the glass panel, cheeks flushed.

"You didn't waste any time," Emily said, laughing with relief.

"Neither did you," Francine replied, looking at the documents strewn over every available surface. "How long have you been at this?"

"I barely started. Can you believe how much he kept?" Emily waved her arms, indicating the forest of paper. "I didn't imagine you'd be back so soon. What did you find?"

Francine sat and reached into her bag, pulling out what looked like newspaper articles. "Do you have coffee, or something stronger?"

"Check the carafe on the coffee bar. If it's empty, we can make more," Emily said. "So, start at the beginning—what's all this?"

Francine crossed the room and came back a minute later, a mug in hand. "I went to the newspaper office, figuring the Treasure Tours operation might have run some advertising when they first arrived in town. There was a half-page ad, yes, but they also ran a brief business profile and a photo taken at some kind of gala party for investors."

She flicked open the paper and folded it back. "Look at these names in the photo caption: Davis, Huntington, Spenser. And that—" she stabbed a finger at the photo— "that is Russell Pinkney. All the rest are Albuquerque people, and every one a contact Cliff had listed in his notes, people he believed were contacted to invest in a treasure retrieval scheme. It's the last name that gets me, though. This Anders Spenser fellow. I called him, just on a hunch, and guess where he lives now?"

Emily studied the faces. She recognized the prominent faces: a stock broker, a car dealer, and the owner of one of the most successful restaurants in the state. Pinkney seemed the odd one out, a pudgy man with thinning hair and a ruddy complexion, compared to the others who looked as if they spent their days on the golf course or a yacht somewhere.

"Taos," Francine said, pulling Emily's attention back to the fact she'd posed a question. "When I talked to Anders and asked what he knew about the treasure tour outfit, he got really cagey. He's got some connection—I'd bet on it—but I don't know exactly what. The names on this list, they're all people with money. A couple of them even fund endowments for the university."

Emily blinked, wondering. "Is it all for real, then, all of these people believe there's gold nearby? Or … do you think they showed up here, establishing a connection with the treasure tour guy, because of Cliff's prestige and university connection?"

"Either is conceivable," Francine admitted. "Or maybe we're being strung along, like everyone else. I tried several of the other contacts—no one has responded."

"They're staying lowkey, like Cliff," Emily said softly. Her eyes held Francine's for a long moment before dropping back to the paper.

"We can connect a few things, and Pinkney is definitely in the middle somehow," Francine said. "Someone knows how to tap people's interest. Cliff was interested. What if he actually found something?"

"Maybe something too top-secret to put into words," Emily said, thinking of the various symbols within his notes. The idea made her uneasy.

"Remember what you said about this Vince Hutchins? How he has convinced people there's gold? I'm beginning to wonder if we have it backwards. Someone convinced Vince, instead."

"Like who? Professor Pinkney?"

"That's the question." Francine drew out another sheet of paper. She seemed to have notes ready for every angle of their conversation. "If someone in Taos knows the real story, we'll find them. Maybe there's another connection here that's worth more than the gold itself."

"What if we don't find out in time to locate Cliff?" Emily asked.

"Would you give up?" Francine answered, her tone making it clear she wouldn't.

Emily smiled, grateful for the insistence in Francine's voice. "No. I wouldn't give up either."

Francine leaned back in her chair, surveying the table. "What are we missing?" she said, directing the question more at the research than at Emily. "Look at this material. Half of Hutchins's story comes from your family's library. The dates and records and everything else—he made up his version based on actual history."

Emily took the papers from Francine, reviewing the names and places and all the lines they formed. She hadn't thought of it like that before. Maybe it was her family's version, in a way.

"So where does that put us?" she asked.

Francine was staring out the window, a glint of mischief in her eyes. "We're right where we want to be, even if we don't know it yet." She turned in her seat, surveying the library, taking in the massive bookshelves, the adobe architecture, the history that saturated the space. "The answers are here. But there's one more thing, something I can't get here."

"What's that?"

Francine winked, a new plan already forming. "I'm going to confront Vince Hutchins, even if I have to camp out in front of that blasted tour office until he shows up."

"You shouldn't go alone. I'm coming with you."

Chapter 18

After two hours of watching from the parking lot of the Walgreens across the street, and no sign of Hutchins, Emily had a better idea. "I know a guy who works here. How about if I ask him to text me when someone shows up at the Treasure Tours office? Meanwhile, we could grab some lunch—I'm starving."

Francine was about to agree when she spotted a sleek, dark blue sports car that whipped into the space across the street. She nudged Emily. "Is that him?"

"It is." Emily started her Jeep and negotiated through the traffic to get there. She pulled in at a neighboring driveway and parked at the south end of the property, out of sight of the plate glass window at the front.

"Okay, let's do this thing." Francine was out of the vehicle in two seconds.

Emily followed along, reminding herself of what they were here for, to learn what they could about Cliff Littleton's disappearance.

As she approached the door, Francine paused, taking a deep breath and giving Emily a wan smile.

"You can do this, Francine," Emily whispered. With a gentle twist, she pushed the door open and the women stepped inside.

Although Emily had been here the night of her tour, the place was crowded then. She noticed more of the details now. The lobby area contained a carefully planned display of adventure and mystique.

Francine's eyes darted around, taking in details. Ornate maps covered the walls, their edges deliberately aged to pretend antiquity. Glass cases housed cheap copies of ancient artifacts — arrowheads, pottery shards, and weathered coins — mostly irrelevant but labeled with dramatic descriptions of their supposed significance.

A reception desk dominated the center of the room, its surface cluttered with a rack of brochures, some posters for sale rolled up in tubes, and a state-of-the-art laptop that seemed at odds with the rustic decor. Behind the desk, a rectangular map dominated the wall, purporting to show the route of the conquistadors and how they had ended up just outside Taos, their pack animals laden with chests and chests of gold treasure.

And there, lounging in a high-backed leather chair, was Vince Hutchins himself. His dark locks were artfully tousled, and his rugged good looks were accentuated by a carefully trimmed beard. He wore a crisp white shirt with the sleeves rolled up, revealing tanned forearms that showcased an expensive-looking gold watch.

Vince gave Emily a cursory glance, showing no sign

that he recognized her, before his eyes met Francine's, a slow smile spreading across his face. "Dr. Morales," he drawled, his voice smooth as honey. "To what do I owe the pleasure of this unexpected visit?"

"You know who I am?"

"It's a little town. Word gets around."

She squared her shoulders. "Mr. Hutchins," she replied, her tone cool and professional. "I hope I'm not interrupting anything important."

Vince stood and gestured expansively, his smile never wavering. "For you, Dr. Morales, I always have time." He moved over to stand at the desk, casting his eyes downward at Francine, although his height barely matched Emily's.

A subtle power play, she realized. Despite his slick attitude, her estimation of Vince's cunning notched up a tiny bit.

"I must say," Vince continued, leaning forward with an air of conspiratorial excitement, "I've been hoping we'd have a chance to chat. Your work on Southwestern folklore is fascinating. I'd like to pick your brain about some of the local legends."

Francine's eyes narrowed slightly. Emily could see the trap he was laying—draw Francine into a scholarly discussion, flatter her ego, and deflect from the real issues at hand. She pretended to study one of the brochures, watching him closely.

"I appreciate the interest, Mr. Hutchins," Francine said carefully, "but I'm here on a more ... specific matter."

Vince's eyebrows raised, a picture of innocence. "Oh? And what might that be?"

Francine took a deep breath. "Dr. Clifford Littleton."

The change in Vince's demeanor was subtle but

immediate. His smile didn't falter, but something in his eyes hardened, like a steel door slamming shut behind them.

"Since Dr. Littleton came here to check out your claims about the conquistadors and their gold, my colleague has disappeared."

"I'm not sure I follow, Dr. Morales. What does your missing friend have to do with my work?"

Francine leaned forward, her voice low and intense. "Cliff had concerns about the authenticity of your claims and about the impact your treasure hunts were having on local historical sites."

Vince's laugh was warm and disarming, but it didn't reach his eyes. "Dr. Morales, I assure you, my work is entirely aboveboard. Every artifact we've found has been properly documented and verified by experts. As for your friend …" He shrugged in a gesture of helplessness. "I'm sorry to hear he's missing, but I fail to see how that's connected to me."

Emily felt a surge of frustration. She had expected denials, of course, but the ease with which Vince dismissed Francine's concerns was infuriating.

"Mr. Hutchins, I've seen Cliff's notes. He had evidence of inconsistencies in your reports, of damage to protected sites. And then he vanishes, just as he's about to go public with his findings? You have to admit, it's suspicious."

Vince's smile finally faded, replaced by a look of concern that seemed just a touch too rehearsed. "Dr. Morales, these are serious accusations you're making. I understand you're worried about your friend, but jumping to conclusions won't help anyone. Have you spoken to the police?"

"Of course I have," Francine replied, her voice tight.

"But they don't seem to have any leads. They think he just ... wandered off on one of his research trips."

Emily noticed that Francine didn't mention Cliff's car or the bloodstains.

Vince nodded sympathetically. "Well, that does sound like something an enthusiastic researcher might do. I'm sure he'll turn up soon, safe and sound."

Emily felt her temper flaring. "Mr. Hutchins, Dr. Morales is not some hysterical friend jumping at shadows. We're both trained historians, and I know when something doesn't add up."

Francine clenched a fist on the desk top. "Cliff was onto something, and I intend to find out what it was."

For an instant, something dark emerged in Vince's eyes, a glimpse of fury beneath the charm. Then it vanished, replaced by a look of gentle concern. "Dr. Morales, I can see you're upset. And I understand. Truly, I do. But I think you're barking up the wrong tree here. My work brings joy and excitement to people's lives. It celebrates the rich history of this region. I would never do anything to jeopardize that."

"You can dress it up however you like, Mr. Hutchins, but what you're doing is exploiting people's hopes and dreams. You're twisting history to suit your own ends. And if Cliff got too close to exposing that, well ..." She left the implication hanging in the air between them.

Emily held her breath, hoping Francine hadn't gone too far.

Vince stood straighter, his height allowing him to tower over Francine. His voice was still smooth, but there was an edge to it now. "Dr. Morales, I've been patient out of respect for your reputation and your obvious distress.

But I won't sit here and be accused of … what? Fraud? Kidnapping? This is absurd."

Francine met his gaze unflinchingly. "Is it, Mr. Hutchins? Then you won't mind if I pass along our conversation here to the sheriff. I'm sure you have nothing to hide."

For a long moment, they stood there, the tension between them sparking like lightning. Then Vince's charming smile returned, though it seemed more like a mask now than ever before. "By all means, Dr. Morales. Investigate to your heart's content. Now, if you'll excuse me, I have a conference call in a few minutes."

As the women turned to leave, Vince's voice stopped them at the door. "Oh, and Dr. Morales? Do be careful in your … investigations. The mountain can be a dangerous place."

Behind them, the door closed with a soft click.

Chapter 19

By the time Emily dropped Francine off at her vehicle and said goodbye, she was twitchy and irritable. The morning together in research, the hours of watching the tour office, and then the confrontational encounter with Vince Hutchins—all of it had drained her. Missing lunch was probably a factor, too, she admitted. She walked through the library, with Moonbeam vocally letting her know she'd been gone too long. The two of them crossed the courtyard and entered the kitchen.

A snack of cheese bites and turkey slices, along with an apple, perked her up.

Francine had reiterated that her next move would be to visit the sheriff's office once again, hoping to put more urgency on an investigation into Vince Hutchins and his shoddy operation. There was more to this than simply busing people out to a cave, projecting some fancy graphics around them, and tossing a few glittery bits on the ground for them to find.

Emily and Francine agreed on that point. If Hutchins's past had any bearing (and how could it not?), he was after deeper pockets and some kind of huge payoff. They'd found some names and had an idea these wealthy men were somehow involved, but so far, they'd not connected the dots. Emily hoped Sheriff Beau would be able to.

She tossed a tidbit of turkey toward the cat, then carried her plate to the sink. Frankly, she hoped Beau would locate the missing professor soon. She wanted to get back to her own organizing efforts in the library, and was a little weary of Francine taking up so much of her time.

"What would Grandma do?"

Mrroww.

"You're right. She'd tell me to follow my heart. And that means not letting someone else completely highjack my plans."

Mrroww. This time, the cat's response seemed to affirm her human's words. *Am I actually learning to interpret 'cat'* Emily wondered.

She brewed a cup of English tea and wandered into her grandfather's study. Moonbeam followed closely, and Emily noticed the first thing she did was to walk over to the bookcase that led down into the tunnels. Fur rose on the cat's back and tail as she sniffed the almost-imperceptible crack to the doorway.

Okay, that's eerie. But then she remembered that this cat had lived here before, had spent her earlier lives with the grandparents and may have had access to parts of the home that Emily was only beginning to discover.

"It's okay, Moonbeam. Relax."

The cat gave her a quizzical look, sniffed the bookcase once more, then slinked over to the sofa across from the desk and settled onto an earth-toned woven blanket.

Emily set her red tea mug on a coaster and switched on the desk lamp, intending to return to a project she'd begun a couple of weeks ago, before Francine and Spanish conquistadors entered her world.

When she moved permanently into this house, she had decided to create a visual display of Plankhurst family history, complete with framed photos and vintage letters. Choosing what to include for her own enjoyment—as opposed to those items that should be a part of the library collection—had consumed most of her free time in recent months. Those items had become scattered across the wooden desk. Sepia-toned images of various ancestors, their solemn faces framed in intricately carved wood, patiently regarded her.

Only a few of the items were ready; more were waiting as she decided which of them to take to the frame shop. There were so many treasured images, and only so much wall space. She sighed and began to spread them out, the sounds merging with the gentle ambient sounds from outdoors. Emily felt a subtle stirring around her, and a faint smile played on her lips as she glanced over her shoulder.

"Hello, Grandma."

Valerie's ghost appeared, her shimmering fingers giving Moonbeam a tickle behind the ears before settling over an opened box of photos and letters tied in bundles with ribbon. She wore her favorite flowing skirts and bead necklaces, ghostly yet vibrant against the earthy warmth of the library. She drifted closer, the edges of her ghostly figure wavering as if in a warm breeze. The cat squeezed her eyes shut, completely contented.

"I'm so happy to see you back here, working on our own family history again." Valerie's voice was calm and melodic, echoing against the adobe walls.

Emily pushed up her dark-rimmed glasses, regarding her grandmother with a look of affection. "I know, Grandma," she replied, carefully turning over a page. "I've felt guilty about taking time away from this, but Francine's mission is essential. Finding her missing colleague may also expose these tour operators as charlatans, and everything we can do to keep history accurate will help protect our legacy as librarians."

Valerie hovered near the table; the translucence of her form seemed almost tangible in the gathering twilight. "And are you certain, Emily," she said, her voice carrying gentle authority, "that she's prepared for all she might find?"

"I have no idea what she's prepared for, but I trust her and I want to help her," Emily sent a smile toward her grandmother. She had grown accustomed to these moods, knowing that Valerie would gently admonish, nudge, and perhaps even scold her in that firm but affectionate way.

Valerie floated near the photos. "I like what you're doing with these, sweetie. The frames are nice." She lingered over a particular letter, its edges frayed with age.

"Thanks. I'm going for a combination of historical, contemporary, and whimsical." Emily squinted at the photos that were already in frames. "I hope it's not too odd a combination."

Valerie was silent for a moment, the air settling as her apparition seemed to glimmer slightly. "Perhaps her colleague wants to stay lost," she ventured. "Have you considered that, dear?" Shifts in subject were not unusual with this ghost.

Emily looked up with patience and confidence. "I

suppose … but somehow I think he wants to be found."

Valerie ran a ghostly hand over one of the letters Emily had set aside and appeared to falter, a sign of agitation Emily hadn't seen before. Moonbeam looked up, following Valerie's tense movements. She drifted away from the desk and moved back again, gliding more urgently through the room. "Don't be so certain. Bringing up the past can involve risk."

Emily set the photos down and gave her grandmother a firm look. "What risk are we talking about here? Are you still talking about Francine Morales or are we back on the subject of my little project here? I see *this* as a part of preserving our family's legacy. You told me yourself that it was important to honor our past."

Emily met her grandmother's gaze. "On the other subject, *if* it's necessary to solving the mystery, I think Francine is the right person to share information with. She'll use it wisely. She's trying to help someone, Grandma."

"She may already know more than you think," Valerie suggested.

"In that case, I wouldn't be betraying a secret, would I?"

Valerie's image lightened, a sure sign her agitation was passing. Her sweet, slightly amused smile showed, and Emily could see she was getting ready to drift out again. "*Perhaps* she is trustworthy," the ghost said, with less hesitation than before.

"And *perhaps* I won't need to share very much information at all." Emily glanced around the library and then back toward her ethereal grandmother, who vanished almost immediately. "Grandma? Trust me. I'm not going to let our legacy be destroyed. I promise."

Chapter 20

Jax had chickened out, not calling the FBI agent right after he took the pictures. Now he crouched over tangled ropes and sacks, muttering to himself in the dim storage room as he pawed through a mess of props. He stacked fake treasure chests against the far wall and turned over a weather-beaten box, grunting at its weight, when Vince's voice filtered through the drywall from the next room.

"Huge profits ... yeah, yeah ... won't be disappointed." Vince, working his charm on someone, was promising an immense payoff. "Hutchins always delivers."

Was this one of the venture capitalists Vince claimed to be meeting with soon? The name of the investor didn't come through, but the words "our cut" did, and Jax pressed his ear to the wall, shoulders tense, listening as hard as he could. The conversation left little doubt in his mind: Vince planned to keep all the money.

Jax tiptoed to the hall, edging toward Vince's office, straining to catch every word through the closed door. There was a pause and then a low laugh, full of confidence and charm. "The ghost bit? Just a way to make it more fun. Pure entertainment."

Jax imagined the look on Vince's face as he played his mark. A wide, smug grin. "You know me. It's about the experience." Another pause, and Jax could picture the dollar signs in his head. If Vince was talking to another new investor, the plan must be coming together.

Jax felt his stomach twist. Vince wouldn't even share the name, this was probably just another number in that ledger book. He edged a little closer, pretending to stack a couple of boxes in the hallway.

Vince's voice rose slightly. "Listen, it's a goldmine. Haha, literally! I guarantee your investment will double."

That word again, the term Vince used with wealthy clients. The promise of massive returns, carefully constructed to sound both reasonable and exciting. A classic Vince Hutchins pitch. Jax shifted again, trying to hear better through the narrow gap in the door.

"Keep this under your hat," Vince added, the tone of secrecy meant to make his listener feel part of something special. "There's a lot more here than meets the eye." A long pause. "No, no split—that's not part of the picture anymore."

The words were barely a whisper, but Jax caught them. Vince definitely planned to keep the real money for himself. The conversation wound down, and Jax knew he wouldn't hear anything else. He gritted his teeth as he moved back into the storage room and stared contemptuously at the clutter.

It was Vince's classic spiel, the same old hustle, with a new twist every time. And here was Jax, left in the dark until Vince needed him to take care of the messy details. He dropped a sack of fake gold coins into a crate, his jaw clenched. How long did Vince think he could pull this off without anyone figuring it out? How long without him, Jax, getting wise?

He heard the chair roll across the floor, Vince getting ready to end the call. "Don't worry," came the final, soothing note. "I'll take care of everything. You can trust me."

Trust me. Jax thought of all the times he'd heard those words before, but never quite like this. Never with his cut being promised to the mark. For him, this time it was different.

Pushing open the door to the office, he fixed his gaze on Vince. Vince barely glanced up, looking more pleased with himself than surprised. He hit a button and ended his call.

"New investors?" Jax asked, trying to keep his voice level. "Heard some big promises."

Vince gave him a thin smile. "Just business, Jax. Nothing you need to worry about." He leaned back, putting his feet up on the desk. "Gotta keep it interesting for the clients. You know how it is."

Jax shifted his weight, unsure of how much to press, how much to say. Vince acted as if Jax wasn't even there, reaching for a paperweight, tossing it in the air, catching it in a loose grip.

"We're partners on this, right?" Jax finally said. "I

thought we were—"

Vince waved off his concern. "Right now we have other problems." His voice was smooth, but with an edge of impatience. "Like that woman."

"What woman?" Jax had to work to keep up with the sudden change.

"The historian. Morales. She and some other young lady popped in here, questioning me." Vince stood, and Jax could see the irritation in the way he moved. "She's looking for that guy from Albuquerque. The professor. You did handle that, right?"

"Yeah, sure. You know I did."

Jax bit back a comment. He knew how this would go, how Vince would sidestep and distract and try to keep him in the dark about the money.

"She's asking questions around town, and it's bad for business," Vince said, heading to the front window and looking out. The streets were quiet and the soft light of autumn made the day seem peaceful. An illusion, like everything else. "She talked about going to the sheriff. If she keeps digging, it won't be good for us. And I'm talking about you and me here, Jax." Vince turned, locking eyes with Jax for the first time.

Jax nodded, letting Vince see he was listening. Letting him think he was still playing the game. "You want me to handle it?" Jax asked, pretending to sound casual.

"You need to scare her off. Now." The words were crisp and definite, meant to close the conversation and the issue.

Jax could do a few things to rattle her cage, make her nervous. But he wasn't taking the chance of doing anything drastic, not this time. He studied Vince for a moment longer, taking in the calm, confident stance, the way Vince seemed so sure of himself, certain that he still held all the cards. Jax would let him think that, for now.

He turned and walked back to the storage room, pushing aside the chaos of ropes and boxes. As he loaded the van with boxes of fake coins and some extra extension cords for the tour site, he had a lot to think about. Vince's phone conversation rang in his ears, confirming what he'd suspected.

It was all betrayal.

* * *

Jax climbed into the van and started the engine, his thoughts as unsettled as the boxes that rattled around in the back. He gunned it past the square tan office building with its flashy sign, pulled onto Paseo, and kept driving, watching Vince's cheesy little world shrink in the rearview mirror.

This wasn't going to be like before. Not for Jax.

Two miles north of town, he parked in the dirt behind a shuttered curio shop and checked the lot for anyone who might see him. A gust of wind whipped fallen leaves around, like little spies. Jax grabbed his phone, made sure the charge was adequate, then pulled up his camera app. Here were the ledger pages that proved his suspicions.

He scrolled through the photographs, selecting the best ones, making sure they were as clear as he'd hoped, pausing on each entry that Vince had carefully noted. Amounts and names, numbers that revealed everything. He checked the surrounding area again. A couple of loose dogs sniffed around a nearby trash bin, but there were no people. Just him and the knot in his stomach.

Jax leaned back in the seat, his thoughts spinning. He was in this deep now. The images had to be enough to get Vince. Enough to free himself. Was he sure about this?

His pulse quickened as he tapped out the number, the keys clicking against his thumbs, loud in the confined space. Vince would never see this coming. Jax glanced toward the street, half-expecting to see Vince there, grinning and ready to shoot him, but the only movement was the relentless swirl of dust and leaves.

He set his jaw, and pressed SEND.

If this didn't work, he was a dead man.

Two minutes later, his phone rang. "Rivera," came the voice on the other end. "Steve Price here."

"Yeah. It's me." Jax tried to sound calm, like this wasn't a huge step. "You getting what I'm sending you?"

A pause, as if the agent wanted to double check. "Got it, Jax. Tell me what I'm seeing."

Jax went through it all, where the ledger was kept, how Vince made his entries.

"You really delivered." The voice had a slight drawl, a slow, unhurried quality that put Jax on edge. "I'm impressed."

Jax swiped through the images again, the photos he'd snapped just before Vince could walk in on him, right after he'd begun to feel certain Vince was playing him.

"Yeah? You better be," Jax said, his throat dry. "There's more. I'll give you more." He scanned the horizon again; the open space felt too revealing.

"We'll need details." The voice came through steady and direct. "Names, locations. We need to know everything." Jax could hear the clatter of a keyboard, the agent holding the phone between shoulder and ear as if Jax's call was just another task in the middle of a busy day. Like Jax was just another informant. And maybe he was. But the next words told him something else: "Can you get me the actual ledgers?"

Jax didn't answer right away.

"Soon," he said, still uncertain, still holding back. "I'm not sure what else is in writing," he went on, the words spilling out in a jumble, Vince's conversation this morning replaying in his head. "He's got new investors, at least two, maybe more. I overheard him setting up a presentation for some venture capitalists. We're talking hundreds of thousands."

In his head flickered the memory of Vince's smooth instructions about getting rid of the woman, the instructions Jax had no intention of following. Not the way Vince wanted.

The agent cut in, "Stay sharp, Rivera. We don't want him getting suspicious. We don't want you tipping your hand."

"Right." This could be it, the moment he'd been waiting for, the one that would turn the game on Vince.

"When can you get me something more?"

Jax hesitated, hearing the way Vince had brushed off his questions and sent him off to deal with the professor and the historian. But he was fed up with making people disappear. He wanted this thing over with—now.

"Give me two days," Jax finally said, knowing he'd have to watch his back the whole time. "Maybe three."

"We'll hold you to it. Don't let us down." The words were cool, confident, a far cry from Vince's false assurances, but they carried their own kind of threat.

The call ended with a click and a dead connection, and Jax slumped back in the seat, the phone loose in his hand. He closed his eyes for a moment, then opened them quickly, as if even that short pause might cost him. He'd made his choice, but technically he was still in Vince's game, and the stakes were higher than ever. A single slip could be a disaster.

He powered off the phone and sat there, letting the tension in his neck unravel, bit by bit. There was no going back now, but his decision felt both terrifying and right.

Chapter 21

Half-full, the cup of coffee sat neglected on Emily's kitchen table, pushed aside by a stack of newspapers and a yellow legal pad filled with notes and doodles. When her phone rang, she reached for it instinctively, without looking at the number.

"Emily Plankhurst," she said, half-expecting to hear a telemarketer's voice. Instead, it was Francine, who was nearly drowned out by the background sound of rushing traffic and car horns.

"Hold on a sec," Francine said, shouting to be heard. "Let me get somewhere quieter. I need to tell you something."

Emily held the phone away from her ear and turned to glance out the window. Her snug adobe house was normally her sanctuary, if only she could find time to relax and enjoy it. Right now, she needed answers—about Francine, Vince, Cliff, and the tangled web that seemed to be drawing her in.

Francine's voice came through again, still layered with noise but less chaotic this time. "Sorry about that. It's crazy out here. I was at the hotel and decided to take a walk. Thought I might run into Vince. Or one of his thugs."

He has thugs now? "Francine, what are you—" Emily said. "Has something happened to you?"

Francine definitely sounded rattled. "There's something going on at the hotel. Last night I heard doors slamming. They woke me from a sound sleep several times. I called the front desk but when they sent someone around, the noises had stopped. And in my room, the lights blinked a bit alarmingly. I think it's Vince's doing."

Emily could picture the classic hotel, a favorite for tourists with a taste for history and a tolerance for eccentricity. "And why do you think Vince is doing it?" she asked.

"It's exactly the sort of thing he stages for his treasure tours. I think he's setting me up, making it look like I've gotten myself spooked. When I confronted him yesterday, he wasn't pleased about me sticking my nose into his tour operation. Said I'd better back off if I knew what was good for me. Then all this started happening." Francine's voice trembled, just enough for Emily to hear it.

"Yes," Emily agreed, keeping her voice steady. "It could be someone who wants you to leave town, and that means you're onto something."

"If Vince gets scared enough to really hurt me, I don't want you or anyone else to be collateral damage."

Emily took a deep breath and sat back, the phone

pressed to her ear, and let the scenarios play out in her mind. Vince, cornered and desperate. Francine, stubborn but at risk. Cliff, out there somewhere, his whereabouts a mystery and his safety a concern. "Did you get the chance to talk with Sheriff Cardwell again?"

Francine's answer was drowned out by traffic noises.

"Come by the library," Emily suggested. "You need the peace and quiet right now." *And a conversation out on the streets is not a smart idea.*

They ended the call, and Emily put her phone on the table, staring at it as if willing it to ring again and offer some instant answers to the dozens of questions filling her mind. She reached for her cup. The coffee was cold, but she drank it anyway, lost in thought.

She wondered how Vince could be so callous toward his customers and why he would stoop to cheap parlor tricks to threaten Francine. The thought circled back to Cliff, to the bloodstains in his car and the uncertainty about whether he was even still alive. Emily had to believe Cliff could be found.

Her eyes drifted back to the yellow pad on the table, filled with her notes on places to look and names of people who might have seen or heard something. None of it had panned out yet, but that didn't mean it wouldn't. Her thoughts were interrupted by a loud crash from the next room—a stack of books and papers she'd left on the end table near her sofa—and she ran to investigate. Emily smiled, in spite of herself, seeing the influence of Vince's fake haunting even in her own home. But no blinking lights or slamming doors were going to scare her off.

"Moonbeam? Did you knock these books off?"

No admission of guilt from the cat.

She gathered up the fallen pile and reached for her lightweight jacket, pulling it on as she headed toward the library. Francine was right about one thing: If Vince thought they were getting too close to uncovering his scam, there was no telling how far he'd go to stop them. She would have to move quickly and carefully. With the sound of Francine's anxious voice still echoing in her mind, Emily locked her door and made her way across the courtyard.

* * *

The warm glow of antique lamps lit the tables in the Morton Library's main room, spilling warm pools of amber light across the tables and creating a cocoon of calm as evening darkness closed around the building. Francine stood near Emily, keeping her voice low, as Emily shelved some returned books.

Suddenly, the lamps flickered once, then steadied. Francine's eyes were wide. Emily gave a nervous laugh. A floorboard creaked as Emily shifted her stance, catching both of their attention.

"Have things settled down at the hotel?" Emily asked.

"For now, apparently. But if I stay there tonight, I'm sure he'll start up again. I think Vince has someone watching me." Her eyes darted toward the front window. "I'm thinking of switching hotels. I can't go another night without sleep, not to mention how unfair it is to the rest of the guests to be interrupted by noises all night long."

Emily nodded slowly. "Let's go one better. How about if you pretend you're switching, but you stay here instead?"

"It's just that I really like the place where I am, and I've got all my work spread out and everything," Francine started to protest. Then she caught herself. "Why not? Just for one night. In case someone is watching, I'll carry a suitcase out and get in my car …"

"Drive to another hotel and walk into the lobby. I'll wait somewhere, maybe near a side exit, and pick you up. Leave your car there. In the morning, we can ask some questions at both places, to see if they've had reports of the things you experienced. If not, ta-da! You're rid of your ghosts."

Emily straightened a stack of research books that lay waiting for one of her patrons. "And if the mischief continues, we can encourage the hotel staff to report it to the law," she said, keeping her voice low. "Maybe we're pushing Vince harder than we thought."

Francine looked at Emily, her eyes a little anxious. "Maybe," she admitted. "But if we let up, it could give him the chance to do something even worse. Such as actually harming someone during one of those tours in the cave."

"Or defrauding investors and skipping town. We can't give him that opportunity." The idea angered Emily. "Sheriff Cardwell can't think it's all just a coincidence," she said, certain that Francine had already updated him.

"I spoke to him yesterday, after Vince's warning." Francine crossed her arms, defiance in the gesture. "I told him everything we've learned about the cons and the fake gold in the tours. But I don't think the sheriff is ready to do anything yet. Not without more proof. He doesn't want to play his hand too soon. He told me that con artists always have some kind of glib reply to every question, and they're notorious for leaving town in the middle of the night if they sense they'll be caught."

Emily nodded. It was pretty much as she had feared.

"I did learn something more about Russell Pinkney. Your Sheriff Beau called in a favor from his counterpart in Maricopa County, whose deputy paid a visit to the university, to see if Pinkney was really taking a sabbatical."

"Oh?"

"It turns out that he is. The deputy didn't simply walk away. She got specifics—Pinkney was in Taos recently, but it was months ago. The timeframe doesn't overlap with Cliff's visit here at all. Right now, he is supposedly on an elk hunt with his son-in-law in Montana. The sheriff plans to track that down and verify it."

The lamplight cast Emily's shadow across the documents on the table. "I wish there was a way to act fast, but we still need to find Cliff," she said. "If, as Beau suggested, Vince gets spooked and decides to leave town—" She didn't finish the thought. They both knew what it could mean. They might never know what happened to the professor.

"If there's a chance of that, it's all the more reason to stop him first," Francine countered, but they both realized they were in risky territory.

"So, what do we do?" Emily asked. "*We* know Vince is running a scam. We know he threatened you. But we don't know where Cliff is."

Francine leaned against one of the bookshelves, her reflection wavering in the glass doors. "Sheriff Cardwell's doing what he can, but you heard him. He won't move on it unless he gets a concrete lead."

Emily considered her words. Another flicker of the lamps startled them, adding to the gravity of the moment. "Then maybe we need to give him one," she said slowly. "Make Vince think he's already lost and see what he does.

He might slip up. He might get careless."

"Or he might get mean," Francine replied. "What if we provoke him, and someone gets hurt? What if I'm the reason we never find Cliff?"

The words echoed in the quiet room, and Francine let out a long breath. "I don't want to endanger Cliff, or anyone else," she continued. "It's the worst thing I can imagine."

Emily walked to the window, watching as an evening shadow crept across the street outside. "We can be smart about it," she said, turning back to Francine. "We can keep the pressure on without risking too much. But if we wait—" She let the thought hang, unfinished.

"If we wait," Francine echoed, looking pained. "Emily, I've already put you in the middle of this. I don't want—"

"I'm in the middle, no matter what," Emily interrupted. "And I'd rather know what's coming than sit back and watch it happen. I'll talk to Vince myself, if I have to."

Francine's eyes widened. "You can't. It's too risky. And if he thinks we're working together—"

"He already thinks that," Emily pointed out. "I was with you when you talked to him. I'm the new librarian, remember? The granddaughter of David Plankhurst. Why wouldn't I be working with the best historian in the state?"

The room was silent for a moment, as Emily's words sank in. "I don't like it," Francine finally said. "But if you're sure—"

"I'm sure." Emily's tone left no room for doubt. She walked back to Francine. "He might not even know I'm onto him. If I play it right, maybe I can get him to slip up without realizing he's done it."

Francine shook her head, but there was a glint of

reluctant agreement in her eyes. "You've got more nerve than I do," she said with a tense smile. "But be careful, Emily. We can't take chances. Not now."

The two women stood in the silent library, listening to the ticking clock. "He thinks he's got it all planned," Francine said quietly. "He thinks he's smarter than anyone else."

"Maybe it's time to show him he's not," Emily replied. She moved toward the door, confident now that they were on the right track. "Let's put Operation Hotel Switch in motion."

"I'll text you when I'm heading to the new place."

"Got it, and I'll be there."

"Thanks for offering your spare room," Francine said.

"No problem at all." Emily made a mental note to check the freshness of the linens and put out extra towels.

She saw Francine out the front door and watched as her friend got safely into her vehicle. But out of the corner of her eye she spotted movement down the street. A dark figure ran toward a sleek sports car, got in, and raced away.

Chapter 22

Morning sun filtered through the lace curtains at Emily's bedroom window, and the previous evening's strangeness came rushing back. The unsteady lights in the library, the dark car racing away when Francine left. And that reminded her she had a houseguest. She quickly showered and dressed, then made her way through her living room.

The smell of coffee greeted her before she got to the kitchen.

"I hope you don't mind," Francine said. "Your kitchen is so well organized, I found everything I needed." She held out a filled mug to Emily.

"Some hostess I am." But she was grateful for the instant gratification in the cup.

Francine waved off the comment. "I called both

hotels, asked if there'd been any strange complaints during the night. Neither of them heard a thing. So, I'm going to gather my things and go back to staying at my first place. All I really packed was a toothbrush and change of undies."

"You know, thinking logically about it, since no other guests reported noises, I wouldn't be surprised if someone got into your room and rigged speakers and lights to startle you."

"Seriously?"

"Think about it. The whole basis of their hokey treasure tours relies on recorded sounds and projected images. How much of a stretch is it to play recorded door-slams and rig the lights to blink on and off?"

Francine gave a rueful smile. "And I fell for it."

"Vince's helper could have posed as hotel maintenance and got the maid to let him in when you weren't in the room. Placed a few unobtrusive objects around. He could have even been sitting out in the parking lot to watch for you to turn out your lights at bedtime."

"Or set them up on timers." Francine's phone rang, interrupting the thought. "Sheriff Cardwell, hello. No, I'm at Emily's house right now."

She put the phone on speaker, and Beau's voice came through. "We got DNA results back from the Albuquerque lab that tested Deandra Littleton. The expert compared them and says the blood from the car is a close enough match to indicate they're related. It's most likely the professor's."

"Oh no."

"As I told you before, we don't believe it was enough blood to indicate a fatal wound. And we are still on the lookout. Once we find him, there is probably a reasonable explanation."

"Thank you. I feel better about that," Francine admitted. "And I'm glad you are keeping the search active."

When she ended the call, she turned to Emily with a timid smile. "Well, at least it wasn't bad news. And now I'm going to get out of your way."

"Don't feel like you have to rush off. I have a lunch date, but nothing else this morning."

"You have your regular routine and your library patrons. I've already completely disrupted your life."

"But, for a cause we both want—finding out what's happened to Cliff."

"True. Which is why I'm going back to devote myself to his notes. I still haven't read every single thing Deandra gave me. I'm thinking something among his papers will tell us what trail he wanted to follow when he came here."

"You're sure you don't want to come back here again tonight?"

"I don't think so. It's amazing how much clearer I feel after last night. I slept like a dead person." She halted. "Sorry, with what's going on, I shouldn't joke about that."

"Your bed's here if you want it," Emily assured her as Francine placed her own mug in the sink and picked up the tote bag she'd brought with her.

"Thanks. For now, I'm going to walk down to the bakery, and once I've gorged on an almond croissant, I can walk to the hotel where I left my car. So handy that it's only three or four blocks."

"Keep me posted. I should be back from lunch by early afternoon."

Emily toasted a bagel and finished her coffee, but her mind was still filled with fragmented thoughts of Beau's investigation and the growing pressure to uncover a lead on finding Cliff. She'd thought of a few more documents in the library that might give clues, so she carried her half-eaten bagel and walked over. Moonbeam raced ahead and waited for her at the back door.

She went through her morning routine, switching on lights, booting up the computer, turning the Open sign around. An early-bird patron drove up and greeted her happily when he saw that she'd found the books he wanted. She finished the checkout process and went in search of the documents she wanted, settling with them at the table.

"There has to be something we're missing," she muttered, pushing her glasses up the bridge of her nose. "Some clue hidden in plain sight …"

The problem with research was how much time it eats up, she realized when Kevin walked in, startling her from her reverie. Emily's eyes widened as she glanced at the time.

"Oh no, I'm going to be late!" she exclaimed, hastily grabbing her shoulder bag from under the desk.

As she stepped out onto the sun-drenched streets of Taos, Emily took a deep breath of the crisp autumn air. The adobe buildings seemed to glow in the golden light, their earth-toned walls a gorgeous contrast to the vibrant blue sky above. She hopped into her Jeep and made her way toward Riki's shop.

"I hope this lunch helps clear my head," Emily thought, pausing at a stop sign. "Maybe Riki and Kelly will have some fresh perspectives."

The aroma of freshly baked brownies wafted from the bakery next door to Puppy Chic, making Emily's stomach growl. She stepped inside, deciding that she would provide the lunch. This would be quicker than fast food and so much more nutritious.

"Hey, Jen, how's it going? I need three slices of quiche,

please," she said to Jen after a quick scan of the display case. As she waited, Emily's mind drifted back to the investigation. What if they were looking at this all wrong? What if Cliff's disappearance wasn't just about the present, but somehow connected to the past?

Jen's voice pulled her back to reality. "Here you go. Enjoy!"

Emily thanked her, carefully balancing the warm paper bag as she stepped back out into the sunlight. The quiches reminded her of the simple joys amidst the complexity of the mystery she was trying to unravel.

"One step at a time," she whispered to herself, a tiny smile tugging at the corners of her mouth as she approached the colorful facade of Puppy Chic. "Who knows? Maybe the answers we need are waiting just around the corner."

As Emily pushed open the door to the grooming shop, a cacophony of barks and yips greeted her. The cheerful chaos enveloped her—the earthy scent of shampoo mingling with the unmistakable aroma of dog, the sight of wagging tails, and the feel of fur brushing against her legs as an excited retriever bounded past.

"Yay, look who's here!" Riki's warm voice rang out above the din. "If it isn't our favorite bookworm!"

Emily's tension melted at the sight of her friend's beaming face. Riki's curls were pulled up in a messy bun, a few strands escaping to frame her smiling face.

"Hey, Riki," Emily called back, carefully maneuvering through the furry obstacle course. "I come bearing gifts of the quiche variety."

Riki's eyes lit up. "You're a proper lifesaver, you are! I'm famished."

As Emily set the bag down on the grooming counter,

she heard the click of a door from the back room. Kelly emerged, her arms full of freshly laundered towels.

"Emily!" Kelly exclaimed, her face brightening. "Perfect timing. I was just about to ask what everyone would want for lunch."

Luckily, I'm a born planner. Emily grinned, gesturing to the bag. "Great minds think alike. Shall we head outside? It's too nice a day to stay cooped up."

The three friends gathered their lunch and stepped out onto the sidewalk. A small wrought iron table waited for them, bathed in the warm sunlight. As they settled in, Emily couldn't help but think, *this is exactly what I needed— excellent food, great friends, and a chance to clear my head.*

Riki took a bite of her quiche and sighed contentedly. "This is brilliant. So, Emily, what's new in the world of dusty tomes and hidden treasures?"

Emily chuckled, her hand instinctively reaching up to adjust her glasses. "Oh, you know, just the usual. Uncovering centuries-old secrets, chasing ghosts of the past … all in a day's work at the Morton Library."

The others laughed at her description, maybe with a little envy.

As they ate, Emily found herself relaxing, the warmth of the sun and the company of her friends providing a welcome respite from the intensity of the investigation. Yet, even as she laughed at Riki's jokes and listened to Kelly's latest anecdotes about Ana and her escapades, a part of her mind continued to turn over the puzzle pieces of Cliff's disappearance.

Maybe, she thought, taking a sip of her iced tea, *the answers I'm looking for are closer than I think. Sometimes it takes stepping away to see things clearly.*

Riki was the one who brought up the question about Francine's missing colleague. Emily set her fork down, suddenly serious. "Actually, there's been almost nothing new." She leaned in, her voice dropping to a hushed tone. "Francine's been working tirelessly, but we're hitting dead ends at every turn."

Riki's eyebrows furrowed with concern. "That's rough. Poor Francine must be going a bit mad."

"You have no idea," Emily sighed. "It's like he vanished into thin air. Sheriff Beau located his car, abandoned, but otherwise we've exhausted every conventional lead. An academic competitor was here in town for a while, but we can't seem to locate him now, either. We're running out of options, and I can't help but feel like we're missing something crucial."

Riki glanced at her watch and stood up, brushing crumbs from her jeans. "I'd better get back to the shop. Marcy Jones's poodle won't groom itself, you know." She squeezed Emily's shoulder. "Keep your chin up, love. You'll crack it yet."

As Riki disappeared into the cheerful chaos of barking dogs, Kelly turned to Emily with a thoughtful expression. "Have you ever considered … alternative methods of investigation?"

Emily tilted her head, curiosity piqued. "What do you mean?"

Kelly leaned in, her voice barely above a whisper. "I have a book of runes. Ancient symbols that can offer guidance, reveal hidden meanings. They might provide insights we've overlooked."

Chapter 23

Runes? I've never thought about using anything like that in research." She'd wondered if Kelly and her mother were believers in some unconventional things. Now she felt pulled between skepticism and desperation. "Do you really think they could help?"

Kelly nodded earnestly. "It can't hurt to try. Sometimes, when normal methods fail, we need to open our minds to other options. The runes have a way of illuminating paths we didn't even know existed."

What do I have to lose? If there's even a chance it could help Francine find Cliff …

Emily's eyes sparkled. "All right, I'm willing to give it a try. Where do we start?"

Kelly beamed. "If you have time now, let's head to my place. I keep the book in my attic studio."

Why not? She'd left Kevin in charge of the library for the afternoon and wasn't expecting any visitors who would need her attention. The only person on the appointment schedule was a tribal elder who wanted to go through some documents. Kevin was much more qualified to help in that area.

The two women climbed into their cars, the warm autumn sun highlighting the crowds of tourists as Emily followed Kelly past the plaza and several galleries. Emily couldn't help but think of Francine and the urgency of their mission.

"I hope she won't think I've lost my mind," Emily murmured, tapping nervously on the steering wheel when she got caught by the red light at Civic Plaza Drive. "On the other hand, I really don't need to tell her about this, do I?"

She watched Kelly's little car continue ahead, but within a few blocks she had caught up. They pulled up to Kelly's Victorian home, its gingerbread trim looking fresh and crisp in the afternoon light, and Emily felt a flutter of excitement in her chest.

"Scott took Ana to her pediatrician appointment and promised her ice cream afterward, so we should have plenty of time to ourselves," Kelly said, unlocking the front door and ushering Emily into the spacious foyer.

Emily had always been impressed with the beautiful old house and the restoration work done when the Sweet family had bought the place from the estate of the famed author, Eliza Nalespar. The same author whose legacy endowment now funded operations of the Morton Library. Taos really was a small town.

They bypassed the wide doorways to the parlor on the right and dining room on the left, climbed the sweeping staircase to the second floor, and proceeded to the narrow stairs to the third-floor attic.

"Would you like tea?" Kelly offered, as she rummaged through an oak cupboard. "Just hit the button on the kettle over there. Teabags are in the tin beside it."

Tea sounded ideal. Emily found a hearty assam and dropped a bag into a mug she spotted on the neatly arranged shelf above. She did a second one for her friend.

"Ah, here we are," Kelly said triumphantly, pulling out a leather-bound volume and a carved wooden box.

While Emily waited for the kettle to boil, she noticed that Kelly held the box, closing her eyes. By the time the two steaming mugs were ready, Kelly had settled at a worn trestle table with the book in front of her. She indicated the chair beside her. Emily perched on the edge of it, leaning in to get a better look. She saw pages of symbols and letters that made no sense to her.

"I usually pose a question and then let the book take me to the answer." Kelly held the book between the palms of her hands, its spine resting on the table. She lightly closed her eyes again and said, "Help us find a missing professor who was here in Taos a few weeks ago."

Kelly allowed the book to fall open to a random page. "These ancient symbols have been used for centuries to divine hidden truths," she explained in a hushed voice. "Each rune carries its own meaning and energy."

Emily's eyebrows furrowed. "Does it really work?"

Kelly's eyes twinkled. "You'd be amazed. Once, I used these runes to locate a friend's lost wedding ring. The symbols led us right to it, tucked away in a place she'd never thought to look."

As Kelly ran her fingertips gently over the symbols on

the page, Emily found herself drawn in despite her initial doubts. The heady scent of herbs and the warm glow of the sun filtering through the attic window created a serene atmosphere.

"Can you read the markings, Kel? They all look like hieroglyphics to me."

Kelly began to read aloud. "There are random words ...*wandering* and *lost* but there are more: *darkness, trickery, deceit*, and some type of a *find*. Here's one full sentence: the lost object has been stored in a safe place ..."

"Lost object? Lost person?"

"Probably. It's not really an exact science." Kelly turned her attention back to the page. "Okay, it also says, 'The safe was breached.' At least I think that's what it says. I'm not sure the translation of 'breached' is exactly right."

Emily nibbled at her lower lip. "I wonder where this safe place is? What else does it say?"

Kelly started to touch the page again, but the writing had vanished. Both of them stared at the now-blank page.

"What the—" Emily felt her chin drop.

"Okay ... that appears to be all it has to say on that subject."

"What about on another page, phrasing the *where* as a separate question? Do you suppose the runes could create a map of sorts?" Emily suggested, her voice quickening with excitement. "Could it work that way?"

Kelly's face lit up. "Oh, that's brilliant! I can also try to incorporate them into a timeline of events."

".... to help us think outside the box about potential leads we've overlooked."

When Kelly posed the question about where this *safe place* might be, an image appeared. Unfortunately, it showed only a forest. Tucked among the trees was a wooden house, maybe a cabin. She tried rephrasing the question, being more specific in her query, even asking for a map or a timeline, but it seemed the book was finished.

"Can I take a picture of that image on the page?" Emily asked, reaching for her purse.

"Try it. I really don't know."

But by the time she'd retrieved her phone, the page had gone completely blank.

"Okay, I guess it doesn't want its picture taken," Emily said with a rueful grin. She pulled out her notebook and quickly jotted down the information they'd received. "You know," she mused, pausing to adjust her dark-rimmed glasses, "Francine might be skeptical of this at first, but I think she'd appreciate the systematic approach and the answers we got."

Kelly grinned. "That's what's so great about you, Em. You always find a way to bridge the gap between the mystical and the practical."

Emily gave a nervous smile. *You don't know the half of it. Wait till you meet my grandma.* She stood to leave, giving Kelly a hug. "I can't thank you enough for this. Your insights, this book—I really do think we learned something."

Kelly smiled in return. "We did. Not sure what, exactly, but we did learn something."

The Victorian house creaked comfortingly around them as they made their way downstairs.

"You know," Emily said, pausing at the front door, "there's something oddly fitting about using runes to solve a mystery here in Taos."

She walked out to her Jeep. The sun was already low on the horizon, and her mind whirled with what she'd learned. Maybe something in the library would connect it all together, and Francine might have ideas to add.

"Francine might actually be intrigued by the historical angle. Or she might think I've lost my mind." She giggled at the thought as she turned onto her street. "Even if the runes don't pan out directly, they've given us new ways to approach the problem. That has to count for something."

As she pulled into her driveway, Emily took a deep breath. "One way or another," she murmured, "we're going to find you, Cliff. And these runes just might be the key to unlocking the whole mystery."

Chapter 24

Jax shoved his worries aside and stood apart, letting the shadowed corners of the private dining room conceal him as Vince Hutchins spun his tales to an audience of gullible, well-heeled potential investors. As he walked among the tables, Vince leaned toward his listeners, his voice low and compelling.

"What we have for you folks tonight, is a rare— You know, I have to say, an *unheard of* opportunity." He wore a confident grin.

"My team and I have researched meticulously. We've talked with the brightest minds in the academic world, the top historians from the university ..."

Talked with, yeah, but the guy shared nothing of use to us. Jax pushed back the knot of anxiety over that particular debacle.

"And what we have now, is the chance to bring in a few—mind you, only a *select* few—investors to share in the capture of ... the Conquistador's Gold. This treasure was assumed to be a mere legend here in the Southwest."

Which none of you ever heard about because you're not from around here. Jax had noted the out-of-state plates dominating the parking lot when he arrived.

"The famed Seven Cities of Cibola were where the Spanish king sent his troops to capture these cities actually built of gold!" Vince's tone capitalized the prestigious title before he paused to let that sink in. "Those very conquistadors rode right through here, through this little town when it was even littler than now ..." strategic pause for laughter "... and they hid that gold in the hills. Back then, you see, Indian attacks were common. And these men knew they needed to hide the king's treasure. But they would come back for it. And then they didn't."

Three long beats, while that sank in.

"And we *know* where that gold is."

The entire story was pure b.s. but Jax could see the diners' cynicism melt. Couples exchanged glances. Jax watched them warm to Vince's pitch and saw the glimmer of greed in their eyes, a familiar, shared hope that the next time Vince spoke they might be included in whatever marvelous plan he had in mind.

At a subtle signal from Vince, a waiter appeared and refilled wine glasses. The warmth of the room mixed with the smell of sage-roasted prime beef and the expensive wine, creating an illusion of comfort and camaraderie.

From his corner, Jax tracked every move, each animated gesture and well-timed pause, and he knew exactly when Vince had them hooked. It was all part of the performance.

"Of course," at this point, Vince ducked his head

slightly, as if admitting to a fault, "of course, it's not cheap to get into these places or to bring out a treasure of this magnitude. It will take a whole crew—all of whom must be thoroughly screened for security risks—and we'll probably need trucks and trucks, to get this treasure out of the hills and transported to the safety of bank vaults."

Again, the almost-shy tilt of his head. "And that's where I'm asking for your help. But—" one index finger raised "—but I'm not asking for a freebie, no sir. Every single one of you who pitches in to help us out with the cost … every one of you is a fully invested partner."

Like me, the guy who's about to get screwed out of everything I was promised? Jax gritted his teeth.

"You will *all* receive a just percentage, based on your investment. And from the preliminary figures I've obtained from the *certified* gold assayers named in *your* prospectus there, each of us will probably quadruple our money. And yes, that's me too, folks. I've invested *every* penny I've got in this operation." His voice was taking on the cadence of a televangelist now.

Jax had already slipped one of the made-up prospectuses into his inner jacket pocket, more evidence for his contact guy.

"The only thing, folks, this is a limited engagement. I mean, we gotta act now," Vince announced to the group, his tone making the cliché sound sincere. "No guarantees for tomorrow. This is an exclusive, ladies and gentlemen. You'll be the first, the very *first*, to discover what treasure lies within the hills of Taos. I want you to imagine the adventure. The gold. And it's all here, just waiting for you."

He gestured toward the easel at the front of the room, where one of his cheaply printed treasure maps had been dressed up with some color and a few extra symbols to make it seem as if a geological survey firm had checked and endorsed it.

Jax crossed his arms over his chest. *Yeah? So, when were these rubes going to actually start writing checks?* He'd heard the pitch so many times before, but this time Vince was going all out. The dinner invitation, the upscale venue—he had brought out his A-game, a sign that he was a little desperate to close the deal and get moving.

This time, at least, the guests were eating it up, literally and figuratively, sharing stealthy smiles over candlelight and weighing their greed against the lure of the promises.

One of the wealthier-looking couples at the table glanced at each other, and Jax saw the exact moment they decided they would go for it. They were a plant, of course, someone he'd hired to dress up and play the part of first-in. Their nod to Vince, as if confirming a pact, marked their assent to get in on the deal.

"Don't let someone else find your treasure," Vince teased. "From experience, I can tell you, no regrets for the bold and brave."

The couple Vince had pointed to laughed as if sharing a joke with the others. With luck, they would now become Vince's promotional team. Jax understood how these things worked. He'd watched it before. Someone leaps in. Somebody else sees them go and they join. This encouraged rubes number three, four, and five to go ahead. And shortly after that, it would be everyone in the room. They just needed that safety of seeing somebody else be the first to sign up. The tipping point always seemed to be three.

But now, no one else was jumping. What was wrong?

"Finders keepers," Vince quipped with a wide grin. "And, of course, it's our secret. Just us treasure hunters in the know." Vince Hutchins was never more sincere than when he was lying.

That 'in the know' bit had grabbed some attention. A few eyes sparkled, but a few more still held that wait-and-see look.

Jax stayed in his shadowed spot, observing the small change in Vince's face. He'd known Vince long enough to read the subtle shift, the way his charming smile widened when things weren't quite working. The presentation ramped up, with Vince promising early access to maps and leads, clues he would give only to them.

"Imagine the payoff," he urged. "Think of the bragging rights. You can go home with the investment potential of a lifetime."

One of the listeners, a skeptical woman in a designer dress, raised a question. "How close by is this treasure? You've been there and seen it for yourself?" she asked, raising one perfectly shaped eyebrow.

Vince laughed easily, waving a hand as if batting away a fly. "I do know exactly where it is. A smart investor like you knows the best returns come with risk. You can't get gold from a damn ATM."

The group chuckled. Jax saw the woman nudge her partner and caught the glint of the enormous diamond on her hand. These were people who were used to spending money. Another half million wouldn't be a big deal to them, would it?

Jax shifted his weight, uncomfortable as he thought of the millions Vince hoped to bring in tonight.

Another couple gave Vince the nod. "You can put us

down for it," the man said.

That was two. Jax could hardly stand to watch, but he couldn't look away. He couldn't breathe. If a third, and then a fourth, investor spoke up, soon the inevitable end was coming and they would have to beat it out of town—fast. Because in the eyes of the law, Jax would be every bit as guilty as Vince, whether he actually received a penny for his involvement or not.

Suddenly the room was too hot, too full of his own resentment, so without a word to Vince or anyone, Jax slipped away. But even as he was seeing Vince in a clearer light, his own problem loomed larger. He would soon have to admit that he'd lost their hostage.

Chapter 25

Jax's fists clenched, tight and furious, as he left the restaurant and stepped into the dark street. The crisp autumn air nipped at his skin. Vince's slippery pitch still rang in his ears, the empty assurances to the marks, the promises that would never come true.

Because, he realized, everyone was a sucker, including himself. A weakness, Jax thought, that Agent Steve Price would try to exploit. He had to do this right. Get ahead of Vince's game. Get out while he still could. But he had no access to all the money that would soon roll in. He had only one choice.

He pulled out his phone and tapped the number he'd memorized.

"Price."

"Yeah, Jax. Whatcha got?"

"Everything's coming down. Soon. He's got maybe five million dollars sitting in a room with him right now. Once that comes through, he'll be outta here. You need to make your move now."

"I can have a warrant in an hour. The judge already approved it and knows we're nearly ready to move."

"Didn't you hear me say *now*? Look, I'm just saying … I need to get out clean."

"Right. Right. Okay, look. I'll make the calls. Meet me at Vince's office. Ten minutes."

"I ca—never mind. I'll be there." He had no idea what story he would cook up when he next saw Vince, but he reached into his pocket and pulled out the keys to the Ferrari.

During the longest ten-minute drive of his life, Jax relived his prior conversation with Steve Price. It was only two days ago, in a coffee shop out by the pueblo. Price had the local look nailed, leather jacket and a turquoise bolo tie that might have been real. He wanted stories, and Jax had plenty of them—how things went down, how Vince always structured the hook, the grab, and the escape. Price already knew a lot, how he'd been chased out of other towns, that he'd done it all before. Clearly, the FBI had been watching Vince Hutchins since way before he came to New Mexico. And they knew Jax had been a part of it before, back in Arizona.

In that coffee shop, Price had taken a new tack. "Know anything about a university professor, Clifford Littleton?"

"Maybe." Jax had grunted.

The agent nodded, not pushing. "Look. You might already have figured this out, but Vince is about one step away from screwing you over. We hear he's lining up more than he can deliver, taking on more investors and planning to leave you holding the rap for a dead academic. That's a forever-sentence in prison, you know."

The accusation sent an electric jolt through Jax.

He'd thought about those words for the last forty-eight hours. They rang true, especially tonight. Vince had promised those rubes the world. Jax saw how fast Vince moved, taking the money, minimizing the risk. But Vince had a knack for spinning anything into a win. Even now, Jax couldn't help admiring that.

But within the past month, Vince had grown reckless. When Cliff first showed up, Vince should have been more careful, should have never even talked to the guy. It was clear that Vince was pushing too far.

"He'll run. And you'll be the one in cuffs," Price had reminded.

Jax hadn't said anything to that. But it festered. All of it. Enough that now, as he drove through the quiet streets of Taos, on the way to meet Price again, he knew he had to decide. Do it or don't.

With knuckles white on the steering wheel, the conversation from two days ago played in a loop in his head. The agent made it sound easy, like they'd drop all charges if he could just give them more. Better proof. And if he could provide details that would tie Vince to Cliff, the whole thing could turn into a kidnapping case—or more. A murder rap would put Vince away forever.

It would mean ratting his partner out, a frightening idea. But wasn't it more likely Vince would throw him under the bus first? Vince was never one to let sentiment get in the way of a score. Leaving Jax without a dime, leaving Jax with the consequences? Vince Hutchins took risks, sure, but he always made sure he came out on top.

He paused at a traffic light, two blocks from the office. A full moon peeked from behind heavy clouds, a serene sight. But Jax felt anything but serene. Every nerve tingled as tonight's presentation to the venture capitalists replayed in his head.

Vince had always counted on the volume of the con. More investors. More towns. And the Arizona job actually had paid off. But Vince was changing the game this time. Running tours until he had enough, then cutting out? Probably.

The reality set in, stark and unavoidable. One of these times it wouldn't work. New targets were getting smarter. Better connected. They had high power lawyers; they would go to the police. And then Vince would go underground. But Jax? Jax would end up screwed.

Letting Price and his team into the office was the answer. If they could get copies of the investor list and that new, fake prospectus Jax had in his pocket right now, the FBI might give him a deal. Might keep him out of prison. He thought about the risk. And about Clifford Littleton. Which was yet another mess to figure out.

* * *

"This place is more of a dump than I'd imagined," Price said, taking in the jumble of crap in the storeroom, the cheap metal filing cabinets in the office, and the boxes of brochures. Jax found the tourist lists, credit card receipts, the new contract sheets, and he didn't hesitate as one of the feds ran them through the copier.

They were all there, including the ridiculous new prospectus Vince had printed up with his usual flair for making bullshit sound believable. Price rifled through, tossing aside the duplicates, sorting what he wanted.

Jax's phone buzzed in his hand. "Hell, I gotta go. Unless you want Vince to bail out tonight, try to leave things as you found them. Or get that warrant ready to arrest him."

He could tell the agents didn't yet have enough evidence to make the serious charges stick. He put a hand on the doorknob. "And lock the door when you leave."

"Right. And you—don't admit to anything. We need you to stick with him until we can move in and make an arrest."

"How much longer?"

"A few days, at least."

He couldn't believe he was trusting a federal agent this way, but what choice did he have? The phone buzzed again.

"Yeah."

"Jax, where the hell are you?"

"On the way back. See you in five." If he ran every red light. But he needed the time to come up with a story. Hopefully, Vince would just assume he'd gone outside for a smoke and hadn't realized how long he'd actually been away.

His hopes were dashed when he pulled up in front of the restaurant and saw Vince pacing the sidewalk, his face beet-red. He yanked the passenger door open before Jax was fully stopped.

"What the freaking hell!"

"Are the investors all gone?"

"*No*, but that's no thanks to you. I ordered a stupidly pricy dessert and some ridiculous champagne to keep them going. Now get your ass inside and help me close this deal."

Jax had about four dozen questions but they would

wait. He parked the car and got out, straightening his jacket on the way inside.

The mood in the dining room didn't feel festive, and he could immediately see why Vince was getting nervous. Even though he'd stepped back up to the front of the room and put on his best salesman smile, Vince wasn't wowing the crowd as before.

Using their own inside sign language, Vince let Jax know which two couples had pledged money. He was expected to sit with them and talk up the potential find and how he, himself, had money at stake and was so excited for the retrieval of the gold to commence. Since the guests hadn't seen much of Jax earlier in the evening, they had no way of knowing he was Vince's partner.

One by one, the couples began to say goodbye, telling Vince they would certainly consider the investment offer and would get back to him in a day or so. It was basically the kiss of death to the whole enterprise.

While others jabbered on, Jax was glad he hadn't eaten any of the meal. It would be all over the floor by now. He still had to come up with an explanation for Vince, for how Cliff Littleton had vanished (he had no clue), and why despite driving the streets of Taos during every spare moment of his time, he hadn't been able to find the missing man.

Talk about the kiss of death.

Chapter 26

All night long, Emily's dreams were filled with what she'd learned during the rune reading at Kelly's house. Among the words that had come up were 'wandering' and 'lost' but there were others—darkness, trickery, deceit, and some type of a 'find.' She understood how some of those could relate, but others made no sense. And what was that image in the rune book, the one depicting a house in a forest? The mountains around here were solid with trees and lots of cabins and houses. How was she supposed to make sense of it all?

After tossing and turning into the morning's wee hours, at daylight she decided to get up. Writing down all her thoughts and impressions would help solidify and define what she'd seen. And give her mind some peace.

She brewed a cup of tea and then settled into a spot in

the corner of the living room sofa, a woven blanket over her legs and Moonbeam snuggled onto her lap. For a long moment she closed her eyes and breathed deeply, recalling the images of the runes on the pages. Without dwelling too much on specifics, she picked up her notebook and pen and began writing—any and every thought that came into her mind. It all went on the page.

When she glanced at the clock across the room, she realized that more than an hour had passed. Setting the notebook aside, she went back into the kitchen where she made a hearty breakfast—omelet, bacon, and toast. She found her eyes traveling to the kitchen window, thinking of Francine arriving, but then remembered the professor had said she planned to burrow away in her hotel room and go, page by page, through all of Cliff's materials again.

When Emily looked down again, she saw that Moonbeam was sitting beside her chair, attentively waiting for a morsel of egg from her plate.

"Am I selfish for thinking this, but isn't it nice to have the place to ourselves again for a while?" She posed the question as she handed the cat a tiny morsel.

Mrroww. It must have meant *I agree* and *thank you*, at the same time.

Emily took her time clearing the dishes and tidying up the kitchen, heading back to her bedroom, and dressing for the day. Kevin would be at the library again this afternoon, but she had the morning fully to herself. And while her initial thought was that it would be the ideal time to really dig in and organize another box or two of those new donations, the idea that jutted into her consciousness was more along the lines of walking down to Sweet's Sweets to see if they had any more of those bear claws.

"No," she told herself aloud. "I just had a big breakfast

and I do not need a huge pastry."

"But they taste *so* yummy," said her bad-girl side. Or was it?

She tugged a cotton t-shirt over her head and spotted a familiar shape—gauzy skirt, beads, and all—in the corner of her bedroom. "Grandma ... are you trying to tempt me with a sugar high?"

The enigmatic smile hinted that perhaps sugar was no worse a high than Valerie's generation used to enjoy.

"Stop it, right now! I need to do something productive."

"And why is that?"

"Well ..."

"Exactly." Valerie floated toward the bed and reclined among the tousled covers. "Sometimes our greatest moments of insight happen when we're least pressuring ourselves."

"Okay, point taken. I promise I will spend a little time outside today." Emily picked up her pillow and plumped it. "Now scoot. I need to make up my bed."

Valerie sent her a loving smile and faded away.

Morning sunshine tracked across the courtyard when Emily glanced out the kitchen window. She spotted Victor Martinez's pickup truck and walked out to say hello.

"*Buenos dias*, Victor," she called out.

"Ah, Señorita Emily! What a beautiful day, no?"

She glanced at a large canvas bag on the tailgate of his truck.

"I brought mulch, for the flowerbeds," he said. "I water them a little, then mulch, then water again. Everything will be *muy contento* for the winter."

She smiled, noticing how the spray from the hose created a rainbow mist. "Victor, are you doing all right? I mean, after …"

He nodded vigorously. "*Si. Todo esta bien.*" He turned away, adjusting the water flow and moving the hose.

The poor man had gone missing last spring, and everyone in the community had been concerned for his safety. It was no wonder he didn't want to talk about it. Emily made a show of unlocking the library door and waving to him as she went inside.

As she switched on the overhead lights and measured coffee into the filter basket, a vivid memory came into her mind—her grandfather doing this same task, his eyes twinkling as he teased ten-year-old Emily about how she took her coffee. Moonbeam slithered between her legs and jumped up to a bookshelf, sitting eye-level with Emily. The cat stared, unblinking, as Em filled the coffee maker with water And in her head, her grandfather's voice came through once again. "The Spanish Conquest."

Emily scanned the room, but the only one here was the cat. She remembered young Ana's interaction with Moonbeam recently. Was Grandpa somehow speaking through a feline, steering her toward something specific? "The Spanish Conquest, Grandpa? What aspect of it?"

What had Grandma said this morning—answers will appear at unexpected times? The cat, after all, had lived here before, had interacted with both grandparents.

She quieted her mind and let David's response come. "Map. In the book."

"Okay … Can you show me?"

And without hearing a verbal answer, she walked toward the bookcase where Moonbeam sat. Her fingers moved along the spines until she thought she heard *stop!* It was one of the oldest books in the collection—she knew that much. But the title indicated it was a guide to Indian pottery, not about the Spanish Conquest at all.

Emily pulled the volume from the shelf and opened it, her pulse quickening as a faded piece of parchment fluttered to the floor. The distinctive shape of it practically screamed at her. Could this be the missing fragment of the map she had found a few days ago?

"Oh my," she breathed, carefully retrieving the delicate map. "Grandpa, what secrets have you been keeping?"

Mrroww. And with that, the cat departed into another room.

Emily carried the map to the table and placed it in a clear, protective sleeve before setting the map alongside the historical texts Dr. Francine Morales had been poring over.

"Okay, let's see what we've got here," she said to herself.

Starting at one edge, she began meticulously cross-referencing markings and names with passages from the texts, making notes on a notepad in her neat handwriting. Her eyes darted between the various sources. One word, *cueva,* caught her attention.

Almost immediately, she knew that the notation on the map was not the same cave where she'd been taken for the so-called treasure tour. That information didn't really surprise her; the tour was a touristy sham, and she'd known that from the beginning. But this … this map was genuinely old. It was the kind of document that probably would have ended up in the Spanish National Archives if it had been carried back to its creator's home country.

She laid the book open to the page the map had fallen out of. "Grandpa? This can't be a coincidence," she muttered, copying a particular passage into her journal. "It mentions a hidden location, but where? On this map?"

What if this map held the key to unlocking the mystery of the rumored Spanish treasure? This just might be the type of find that would make a believer of an eminent historian like Dr. Littleton.

And what about his disappearance? Had he known about this document?

Perhaps most importantly, how did an ancient map like this tie in with what was currently going on, those men arriving and claiming to know exactly where the real riches were to be found? Clearly, they had not gotten hold of the original map—they would have never returned it to the library. But maybe they had convinced Cliff to talk. Was that where the words trickery and deceit had come from, in Kelly's rune reading?

Emily squeezed her eyes shut. *Please don't let them have tortured him.*

"I need to talk to Francine about this," Emily decided, closing her notebook with a satisfying thump. "She'll know how to approach this rationally."

She was about to return the books to their rightful places, but something stopped her when her eyes landed on a passage that perfectly described the map's intricate markings. A deep ravine, a draw that led higher into the mountains.

She pulled her laptop over and brought up a topo map of the area, comparing it with the ancient parchment. It matched.

Another search came up with a report, written about ten years ago, by two geologists and published in the university's guidebook to minerals. The authors concluded that the Spanish probably prospected in northern Taos County, although they did not definitively state that any impressive amount of gold was found. This map might overturn it all.

"Oh my gosh," she whispered, her voice barely audible in the quiet library. "This really could be it!"

She leaned back in her chair, running a hand through her blonde hair as the realization hit her. "An inaccessible ravine, a cave there? That's where the treasure might be!"

What if she was on the cusp of something big— something that could change everything they thought they knew about the county's history.

"I can't believe it," she muttered, her blue eyes wide behind her glasses. "Francine's going to flip when she hears about this!" She began typing a text, urging her to come to the library.

As she impatiently waited for Francine's response, Emily couldn't help but imagine the implications. Beyond any thoughts of treasure—this location might be where Cliff had gone.

"Focus, Emily," she chided herself, shaking her head. "One step at a time."

She fidgeted, tapping her nails on the desk. "I wonder if Grandpa knew about this all along." Moonbeam wandered into the room and jumped up on the table. Her paw gently touched the map fragment. "Was that why he showed me that book?"

Mrroww.

Her phone pinged with a text from Francine: I can be there in an hour.

Perfect. Emily forced her breathing to slow down. She wanted to get her documents and notes in order before her friend showed up; otherwise, her thoughts would come rushing out like a geyser. She walked to the counter in the back, realizing she never had started the coffee maker. She pressed the button.

When the front door opened, Emily visibly jumped.

Kevin. She'd forgotten all about him. How could it be noon already?

"Hey, Em." He set his backpack behind the desk. "What's on the agenda for today?"

She noticed he'd spotted the map fragment and she got an idea. "Your grandfather is a tribal elder, right?"

"Um, yeah."

She walked over and pointed to the map where she believed the hidden cave might be. "Has anyone in your family ever talked about this area, like whether there are caves, maybe whether Spanish explorers were ever in this region?"

He studied the map for a long time, his eyes darting back and forth between the topographical map and the yellowed piece of paper. "Well, Spanish explorers, yeah. It's a fairly sure bet. They were all over the place."

She nodded, letting him think.

"And caves … I don't know. This isn't on tribal land, and it's not one of those places I ever poked around as a kid, you know."

"What about the elders? Parents, grandparents, any others ever talk about this kind of thing?"

He shuffled a little from one foot to the other, and she sensed there was something he wasn't saying.

"Okay, no problem. I know there are sacred things the tribe keeps to itself, and I don't want to pry where I shouldn't."

When he visibly relaxed, she knew it was time for a change of subject. And maybe that was best. She felt sure Kevin could keep secrets, but maybe this conversation was best kept between herself and Francine. She invented a bit of research that would take him to the campus south of town for several hours, and he happily grabbed his backpack and headed out.

The library settled into a hush. A glance at the time told Emily that Francine would be here in fifteen minutes or so.

She organized the documents she'd found, setting the map pieces in place so they matched with the modern-day map she'd found online. Maybe that wasn't the right thing to do. Perhaps she should let Francine make the discovery, much as Emily had, on her own. But they were also in a rush to locate Cliff, and the quicker they could put their findings together, the quicker they could reach that goal.

Her hands caressed the edge of her blue leather-bound journal, a gift from her grandfather the summer before his Alzheimer's had become too advanced, before she'd first taken over as caretaker of the library. She recalled his own notes about the conquistadors and his belief that some of the legends were true.

"What would you do, Grandpa?" Emily murmured, her brow furrowing as she considered her discovery. "You talked about the ethics of history when I was just a little girl. Is this something that should be shared, or kept hidden?"

She glanced at the faded map, then back to her meticulous notes. The location of the treasure—if it truly existed—was now within their grasp. But was finding it the right thing to do?

Emily's thoughts drifted to Cliff Littleton, Francine's missing colleague and friend. "This is what you were looking for, wasn't it, Cliff?" she whispered, a pang of worry tightening her chest. "But at what cost?"

She closed her eyes, centering herself. When she opened them again, her gaze was firm. "No, the real mission here is finding you, Cliff. The treasure … that's secondary."

The coffee maker gurgled and Emily nodded to herself, decision made. "I need to tell Francine about this. Together, we can figure out the best way forward. If we find Cliff, we might just find the treasure too."

The crunch of gravel outside told her that Francine had just pulled into the parking lot.

"Grandpa," she whispered, "I wish you could see this. We're so close to unraveling the mystery you always talked about."

Through the front window, Emily spotted Francine's familiar figure approaching the door, the professor's no-nonsense bun, her button-down shirt, and well-fitted jeans looking comfortable in the afternoon sun.

"Hey, what's up? In your text you sounded excited."

"You're not going to believe what I found!"

Francine turned, her eyes lighting up with curiosity. "Okay? What is it?"

Emily couldn't help but grin. "I think I've cracked it," she said, slightly out of breath. "The map, the Spanish treasure—it all fits together!"

Francine's eyebrows shot up. "Show me," she said, her usual skepticism tinged with a hint of excitement.

"If this map leads us to the place where the gold was hidden," she mused aloud, "we might finally understand where Cliff headed. But what if—"

She stopped abruptly, interrupted by the sound of the front door opening again.

"Dr. Littleton?"

"Cliff?" Francine looked as if she might faint.

Chapter 27

The missing professor stumbled slightly as he crossed the threshold. Francine rushed to his side, steadying him.

"Oh, thank goodness." Everyone said it at once.

Emily pulled out a chair, and Francine helped Cliff over to it. There was a minute of complete silence. It really was him. His corduroy pants and button-down shirt were filthy with caked dirt, and his hair lay in greasy tangles. She couldn't imagine the last time he'd had a bath.

Francine was the first to find her voice. "Cliff, what the—we were so afraid you were dead."

"Why would you think that?" He sat up straighter in the chair and ran grimy hands through his hair. It didn't help much.

"Well, for starters, no one has been able to reach you by phone in more than two weeks! Deandra is worried sick, and half the history department is lining up to take over your job because you haven't reported in." Francine was just getting wound up. "Emily says you quit coming into the library, just as your research was getting started, and the ladies at the bakery have way too many leftover chocolate croissants right now."

And with that she burst into tears.

Cliff huffed. Emily pulled Francine into a hug, patting her back and making soothing noises. She gave Cliff a pointed look.

"Okay, okay, *sorry*," he murmured.

"Sorry! That's it?"

"Well, if you weren't always so damn—"

Emily stepped between them. "Look, I can see that emotions are really running high. Let's all back away a little. How about some tea?"

The others both shook their heads. Okay, it was a trite suggestion for a highly charged moment.

Emily paced to the rear of the room and back. "Maybe I should just leave you two alone to sort this out?"

"No." Francine was adamant. In a lower voice she said, "I'd probably just kill him myself."

Emily took a long, slow breath. "Okay, then, let's see how we can move forward." She turned toward Cliff, who had found some strength in his legs now and was standing. "Professor Littleton, you can surely understand why your disappearance has caused a lot of concern?"

"How about if you call your daughter first?" Francine suggested.

Cliff blanched a little. "There are some men—they're probably looking for me." He gave a nervous glance toward the windows. As the daylight waned, the illuminated interior felt more exposed.

"Ah, right. Yes, we know about them." Emily stepped over to lock the front door. She began to gather the map pieces and her laptop. "How about this? We'll close up the library and go to my house."

While Cliff looked a little muddled and Francine's mouth was pinched in a tight line, Emily hustled through her evening closing routine. Within four minutes they were making their way through the courtyard and into the cozy confines of the house.

"Now, Cliff, please call Deandra." Emily handed him her phone. "And Francine, if you'll look through my cupboards and find a couple cans of soup? I'll figure out something ..."

She looked at Cliff's clothing, which she didn't exactly want shedding dirt all over her furniture. The guest room closet still contained a lot of Grandpa's clothing, things she couldn't bring herself to give away, even though it was clear that David would probably never need them again. She rummaged for a selection of slacks and shirts that were similar enough in style that Cliff would probably accept them. She could only hope the sizes would work. Cliff was about four inches shorter.

As soon as he finished his phone call, she pointed him in the direction of the guest bath and the clothes she had laid out on the bed. Back in the kitchen, she was glad to see that Francine had taken charge. Soup was in a pot with a medium flame under it. Bread and sliced roast beef waited on the counter.

"He told Deandra he'd just been tied up and that he'd lost his phone," Francine said. "Yes, I listened."

"Tied up? Like, literally?"

"I have no idea, but I'm guessing we'll get that story over supper."

"What about the sheriff? I think we need to let him know the hunt is over."

"Can that wait until after supper too? I don't think Cliff can handle a whole lot more right now."

Emily agreed. She assembled sandwiches on a plate, and by the time her surprise guest emerged, wearing pants with the cuffs rolled several times, she had a reasonable meal on the table.

Cliff gobbled food like a starving man, and Emily noticed that his color improved a lot by the time he'd put away two bowls of soup and three wedges of roast beef sandwich. Francine merely nibbled at hers, clearly impatient for Cliff to stop eating and start talking.

When the moment came that Cliff set his spoon down and leaned back in his chair, Francine leaned forward. "Okay, spill it. Where were you and what did you mean by 'I was tied up'?"

He gave her an indulgent smile, and Emily could see that these two had both a cordial working relationship and a caring friendship.

"Short answer: Only at first."

"Maybe start at the beginning, or rather, after you quit coming to the library and the bakery. We've pieced most of that together already."

He settled back in his chair, crossing his legs at the ankles. "I found a map here in the library—impressive collection, by the way. It showed me something I'd long suspected. That there are records of Spanish exploration and the discovery of gold in this area. There's a map, which I tucked away in an old book so I'd know where to find it again …"

Emily held up one finger to pause the story while she went into the living room and picked up the materials she'd been studying this afternoon.

When she spread it out on the kitchen table, Cliff exclaimed, "Yes! Exactly!"

Francine held up one palm. "Before we go off on a tangent, I still want to know where you were, what happened. Condensed version is okay."

"There probably isn't a condensed version. I had copied the map and I took the copy, intending to drive up to the spot shown on it, to scout around and see if I could see any reasonable place for a Spanish treasure to be hidden. I got a little north of Questa when my car conked out. Well, it was a flat tire. But I'm embarrassed to admit I've never changed a tire in my life, so I was stuck needing to reach a garage or tire shop."

Francine rolled her hand in a 'hurry up' gesture.

"All right, all right. A guy stops and offers to give me a lift, but the next thing I know, I'm in the back of his van with zip ties around my wrists and ankles and a nasty bandanna over my eyes. And soon after, I woke up in a cabin somewhere with high mountains all around."

"Whoa." Emily couldn't help it, the word just slipped out. The rune book had been right!

"Turned out he was a nice enough chap—almost looked a little familiar to me, but I didn't know why—he said I was going to stay here in his cabin for a while. Brought me groceries every few days, the place had electricity and all that. I said I wanted my car and he told me he was having the tire fixed, just be patient."

Emily had a suspicion. "Can you describe this man?"

"Yeah, sure. Young—maybe thirty-five or so, muscular, in great shape. Buzz-cut, sort of military. Never did tell me his name. But he'd say he had to get back because his partner needed him."

Jax.

"Did he get any phone calls while you were around him?"

"Once, in the van right at the beginning. A male voice was on the line, mumbled mostly, but the guy driving said something like 'no way, I'm not doing that' and he said something about the gorge bridge. I guess that would be the one over the Rio Grande Gorge."

Emily swallowed hard. It sounded like Vince had ordered Jax to kill Cliff but, for whatever reason, Jax refused. She looked at Francine, who seemed to have reached the same conclusion.

"They still needed him for something," she offered.

"So, Cliff, this was about two weeks ago?" Emily asked.

"I guess. Really lost track of time. I'd lost my phone and there was no TV or radio in the cabin. So, I did what I suppose every captive prisoner does, thought about how to escape. Little hard to plan, though, when you're locked in somewhere and you've got no idea where you are."

"How did you do it?"

"Found a window with a wonky latch. I was able to get it open and I could close it back so it wasn't evident. After I'd saved up a couple days' worth of food, I made a break for it. Started downhill, as that seemed most logical. Spotted other cabins, also empty, didn't want to be walking along a road, in case he came driving up, so I just wandered through the woods. By the second night I could see the lights of town, kept heading that direction. It gets darned cold outdoors at night up at this elevation."

"You didn't stop at any of the houses, ask for help there? Or try to find a law officer?"

Cliff's brow wrinkled. "Guess I didn't think of that. All I knew was that the guy had taken the map copy. I had no wallet, no phone, no money or ID. Even lost my watch. I kept thinking that if I could get to the Taos Plaza, I could find my way to the library and I knew I had a friend here."

Aww… Emily felt herself tearing up.

Francine reached over and clasped Cliff's hand. "Do you want me to take you back to Albuquerque? We could leave now, or in the morning."

"Heck no. I didn't come all this way just to go right home. I want to see those guys caught. They've got my treasure map, and they sure as hell won't be turning it over to anyone."

He definitely had that right.

"May I ask one question? The copy of *The Secrets of Monte Sagrado* and the original map of Twining that you checked out?"

From the blank look on his face, she feared she would never see those two rare items again.

Emily stood up, turning to hide her disappointment. But she didn't dare let him go until she had the chance to ask the question again when he felt rested. "I want you to stay here, for as long as you want. We can go to the pharmacy in the morning and get more of your medication. While I get the guest room freshened up, Francine can tell you the rest of the news. Your car was found, and it was miles from where you left it."

Within the hour, Cliff was visibly fading. With a full tummy and a safe, warm place to sleep, he was crashing fast. Emily showed him where everything was in the guest room, wished him a pleasant sleep, and returned to the living room where Francine waited, poring over Emily's notes and the map fragment.

"So," Emily said, her voice barely holding steady, "what's our next move?"

Chapter 28

The white van cruised slowly down Paseo del Pueblo and made the turn into the plaza. Jax's eyes darted every which way, hoping to catch a glimpse of the professor. Somehow, he'd gotten by without telling Vince their hostage had escaped several days ago. He'd already covered most of the Taos Ski Valley territory, although he had to admit that the chances of spotting anyone through the thick trees was nearly impossible. But he had asked at a couple of the gift shops and restaurants, and no one recalled a man matching the professor's description.

Now, he was desperately grasping for ideas. As he took the narrow side street out of the plaza, he spotted a bakery with a purple awning. When Jax was bringing him groceries, Cliff had asked every time if he'd got chocolate croissants. Maybe he'd made it to town and found this place?

Jax pulled into the parking area, noting there was a dog grooming salon on one side of the bakery and a bookstore on the other. Neither of those seemed likely. He walked into the bakery. An attractive woman in her late twenties looked up and greeted him with a warm smile.

He should buy something. "Got any chocolate croissants?" he asked, reaching into his pocket for cash.

"Just one?" She reached into the display case with a sheet of flimsy paper and picked it up.

"I got a buddy who loves these things. Maybe he's been in here?"

Her eyes narrowed just a little. "Would you like a bag for that?"

She knew something.

"Nah, the paper's fine. So, yeah, this friend's an older guy who cannot resist his chocolate," Jax said, flashing his best smile, standing a little straighter. "I was kind of hoping to run into him while I'm in town."

The woman shrugged. "Haven't seen him."

He didn't detect any deceit in that statement. As he dropped his change into his pocket, he noticed her eyes go toward the window and to the left. It was worth driving up that way. He wished her a pleasant day and walked out to the van, taking a huge bite of the croissant along the way. It really was the best pastry he'd had in a long time.

Backing out of the parking area, he steered along the narrow street, munching on his treat, eyes darting in both directions. The street held several art galleries, a library, and a tiny taqueria. Cars lined the street. Nothing seemed out of the ordinary.

He had to admit he was running out of ideas. But Vince was going to have his ass for losing their captive. He needed the old man to lead them to the location shown on the map they'd taken from the guy's car. It wasn't a great copy, and that meant the original was out there somewhere. Which meant someone else could be close on the trail of the treasure Vince thought of as his own.

The whole operation was turning into a hot mess, and Jax just wanted out. But he wanted his share of the investor money before the feds closed in, even if it was less than he'd hoped for.

Chapter 29

Emily ushered Cliff out into the courtyard while she locked the door. The professor had assured her that he'd been taking his medication all along, until he escaped the cabin anyway. He did seem fairly spry this morning, considering his ordeal with his abductors and his days in the forest. She was actually impressed at the distance he'd covered. Now, she was taking him to meet Sheriff Beau and leave him in the capable hands of the law.

"Will I get my car back when we get there?" Cliff asked, for at least the third time since breakfast.

"I don't know. The sheriff told me they were doing forensic tests on it because of the blood inside. I'm sure he'll ask you about that, and he can tell you where the car is now."

Cliff nodded.

Out in the narrow street, a few vehicles whished by. Emily hoped Cliff wouldn't take it upon himself to set off walking again. She'd offered a ride, and really wanted to see him to his destination and make sure he was safe.

"Can we go by the bakery for chocolate croissants? I'd offer to buy, but as you know I came away with nothing on me."

She smiled at his childlike request. "Sure. And it'll be my treat."

They could take an extra five or ten minutes. Beau knew they were coming but it wasn't exactly an appointment. She pulled up in front of Sweet's Sweets, taking in the cheerful autumn display of cookies and cakes in the front window.

Inside, Jen was busy with two ladies who couldn't seem to make up their minds. When she finished filling their order and spotted Cliff, her eyes went wide.

"Professor! We haven't seen you in a while. Em, you found him."

"More like, he found us. Francine and I were really relieved to see him last night."

"Let me guess … two chocolate croissants?"

"And whatever the lady wants," he said with a smile.

Jen asked if they wanted plates or were taking the pastries with them.

"The coffee here is fantastic," Cliff hinted.

"Plates, please, and we'll take two cups of the signature blend coffee." Emily tapped her credit card on the payment terminal and turned to see that Cliff had already chosen a table. Okay, so it might be a little longer than a ten minute stop.

Jen brought their plates over and set them down. "You know, someone else was in here asking about you."

"Since the last time Francine and I were here?"

"Since about five minutes before you got here, just now."

Emily felt a shiver. "Was it a man, maybe five-ten or -eleven, dark hair slicked back and the good looks of an actor?"

Jen pursed her lips. "Um, no. This was more like ex-military, muscles in a fitted t-shirt, buzz cut. He asked about the guy who loved chocolate croissants, but when I said I hadn't seen him, the guy just got in his van and drove away. Headed down the street in your direction."

Emily swallowed hard. "A white passenger van?"

"Yeah, I think so. We got busy then, all at once." Jen smiled as two more people walked in the door.

Emily glanced nervously toward the entrance and parking lot beyond. It had to be Vince's helper, the man who'd been holding Cliff locked up in that cabin. The description fit perfectly. There was no sign of the van now. She looked toward Cliff, but he was so engrossed in stirring his coffee he hadn't registered what Jen was telling them.

When they left her house just now, she'd noted several vehicles driving past, heading west. Was one of them a white van? She honestly couldn't recall, and the five-foot wall around her courtyard blocked most of the view anyway.

Had Vince and his helper been just that close to spotting Cliff?

She suddenly didn't have much of an appetite for the croissant, although Cliff was nearly through his first one. She would have Jen bag it up before they left.

Chapter 30

Jax gripped the steering wheel until his knuckles crackled. That old dude was somewhere here in town; he could feel it. And the minute the guy spilled everything to that lady professor who'd been looking for him, the whole gig was over. His scare tactics at her hotel hadn't worked to scare her away. Her next step would be to report everything to the law.

Jax knew he had two choices: tell Vince what had happened and hope he'd get a share of whatever money his partner had brought in so far, or gas up the van and hit the road and drive as fast and as far as he could.

Both options had their merits. The pull of the money won out.

He hit Vince's number on his phone.

"Yeah, Jax, what's up?"

"We need to talk. Where are you?"

"Almost out here at the tour site. I wanted to check a couple things before tonight's group."

"I'll meet you there." He clicked off the call before Vince could comment. An idea had popped into his head. If he left a few clues or talked to the lady professor, maybe she'd back away and leave them alone.

He reached the north end of town and gunned the van, passing two vehicles filled with gawking tourists, closing the distance out to the cave. When he got there, he spotted Vince's sleek car parked off to the side, in his favored spot, concealed behind a bushy piñon tree.

Jax's feet crunched over scattered pine needles as he approached the mouth of the cave, his phone clutched tightly in one hand. He glanced at the screen repeatedly, but the "No Service" notification blinked back at him.

"Jax, that you?" Vince's voice echoed from the cave chamber. Jax had to weigh his options quickly. Should he try once more to call Francine, or leave hidden clues and hope for the best? Forget it. He'd drop the clues and then call her once he was out of here, if he got the chance.

He took a few more steps, breathing hard from both the elevation and his own frustration. A cloud blocked the sun and a stiff wind cut through his leather jacket; he wished he were back in California where the weather was warm and the jobs were easy. At least back there, he knew who he could trust and how far. Out here, Vince was the only game in town. Jax knew better than to put his full trust in the smooth-talking con man, but trusting his fate to the FBI wasn't a whole lot better option.

He stepped inside the cave, out of the brisk wind. It was now or never. He could still bail. But he remembered the two couples at the presentation last night who'd pledged a half mil each. He couldn't walk away from that.

He pulled in a deep breath, thinking of Francine, the inquisitive historian Vince called "that meddler from Albuquerque." Maybe she wasn't as naïve as Vince assumed. She knew the right questions to ask and was nosing around in places that could do serious damage to their operation. For the first time, Jax began to wonder if, instead of making her go away, Francine could be an unexpected ally in his quest to get paid. Maybe there was a way for him to steer her in the right direction while still covering himself with Vince.

Once last chance. He'd tell Vince about Cliff getting away, make the point that their game was just about up, and demand his share of the money. Now.

He looked around the main room of the cave, hearing Vince rattling around in one of the smaller, side rooms. If Jax wanted Francine to find the clues before Vince found him out, he had to act. His military instinct kicked in. Time to be quick and strategic. He switched off his phone and slipped it into his pocket.

From the other pocket he pulled out the engraved watch. The thing was clearly some kind of heirloom piece that would easily be identified as Littleton's. Jax had swiped it and a dead cell phone from the side table at the cabin the first time he'd gone back to check on the captive. He'd reasoned that it was better if the guy had no idea what day or time it was.

Deep in the inner pocket of his coat, he'd kept the folded copy of the treasure map, the one the professor brought with him the first time he'd met with them. Those three items should be enough to let this Francine woman believe that her colleague had been here in the cave at some point.

Vince's echoing call came again, more insistent this time, and Jax clenched his jaw. He stuffed the map into a cranny in the rough stone wall, then dropped the watch and the phone behind one of the fake treasure chests they used in their act. He knew it was a long shot. Maybe they'd sit undiscovered for days, weeks. But he hoped, crazy as it was, that Francine or someone would stumble across them soon.

With one last glance at his work, he stood and drew a deep breath. It was time to face Vince.

"What the hell, man? How long you been standing there?" Vince had a pistol tucked into the waistband of his jeans.

Jax felt his gut clench. From the look on Vince's face, he knew this was not the time or place to reveal a lapse in his own abilities. Take the stronger position. He knew this.

"We gotta talk. Come on, let's take a ride and discuss the plan." His brain was working overtime, coming up with a way to pivot the story he'd thought he would tell.

He half expected Vince to give him trouble, but Vince merely shrugged. "You want to talk about last night. I'm not surprised." Vince led the way down the path, toward the vehicles. He headed toward the sports car.

"Let's take mine. I got a few groceries for the old guy, need to drop them off." In reality, the bag behind the driver's seat only held a couple bags of chips and some sodas he'd bought for himself, but maybe the ruse would work.

He needed for Vince to be the one to discover their hostage was gone.

"So, you wanna know about your cut now that we have a couple live ones on the line, right?" Vince veered toward the van and got into the passenger seat.

"Yeah, well … you know. We talked about this. Once we got a million or so from some investors, we'd ditch the tours and take the money and run." Jax tried to sound like it didn't matter a whole lot to him. "And well, last night … we got the commitment, right? Two of 'em promising a half mil each."

Vince's response was exactly what Jax expected. "Yeah, but the money ain't in the bank yet. Those were pledges, not cash. But—" he raised an eyebrow "—the minute I get access to those funds, you're right. We'll deduct the expenses and split the rest."

The expenses. All those columns of numbers Jax had seen in the ledger book, the nonsense entries that could mean anything. But he nodded thoughtfully, as if he believed every word.

"That's all set then," Vince said. "My opinion, we'll be out of here within a week, ten days max. That's about how long it takes the bank to clear amounts like that."

Jax nodded again, making the turn toward the ski valley. Somehow, he wasn't all that unhappy he'd shared the ledger contents with Agent Price.

Chapter 31

Emily pulled into the parking lot at the Sheriff's Department offices and turned to Cliff in her passenger seat. "Okay, we're here to report to Sheriff Beau that you've been found, so he can close his file on the report Francine filed. I'm sure he'll have some questions for you."

"I want to get my car so I can go home."

"And that will be one of our questions for him, won't it?" After what she'd observed, she was a little nervous about that. If anything, Cliff seemed even more spacey this morning. "Here we go."

She led the way inside. Beau stood at the front desk, speaking with the officer on duty there. He smiled when he turned and recognized Emily.

"I appreciated your call," he said. "And this is Dr. Littleton?"

"Clifford Littleton PhD, at your service." Cliff held out a hand.

The two men shook and Beau led the way to the back, through the squad room, and into his private office.

"I want to make it clear that you're only here to help us decide what the charges should be against the tour operators, Vince Hutchins and Jax Rivera. We really appreciate your help." He took his seat behind the desk and showed Cliff the visitor chair.

Emily stood in the doorway, appreciating the fact that Beau had chosen to keep this informal. Cliff wasn't suspected of any crime and, as an elderly victim of such, it was only fair to go easy on him. She'd given Beau as much background information as she could, including a description of the van she and Riki had ridden in and the location of the cave where the ghostly tours were conducted.

Beau began with questions about Cliff's encounters with the two men.

"A month or so back, I heard a bit on the news about there being someone in Taos, a Vince Hutchins, who said they'd found the treasure supposedly left by the Spanish conquistadors. New Mexico history is my area of expertise," he preened a little, "and I wanted to find out what they were claiming to have found. Rumors and legends have abounded for more than four-hundred years, but we have yet to actually find such treasure. Still, I'm an open minded man. I really like to follow leads, *if* they seem viable."

Beau nodded. "And the claims you heard from Hutchins—did those seem viable?"

Cliff shifted in his chair. "I was skeptical when I saw the operation. That tour office contained nothing but slick brochures and fictitious maps."

"So, no."

"So, I decided to do more research. This young lady at the library was most helpful, and we were well on our way to unearthing certain original documentation."

"So, maybe there *is* a treasure?"

"Open-minded, as I said. But I do not believe that Hutchins guy cares a whit about history nor does he have a means of finding the treasure, if it exists."

Beau went through the motions of making a few notes. "Let's move ahead to the days of your confinement. Emily tells me you were held in a locked cabin, some miles away from town?"

Cliff nodded. "Slippery Vince Hutchins apparently didn't like my challenging him. Well, I didn't care what he thought, the phony. Once I decided not to have anything to do with him, I headed up toward Questa and got a flat tire along the way."

He told Beau essentially the same story he'd given Emily and Francine last night. "A man stopped to help, younger guy with a military haircut. He offered me some water and must have given me something more ... I got really sleepy and laid down on the seat. Next thing I knew we were inside a rustic log cabin. My suitcase was there. I don't know how *that* happened."

Emily could imagine. Jax must have searched Cliff's pockets, got his hotel key, cleared the room and checked out for him. Probably used some invented story about being a relative or something.

"Do you know where this cabin was?" Beau asked.

A shake of the head. "I felt groggy the whole time I was there."

Emily met Beau's eyes and mimicked drinking something. Francine had suggested the men drugged Cliff's food or water to keep him docile.

"Do you have any idea how long you were there?"

Another head shake. "He wasn't unkind to me, the muscular one. He brought groceries now and then. I said I wanted to call home, but he kept putting me off. Said he didn't have a phone with him and I'd lost mine." Cliff's eyes looked sad. "I don't know how that happened. But people tease me about being way behind the times with technology. The phone and the computer aren't that important to me, I guess."

"I understand." Beau gave a rueful glance toward his own computer on the desk, although Emily knew very well that he was proficient with it. "Tell me about how you got away, and how you found your way to the Morton Library."

"I don't really know … Somehow I must have got out of the cabin, and I remember being in the forest for a long time."

The story he'd told Emily and Francine last night seemed more lucid, but she wasn't convinced it was exactly accurate either. When she laundered his filthy clothing, she'd checked the pockets. In his shirt was a business card from a local contractor, Bravo Electric. She handed the card to Beau.

"This is the person who gave him a ride to the library. I took the liberty of calling last night. Mr. Bravo seemed reassured that he'd done the right thing by bringing him to me. I asked where he'd picked up Dr. Littleton and he said it was on one of the dirt roads in Taos Ski Valley."

Beau's nod told her he would call Bravo Electric and get more details. What Emily had pieced together was that

Cliff had probably spent a night or two wandering on the mountain before this kind soul picked him up.

Bravo told her that the older man was almost incoherent when asked about where he was going, but the man did get the word 'library' from him. Once in town, he'd driven to the public library but Cliff didn't want to go there. When they passed by the Morton Library, he'd become excited.

"When can I get my car?" Cliff asked, sounding a little petulant at all the questions. "I don't want to leave here without my car."

"Now that you're here, alive and well, we hope to get it released for you soon," Beau responded kindly. "It's at the county impound lot and I'll need to make some arrangements."

When Emily's phone buzzed and she saw that the caller was Francine, she stepped outside to take the call.

"How's it going?"

"Well enough. He's very fuzzy about details of his capture and the time he spent under Vince and that other guy's control. And it doesn't seem he's remembering his getaway very accurately at all. But Beau is piecing the story together. Hopefully, he'll get enough to arrest those men on something that will send them to prison for a long time. I have a feeling there's a lot Beau isn't sharing."

"Frustrating. But I suppose that's how lawmen work." Francine cleared her throat. "So, the reason I called was because I want to try to get Cliff's missing items back. That engraved watch, in particular, was really important to him."

"Don't you think the sheriff will—"

"Actually, I don't. A personal item doesn't seem like it would be high on his list when he's trying to catch criminals who are traveling the country and bilking people out of some fairly lucrative investment money."

Emily squirmed a little. What Francine said was probably true.

"So, we could start with that white van that they transported Cliff in. Maybe the watch dropped there."

"A lot of people have ridden in that van in the last week or two …"

"Then their office? If Vince found the watch, he'd probably hang onto it."

Emily felt herself being torn in two directions. She should stay with Cliff until she knew what would happen to him. On the other hand, she shouldn't let Francine barrel in and confront Vince alone. That had not gone well the last time. She told Francine to wait at her hotel and she would pick her up.

They ended the call and Emily walked back inside, retracing her steps to the squad room. Cliff was chatting with Deputy Rico, a paper cup of coffee in one hand and a huge donut in the other. The man's blood sugar must be off the charts.

She saw that Beau was in his office, a phone to his ear, but he had the faraway look that told her he wasn't talking to anyone. She tapped at the doorframe.

"Dr. Morales wants my help with something," she said. "Will Cliff be all right here for a while?"

"Sure. He's having a good time with Rico, and I should be able to get his car released by this afternoon. I'll give him a ride out to the impound lot when it's ready. I think I've figured out the bloodstains in the car—Cliff has a cut on the back of his hand that's nearly healed now. He doesn't seem to remember how or when he got it."

"What are the next steps, Beau?"

"Gathering more evidence against Hutchins and Rivera, making sure we have a case, and nabbing them before they skip town." Again, Emily wondered whether there was a lot he wasn't saying.

"We heard that Vince's main goal was to secure investors for his treasure hunt. What if I pretended to have money, to be interested in the investment? Maybe I could get some kind of admission from him?" She squirmed a little at the thought. "There are some missing items I'd like to retrieve, Beau. Cliff had borrowed an extremely rare book and a map from the library. I really need those back. And he's mentioned his wristwatch, which I gather is a family heirloom."

Beau shook his head. "Be careful, Em. If Hutchins gets desperate … I'd rather you didn't talk to him. We'll put together a team and we'll be able to search his offices and that cave site, all at once, in a concerted effort."

"Yourself and five deputies? Is that going to work, Beau?"

"You'll have to trust me on this." His attention snapped back to the phone. "Yeah, I'm still here," he said into the receiver.

Emily walked over to Cliff and caught his attention. "Beau's working on getting your car released. I'm going to meet Francine for a little errand. Once you have your car, please go back to my house rather than trying to drive all the way back to Albuquerque tonight."

"Oh, I'm not leaving for Albuquerque just yet." A complete switch from what he'd been saying earlier. "I need to find my missing watch."

Oh boy. The watch really was that important to him. "Okay, but wait for me. Francine and I will help you." She left, hoping Beau could keep the older man entertained while she worked on getting Francine to let the lawmen do their work.

She parked in front of Francine's hotel and texted to say she'd arrived. Within two minutes her friend emerged, signaling for Emily to come with her. "I figured it would be better to take my car since yours sort of stands out in a crowd."

Okay, whatever. Emily didn't want to admit she was losing patience. "What do you intend to say to Vince?"

"Hopefully, nothing. I'm hoping the van is sitting outside their office, unlocked."

"And you'll simply climb in and start looking around?"

"Maybe so. A little thing like a watch or phone could have easily slid under the seats."

"Cliff told Beau that he fell asleep on one of the back seats—I'm thinking he was drugged—so it could be exactly as you said. Items fell out of his pockets, he never noticed until the van was gone again."

"It's worth a look." Francine drove as aggressively as she talked, taking the left turn from the hotel's driveway with a squeal.

"Now that we know Cliff is safe, what's your plan? He told Beau he wants to drive back to Albuquerque. But he told me he wants to find his watch first."

Francine gave her a see-I-told-you-so look about the importance of the watch. "With luck, we'll find the missing things, and then I suppose it's time to pack up and get back home. I'll suggest we spend one more night here, so Cliff can be thoroughly rested, and then I'll see if he'll agree to follow me on the drive back."

"That would be a smart plan."

Francine slowed and made the turn into the parking area for the shabby little tan building. There were no vehicles out front, so she cruised to the back, in case the men had parked by the back door. No such luck.

"How about if I just make a special point with Beau, that he should be on the lookout for Cliff's watch and phone when they search the premises? I'm sure he would take care of them and get them back to Cliff." But what about the missing map and the rare book?

Would Beau or his deputies recognize their value, that they were vastly different from the cheap materials Vince had printed up? Probably. But among all the other paperwork and clutter in the office, would her grandfather's priceless map just disappear in the chaos?

Francine was already out of the car. She strode up to the back door of the tour office and put her shoulder to it as she twisted the flimsy knob. It creaked open. "Hmm. Looks like someone didn't properly lock up last night."

Emily rolled her eyes. "We can't just—"

But Francine was already inside. Okay, maybe just a quick look. Emily knew she was the only one who would immediately recognize the map or the book. She turned off the engine and pulled Francine's keys from the ignition.

The back door opened into a narrow hallway that ran straight to the front of the building, with several doors opening off of it. Francine was already in the lobby area, and Emily could hear her going through the desk drawers. "Keep an eye out for a cardboard tube—that would be the map—and a vintage book," Em called out.

She peeked into the first side room she came to. It was stacked with boxes of brochures, several cheaply made wooden 'treasure' chests, some strings of lights, and some rope. She moved on to the next door, which was a bare-bones bathroom with only a sink and toilet.

The third door revealed an office with a wooden desk that was piled high with papers, two used coffee mugs, scattered paper clips, a pair of scissors. She ruffled through the papers but found nothing of value. One drawer held some plastic pens and a little spiral notebook. The other drawer was locked. She ran her hand through the first drawer and came up with a small key, which fit the second drawer perfectly. Great security.

The locked drawer contained two books, which proved to be ledgers of some kind, and a half empty bottle of Jim Beam. No rare book, no map. Beau's men could discover the ledgers for themselves. She relocked the drawer and put the key in a conspicuous spot in the other drawer.

Francine peered around the doorjamb. "Any luck?"

"Nothing we want."

They walked out the back door, taking care to twist the little lock button on the knob before they closed it.

Francine got in the driver's seat again. "I want to drive out to that cave. You know the way, so just tell me where to make the turns."

Emily got a sinking sensation in the pit of her stomach. This could go very wrong. But she couldn't let go, knowing such valuable items from the library's archives were likely to vanish forever.

Chapter 32

Jax let Vince move ahead of him as they stepped up to the front door of the cabin. This needed to be Vince's discovery. Unlocking the padlock on the hasp he'd installed himself, Jax stood aside and listened to the echo of Vince's demanding shouts to the professor. His pulse raced as repeated shouts didn't rouse anyone.

"What the hell! He's not here!" Vince's face was a dangerous shade of purple.

"Look around, he's gotta be somewhere." Jax knew better but it was worth playing out the charade.

"How'd you let him get away? When did this happen?"

"How would I know? I wasn't out here twenty-four-seven. You're the one who thought a senile old man couldn't break a lock or a window, and nobody would come around a vacant cabin and discover him."

"Okay, we gotta figure out where he went." Vince paced back and forth through the two rooms after discovering the malfunctioning latch on a back window.

"Why? We got what we came here for—investors. The tour gig is about up, the dude never heard *my* name, and once we wipe the place down for prints, there's no actual proof we were involved. We simply say that, yeah a professor from Albuquerque showed up when we arrived in town and he seemed real interested in our work. But he never took the tour and he damn sure didn't invest any money. What's the sheriff gonna say to that?"

Vince grumbled, but he started moving. "Okay, gather up everything in here that belonged to him—clothes, papers, anything. And then wipe down anything you've touched."

"You're helping with that part, Vince. Come on, get busy." Jax headed into the bedroom and found a suitcase open on a chair. It didn't look like the hostage ever really unpacked his stuff. He gathered everything personal from the tiny bathroom and checked the closet and a dresser for any other clothes.

In a side pocket of the suitcase was something rolled up in a short tube—a quick peek showed a yellowed document of some kind—and there was an old book in a zippered plastic bag. It looked important, somehow. Jax stuffed both items into his inside jacket pocket. A plan was forming in his mind.

Vince had pulled on his fancy driving gloves, the ones he thought made him look cool in the Ferrari, and was tossing food items into a garbage bag he'd found somewhere. He had a kitchen towel that he was using to polish every handle, faucet, and knob.

Twenty minutes later, they wiped down the hasp and

lock on the cabin door and tossed Cliff's things into the back of the van.

"Okay, we'd better get moving." Vince let Jax take the wheel this time. "It's time to clear out."

"What's the plan?"

Vince had that look on his face, the one Jax recognized whenever his partner was scheming, making up something on the fly. He backed the van down the narrow lane that led to the cabin, turned onto the road, and aimed down the hill.

"We've got what we came for—almost."

Yeah, I think I already pointed that out. But Jax kept his mouth shut.

"We'll grab our stuff from the cave, at least the cameras and equipment. Then we'll get a few other things before we ditch the tour office. Can't leave town quite yet. I've got one more investor who pledged five hundred grand and that's worth sticking around for. I'm supposed to meet with them tonight and get their cashier's check. If we can stuff the important things in my car, we can hit the road by ten or so. We'll leave the van at the lease agent's lot."

"So, to the cave now?"

"Yes, bozo, to the cave."

Chapter 33

Emily hoped she'd spotted the correct turnoff to the cave. It was really just a wide, flat place off the road. There were lots of tire tracks but no vehicles in evidence.

"Grab the flashlight from my glovebox," Francine instructed, retrieving another one from the center console.

They locked the Honda and headed up the trail. Emily began to recognize the way.

"You said this cave only has two chambers, right?" Francine had asked a lot of questions about the layout as they'd driven here.

"That's all I saw. They didn't exactly give us a guided tour through the whole place. We really only stood in the main room when we first walked in. That's where they had the sounds, and some of the projected images were rigged up to appear coming from that second chamber to chase us outside."

The trail turned to the right and the cave entrance loomed before them, a gaping hole in the rugged hillside. Gravel crunched underfoot as Emily approached; they exchanged a glance.

"Ready?" Francine asked, her voice almost steady.

Emily nodded, despite the twinge of apprehension in her chest.

She took a deep breath, inhaling the crisp mountain air one last time before they ventured inside the mine's entrance, leaving the sun-drenched world behind. Cool, dry air enveloped them as the beam of Francine's flashlight danced along rough-hewn walls, revealing glittering veins of quartz amidst the dusty rock.

Emily shivered, pulling her sweater tighter around her slender frame. "During the tour, they had some soft lighting on," she said, her words echoing softly. "I didn't realize the ceiling was quite so high."

Francine nodded, her own leather jacket offering little warmth against the shadowy chill. "Caves can be deceiving."

A faint metallic glint caught Emily's eye. "Francine, look over there," she whispered. "See that wooden chest? Around the base of it was where we *found* the gold. Looks like they've left a few pieces."

Francine nodded. "Be careful where you step." They approached the chest and shone their lights into and around it. Scattered across the ground before them lay a collection of tarnished objects, glinting dully in the flashlight's beam.

Emily picked one up. It wasn't the same as the coin she'd taken during the tour.

Francine knelt carefully, taking in every detail. "Some

of these actually might be old," she mused, picking up a corroded coin, "or they're made to seem like it. Spanish pieces of eight, if I'm not mistaken. And look here—" She gestured to a tarnished metal cross, its intricate design barely visible beneath years of decay.

"But these can't be the real thing. Those con men would have already taken anything that might bring a high price." As Emily surveyed the scattered artifacts, she couldn't shake a growing sense of unease. It all felt ... wrong. Out of place. Like pieces of a puzzle that didn't quite fit together.

She reached into the wooden chest and lifted out some ratty pieces of clothing that were meant to look as if they had come from the Spanish colonial period and some more of the fake gold coins like the one she'd pocketed. Maybe they'd stashed the library's book and map among all this, for effect.

But her hopes were dashed when she discovered that the chest had a false bottom with nothing underneath it. It had been placed there merely to make the chest appear to be overflowing with treasure and artifacts.

"We need to document everything," she said firmly, reaching for her camera.

Standing beside another wooden chest, Francine carefully lifted a tarnished silver pendant, her curiosity piqued. "Emily," she called softly, her voice echoing in the cavern, "look at this craftsmanship. This piece may actually be quite old, but ... not exactly what we expected. Some of these items are definitely old, but they don't date back to the conquistadors. The style, the metalwork—I'd place these in the late nineteenth or early twentieth century at the earliest."

"But that's still incredible, isn't it?" Emily's voice held a hint of disappointment, but she held onto a little hope that the men who'd been here had at least some respect for history.

"I don't want to get my hopes up," she said, dropping the piece into her pocket. "The lab at the university can test it and tell us exactly what we're looking at. It could be that these guys picked up a couple chests full of stuff at an estate sale or somewhere like that."

While Emily snapped a few photos of the chests and their contents, Francine's flashlight swept across the cavern floor, stopping on something out of place among the scattered valuables.

"Oh no," she breathed, reaching for it. "Emily, I recognize this. It's Cliff's." She held up a battered leather-bound notebook.

The pages were filled with Cliff's familiar, hasty scrawl. "He was definitely here, which means he met with Vince Hutchins."

"He admitted to Beau that he'd met with Hutchins, but I'm fairly sure it was not here at the cave."

Francine's brow furrowed as she flipped through the notebook. "Based on the dates in his entries, they were written shortly after he stopped coming to the library. But Emily," she paused, her eyes meeting Emily's, "these notes … they're odd."

"Look at this entry: 'V says the map points to a hidden chamber. Must find it before the full moon.'"

Emily's eyes widened. "The full moon? That doesn't sound like the kind of thing Cliff would say."

"Exactly. It must have been a thought those men planted in his mind."

"It goes along with what we've been thinking, that this Hutchins guy is using the town's legends, Cliff's disappearance, even our investigation—all to keep attention away from whatever is really at stake."

Emily felt a chill that had nothing to do with the cave's cool air. "We have to show these things to Beau, tell him what we've found," she said. "And we need to stop whatever Vince is planning."

They heard a sound. "Stay close. We don't know if they've rigged up traps."

Emily strained her ears, catching only a faint, repetitive sound. Was it the shifting of rocks, or something more sinister? She thought of the many legends in the area and her own personal encounters with the supernatural. Was it a whisper, perhaps, carried on the stale air?

"Maybe we should head back," Emily suggested, her bravado fading.

Francine hesitated. "We've found Cliff's diary. I'd like to look further, see what else we come up with. He's counting on us. And what about your missing book?"

Francine leaned over the top of the two treasure chests, the beam of her flashlight sweeping behind them. The beam caught on something shiny, half-covered in dirt.

"Wait," she called, kneeling to investigate. She carefully extracted a battered item from the grime. She brushed the dirt off and recognized a familiar cell phone case. "Uh-oh. And there's more."

The gold trim on the second item gleamed through the dust.

Emily crouched beside her, pushing her glasses up her nose as she peered at the object. Her eyes widened in recognition. "That's Cliff's watch," she breathed. "I remember him wearing it when he arrived at the library, the first day he was in town."

Francine blew gently at the dusty timepiece and turned it over, revealing an engraving on the back. "To Cliff, may you always find time for adventure. Love, Mom." She carefully brushed off the rest of the dirt and looked up at Emily with a smile. "We found it."

"He'll be so relieved. And this will be further proof for the sheriff. Do you think it's enough, though?" Emily asked, biting her lip. "I mean, finding Cliff's belongings here doesn't automatically implicate Vince, does it?"

Francine sighed, her brow furrowing. "You're right. It's circumstantial at best. But it definitely helps. We'll bring this to the sheriff and see what he makes of it. For now, we should head back. We've found what we came for."

Emily snapped a few more photos, showing the found items in place, then she stashed Cliff's watch and journal in her messenger bag. Somehow, she couldn't help thinking that they were missing something crucial.

A breeze whistled through the opening, the cave seeming to whisper.

"What was that?" Francine stood, facing the cave entrance, senses on high alert.

"The wind?"

"No, I distinctly heard words."

Chapter 34

"Find them and take care of it," Vince ordered.

Jax's eyes darted in every direction as they walked up the trail to the cave, looking for a sign of whoever owned the SUV they'd seen at the bottom of the hill. There were footprints all over the place but that was to be expected; they'd brought nearly a hundred people here in recent days. Not to mention that the little wide-spot parking area they'd begun to think of as their own also led to a couple of trailheads in the adjoining national forest. The vehicle had New Mexico plates; it could belong to anyone.

Vince reached the cave first. "You check in here. I'll search the rest of the area." He headed in the direction where Jax normally set up his little control center for the lights and sound effects.

Jax shrugged, as if it didn't matter, but he was secretly

thrilled. This would be his chance to conceal the book and the tube he'd taken from Cliff's suitcase. If anyone came around, searching for the professor, they'd know he had been in here and wouldn't have a clue about the cabin in the forest.

He wondered how far along the FBI had gotten with their investigation and his skin itched. He really wanted out of here, out of the state, out of the country, if he could manage it.

In the main chamber of the cave, he switched on the lights and walked directly to the fake treasure chest, moved the ratty old clothes aside, and lifted the false bottom. An envelope he'd tucked into his waistband contained papers: one page listed the day's schedule of tours and another had investors' names along with huge dollar amounts. Anyone who got hold of these would figure out the scheme fast. And they would have a list of excellent witnesses.

And if Vince happened to check inside the chest? He would instantly know Jax had betrayed him. Everything felt perilous, but Jax knew he was doing the right thing.

The cave's chill air seemed to seep into his bones as he pulled out the cardboard tube and book he'd found among the old man's things. He added them to the chest, then started to replace the false bottom.

"Jax! What're you doing?"

His heart stopped. Then he realized Vince was still outside. "Coming!" He quickly rearranged the trunk to look undisturbed. He shined his light behind the trunk. Didn't see the watch and phone he'd left there before. Oh shit.

Well, no time to look for them. He was already pushing his luck.

"Jax—where'd you go?" Vince stood silhouetted in the cave entrance.

Jax hated the idea of trusting someone he didn't know, but between leaving clues for Francine and the FBI agent, he'd done all he could. He was out of time to worry about it.

Jax shoved the lid of the trunk closed, praying that everything looked normal.

Chapter 35

Emily held her breath. *Find them and take care of it,* echoed in her head. She was fairly certain the voice was that of Vince Hutchins, except all the charm was gone now.

"We have to hide!" Francine grabbed her arm and pulled.

Emily looked toward the cave entrance where it sounded as if the men's voices were only inches away.

"There's more beyond the two rooms you've seen," Francine whispered frantically. "Come on, now!"

Following the bobbing light from Francine's flashlight, they soft-stepped through the main chamber, into the second room, and headed toward a narrow opening Francine pointed out. Emily had the incongruous thought that this would have been so much simpler if they'd swiped a couple of the headlamps from the Treasure Tours office.

But that was then and this was now.

Francine edged sideways and Emily followed, ducking through a passageway that led to a slightly bigger chamber in the cave system. Evidently, the men had already found this space, too. Trash littered the floor, and she spotted a box filled with the fake gold coins and nuggets.

Male voices echoed through the space. "You check in here, and I'll look outside," came Vince's voice.

Francine turned the flashlight beam to low and put a finger to her lips before switching it off. Sounds carried amazingly well through the space. They heard footsteps crunching over the dirt floor, along with muttering by the man who must be Jax. He seemed to be debating something with himself. When his sounds moved farther away, Emily risked tapping her phone for a bit of light.

"We need to reach Sheriff Beau, tell him to get out here," she breathed, her voice soft as a feather landing on the ground.

She could drop him a pin from this location and he'd know exactly where to come. But she only had a standard landline number for him. She could call Sweet's Sweets and get his cell number from Sam. She could plan all she wanted to, but the fact that her phone showed a solid 'no service' foiled any of those ideas.

She edged her way through the skinny opening into the second chamber. Still no signal. She kept to the edges, pressing her phone against her belly to keep its light from giving her away. From the main chamber came sounds of shuffling and something heavy scooting across the rocky floor. She risked a peek.

The muscular man, Jax she supposed, was kneeling in front of the treasure chest she and Francine had examined earlier, his back to her. In his right hand was a cardboard tube. A tube she recognized. Her map!

How did he—? Never mind. He had it now.

She watched as he lifted the false bottom from the chest and placed the tube and something else inside. Outside the cave, Vince shouted. Jax quickened his pace, replacing the contents of chest, muttering about betrayal and 'I hope they find him', whatever that meant.

Another shout from Vince, and this time Jax yelled, "Coming!"

Emily watched him exit the cave, bearing to the right as he followed Vince's voice. She itched to go and retrieve the tube with the map in it.

"What are you doing?" Francine's whisper was practically right in her ear.

Emily held up her phone. "Hoping to get a signal." But no such luck. She calculated the odds of making a run for it, dashing out of the cave and heading to the left, hoping the men wouldn't see her. But that seemed awfully chancy too.

The men's voices grew louder.

"They're coming back!" Francine tugged on Emily's sleeve and the two of them ducked back through the narrow opening.

Chapter 36

Get anything we can sell somewhere, the little cameras and hidden projectors. I don't care about junk like the ropes and extension cords." Vince stomped ahead, leaving Jax to stack the projectors and light fixtures outside the cave entrance.

All week, Jax had watched Vince becoming more and more desperate as the promised investments failed to materialize. The whole scheme was falling apart, and he'd spent sleepless nights wrestling with his conscience, torn between loyalty to his partner and the nagging voice of his moral compass. In the end, facing up to their deception had pointed the way he should go.

A muttered curse echoed through the cave opening. Jax set down a projector and walked in.

Vince stood hunched over one of the fake treasure chests, his normally impeccable appearance disheveled. He was rifling through the pages of the small notebook he'd carried with him from the office. "I need those account numbers," he grumbled.

Don't let him look in the chest!

Taking a deep breath, Jax squared his shoulders and stepped forward. "Vince," he kept his voice steady.

Vince whirled around, dropping his prized notebook. He seemed confused.

"Jax?" Vince's charm evaporated, his eyes narrowing. "What are you doing?"

Um, getting our stuff. It was your idea ... But what he said was, "I thought you said we were leaving all the props and junk?"

"Yeah, true."

"We were going to get the important stuff and then clear out of here. You said there's still one investor we need to see and then we'll have all the money. Right?"

Vince's eyes narrowed, his usual charisma morphing into something darker. "I'm not quitting. We're on the verge of the biggest score of our lives, Jax. Don't tell me you've gone soft now."

Jax shook his head, struggling with the sudden mood shifts. "It's not about going soft, Vince. It's about playing it smart, about getting what we came for and moving on."

"Getting what *I* came for, you mean. I've been the brains of the operation all along, and what comes of it is rightfully *mine*. *I* created the legend of the gold. *I* brought people out to share in the excitement of it. What did you do—string up some lights?"

For an instant, Jax saw red. Vince didn't see them as equal partners; he never did. Had Vince honestly convinced himself he was doing a community service by scamming tourists out of their money and scaring some of them half to death? Seriously? "Vince, it's about doing what's right. We've crossed a line, and you know it."

"Right?" Vince's voice echoed off the rough-hewn walls. "Since when did you care about right and wrong? You're in it for the money, same as me."

The words hung in the air. *And when will I ever actually see any of that money? Never.*

The tension in the air became charged, like a lightning storm. Vince's gaze traveled toward a pile of rusty tools.

"Vince, calm down," Jax said firmly, his muscles tensing. "We need to think clearly and just finish what we came here to do, to clear out."

With a snarl, Vince lunged forward, grabbing a pickaxe and swinging it wildly. Jax ducked as the tool whistled past his ear. He spun and reached for the handle of the axe, wrenching it from Vince's grasp.

They faced each other, each staring into the disorienting glare of the other's headlamp, both breathing heavily.

Jax sensed the shift in Vince's intentions a nano-second before he reached behind and pulled a gun from his waistband. Without a second thought, he swung the pickaxe. The flat side of it caught Vince's wrist. The gun clattered to the rocky floor.

Vince's eyes widened, a flash of panic crossing his handsome features. In an instant, he shoved Jax aside and bolted toward the second chamber where they'd stored some of the heavier pyrotechnics.

"Oh no, you don't!" Jax growled, his wiry frame springing into action. He lunged forward, blocking Vince's route.

And then the beam of his headlamp cut through the darkness, illuminating Emily and Francine's shocked faces.

Chapter 37

Emily swallowed hard, berating herself. Why had they stepped out of the shelter of their little niche, just to find out what the men were fighting about? Stupid, stupid!

Vince's smooth voice broke the silence. "Well, well. What do we have here? A couple of nosy historians?" He bent to pick up a gun that lay on the floor, holding it with his left hand, favoring the right wrist. He gave a nod to his partner that seemed to carry silent instructions.

If she thought the muscular one might take pity, take their side against his partner, she was sorely mistaken. Jax's iron grip clamped around Emily's arm, dragging her forward. She stumbled as her messenger bag fell to the ground, her glasses slipping down her nose as she tried to maintain her footing.

"I told you to stay out of this, Dr. Morales," Vince

growled, all his charm vanishing. "You just couldn't leave it alone, could you?"

Francine lifted her chin defiantly. "Someone had to stand up to your lies, Vince. You can't rewrite history."

He waved the gun in her direction, ordering her to follow the others.

Emily tried to assess their dire situation. She could feel the rough calluses on Jax's hand as he yanked her toward the cave entrance.

"What are you going to do with us?" Emily managed to ask, her voice barely above a whisper.

Vince's laugh held no humor. "Oh, don't worry your pretty little head about that. We're just going for a little drive."

As they emerged into the sunlight, Emily blinked rapidly, her eyes adjusting as she caught sight of the white van parked at the bottom of the trail.

That's when she felt it—the familiar weight of her phone in her pocket. Her breath caught as she realized Jax hadn't taken it from her. Whether oversight or deliberate, it didn't matter. She felt a tiny glimmer of hope.

"Move it," Jax grunted, shoving her down the trail.

Behind her, Francine continued to rail against Vince. Emily wished she would quit, but the conversation helped cover her own actions.

As Jax roughly shoved the women into the back seat, Emily allowed her body to sag slightly, as if overcome. It wasn't entirely an act. Her fingers inched toward her pocket, praying that neither Vince nor Jax would notice. Her most recent text exchange had been with Riki, and she prayed that her friend would understand what to do. Her thumb hovered over the messaging app. One chance. That's all she had. She took a deep breath and dropped a pin, hoping against hope that help would come before it was too late.

The van's engine roared to life, Jax at the wheel and Vince turning in the passenger seat to keep the pistol aimed at the women.

Emily's eyes darted to the window as she eased her phone beside her right leg, out of Vince's view. If Jax turned around, he might see it. That was a chance she had to take. They approached Taos from the north but turned west before reaching town.

Other than the airport, there wasn't much out here and she really didn't believe the men intended to put them on a plane. The other alternative was to take them far out into the open desert and shoot them, depending on coyotes and ravens to do away with their bodies.

And then it hit her: the Rio Grande Gorge Bridge was straight ahead.

Chapter 38

Y ou won't get away with this," Francine grumbled.

Vince's harsh laugh cut through the silence. "We already have, sweetheart. Now shut up and enjoy the ride."

Emily's hand shook as she carefully maneuvered her phone, shielding the screen from view. She typed out a desperate message to Riki: Tell Beau I'm kidnapped. Headed to the Gorge Bridge. Help!

She hit send, her breath catching in her throat. The soft whoosh of the message leaving her phone seemed deafening in the oppressive silence of the vehicle.

"What was that?" Jax's suspicious eyes met hers in the rearview mirror.

Emily forced a weak smile, her mind scrambling for an excuse. "S-sorry, my stomach. I'm feeling a bit carsick."

Jax's gaze lingered for a moment before returning to

the road. Emily exhaled slowly, her silent plea for rescue echoing in her mind as the miles flew by too quickly.

Emily's eyes flicked between Vince and Jax, noting the tension between the two men. They'd been fighting, back at the cave, and it didn't seem as if anything was resolved. Jax's knuckles were white on the steering wheel, his jaw clenched tight enough to crack walnuts.

"You're going too slow," Vince snapped, breaking the silence. "We need to get there before—"

"Before what?" Jax cut him off, his voice low and gravelly. "Before someone notices?"

"Maybe if you hadn't been so sloppy with the professor, we wouldn't be in this mess."

"And if you hadn't promised people the moon, we'd have been out of here long before now."

Vince's charm evaporated, replaced by a snarl. "Watch your tone, Rivera. Remember who's in charge here."

Emily registered every word, knowing Cliff's side of the story.

As they rounded a bend, the Rio Grande Gorge Bridge came into full view. Emily's breath caught in her throat. The flat metal structure stretched across the chasm like a flat metal band, dwarfed by the vast expanse of the gorge below. The afternoon sun cast shadows, which accentuated the dizzying depth—more than six hundred feet of empty air between the bridge and the river below.

"Oh God," Francine whispered beside her.

Emily swallowed hard, instinctively reaching for the turquoise pendant around her neck. She tried to slow her breathing, to concentrate on what Valerie would advise.

You have to get away, came a soothing voice.

As the van began to slow, Emily's mind raced through

escape scenarios, each one more desperate than the last, as the bridge loomed closer.

Suddenly, a faint wail pierced the air, growing louder with each passing second. Emily's eyes widened behind her glasses as she strained to listen.

"Sirens," she breathed, hardly daring to believe it.

Francine's grip on Emily's arm tightened. "They found us," she whispered, a tremor in her voice.

The sound grew, unmistakable now. Cruisers appeared, ahead and behind them.

Vince cursed loudly from the front seat. "How the hell—?"

He was cut off as Jax slammed on the brakes, the vehicle skewing to a halt. Emily lurched forward, her long hair falling across her face. As she straightened up, she caught sight of the blockade ahead.

Law enforcement vehicles formed a barrier across the road, their lights flashing. Deputies and agents in FBI windbreakers spilled out, weapons drawn, moving to efficiently surround their vehicle.

Shouts filled the air as deputies advanced. "Exit the vehicle with your hands up!"

"We have you surrounded!"

As the van's front doors opened, Emily felt scared and hopeful at the same time. She glanced at Francine, seeing her own emotions mirrored in the older woman's eyes. She slipped her phone back into her pocket and both women raised their hands.

Vince's handsome features twisted into a snarl, the charming mask slipping away to reveal the desperate man beneath, when a deputy ordered him to face the vehicle.

"This isn't over," Vince growled when they cuffed him,

his smooth voice now ragged with fury.

"Yes—it is." The new voice belonged to Cliff, who stood beside Beau's vehicle and gave the two captives a smug smile.

Vince thrashed against the deputy's grip, his dusty clothing even more disheveled. "You don't understand what you're dealing with!"

In contrast, Jax remained eerily calm, his gaze fixed on some distant point as he allowed himself to be cuffed without resistance. Emily couldn't help but notice the resignation in his posture, a subtle shift that spoke volumes.

"Francine," Emily whispered, "I think Jax actually helped—"

Before she could finish her thought, the door beside her came open. A deputy's firm hand took Emily's arm, guiding her out. "You're safe now, Em," Rico assured her, his voice steady and reassuring.

Francine emerged beside her, and without hesitation, Emily threw her arms around her friend.

"We made it," Francine breathed, her usual bluntness softened by the moisture in her eyes. "I can't believe we actually made it."

Chapter 39

Various law officers cuffed the two suspects, read their rights, and ushered them into separate vehicles. Beau walked over to the women, Cliff following in his wake.

Francine stepped over to Cliff. It was hard to tell whether she meant to lecture him or hug him.

"It's lucky the county impound lot is out in this direction," the sheriff said with a smile. "I was taking Professor Littleton out to get his car when we got the call." He turned to Emily. "From Riki?"

"Yeah, that was kind of a fluke. I didn't have a way to text you directly."

"Perfectly fine." Since Riki's ex-husband had been sheriff during an extended absence for Beau, he implicitly trusted that she knew what she was doing.

Emily looked around at the number of cruisers

surrounding them. "So … federal officers, too?"

"Yeah, it's an interesting mix. Seems the FBI received a tip about those two and were in the process of executing a warrant to search both their offices and the cave where the tours were held. They have a long list of charges that go back to other con games in other states, as well as what they were doing here."

"The cave. That's where we were when Vince and Jax caught us. So … you're saying the FBI would have shown up at any moment?"

"Soon enough, hopefully."

Emily let out a long breath. "That does make me feel somewhat better. I wonder who gave them the tip?"

Beau merely shrugged before he was called over by one of the other lawmen.

Emily reached for her turquoise pendant again, thinking of her grandmother, experiencing a profound sense of gratitude. She looked out over the narrow expanse of the deep gorge, the beauty of her adopted home reminding her of why she'd fallen in love with Taos in the first place.

"I wonder what happens now?" she asked softly, more to herself than to Francine.

Francine squeezed her hand. "Now, my dear, we make sure the truth comes to light. For the sake of this little town, and for all the history we've sworn to protect."

"Oh shoot! Speaking of protecting … Excuse me a second." She dashed over to the nearest person wearing an FBI ballcap, a female agent with a clipboard in one hand and a gun on her hip. "In that cave you're about to search, I dropped my messenger bag with some important items in it, and there's a wooden chest with a false bottom …"

* * *

Emily tried going back to work, but the piles of materials at the library couldn't hold her attention at the end of this eventful day. Plus, she knew Beau wanted a statement from each of them—Francine and Cliff had stayed behind to give theirs. She might as well get that over with.

She drove to the sheriff's department, noticing that the streetlamps had come on as dusk approached. The front desk officer buzzed her on through; she smiled at the idea that she was almost becoming a regular here.

In the squad room, Cliff was chatting with the deputies, a donut in his hand. Francine sat in front of Beau's desk, signing something. Several FBI agents were milling about, and the woman Emily had approached earlier, out at the gorge, spotted her and walked over. When she handed her the messenger bag, book, and cardboard tube, Emily almost cried.

"I knew these were important to you," the agent said. "And the sheriff confirmed that you are a vital part of the historic preservation efforts in this part of the state."

"I was scared you would have to hold them as evidence and I might not get them back."

"We took pictures. You might be called on to bring the documents into court at some point. The whole process, and how it will go, is still being decided."

Emily hugged the prized items to her chest and thanked the agent profusely.

Beau walked out of his office, with Francine trailing behind. He smiled when he saw what Emily held.

"I just wonder why Jax hid these in the bottom of that trunk," she said. "From what Vince was telling him, they planned to leave the fake treasure chests, clothes, and other props behind."

"You can ask him, if you'd like," Beau said. "Both men are in interrogation rooms right now, answering to the feds."

Emily demurred. She'd had enough of the two con artists and their deviousness.

"If it adds any insight," the female agent added, "Jax seems to be the one who suddenly got a conscience. He's given us names, photos, evidence, while his partner is still trying to bluff his way out of any wrongdoing. Vince's stance is that nobody invested money they didn't willingly want to."

"We'll see how that plays in court," Beau told the group. "There will be an initial hearing in county court and we'll present enough evidence to secure indictments against both men. You all are free to attend that, if you'd like."

Francine shook her head. "I'm more than ready to get home." She turned toward Cliff, trying to get his attention. Emily told Beau she would think about attending. For now, she was exhausted.

She walked out to the parking lot with her Albuquerque visitors. "I hope you'll consider staying over another night." She tilted her head toward Cliff, who was beginning to look weary again. "A long drive probably isn't the best idea right now."

Francine nodded. "You're right. It will take me a while to pack up all the paperwork I've got spread out in my hotel room, to sort through what goes back to Albuquerque and what must be returned to your library."

"Deputy Rico said he delivered my car to the library a while ago," Cliff added.

"Take your time, Francine. Cliff can have my guestroom again tonight. Let's meet for breakfast tomorrow and we'll get you two on the road."

Francine bade them goodnight, and Emily showed Cliff to her Jeep. They ate scrambled eggs and toast at Emily's kitchen table, and by the time his plate was clean, she noticed he was beginning to nod off. He was tucked in bed by seven-thirty.

Emily cleared the table, tired but way too wired to get to sleep. She settled into her favorite spot on the living room sofa. Moonbeam leapt up to her lap, kneaded the woven blanket a couple of times, and snuggled down, purring loudly. Emily stroked the shiny black fur, letting herself unwind for the first time in days.

Chapter 40

They decided their final breakfast in town should be at Sweet's Sweets. No surprise that it was Cliff's suggestion. To Emily, a slice of Samantha's fabulous veggie quiche and a blueberry muffin actually sounded like just the thing. The three of them settled at one of the bistro tables, savoring excellent coffee while Jen gathered their orders.

When Sheriff Cardwell came walking in, tall and handsome in his crisp uniform, Emily sensed he'd just completed some important mission. She gestured toward the fourth chair, asking if he'd like to join them.

"Early court this morning," he said.

"Tell us." Francine softened the demand with a smile.

"Might as well," Beau said, "since we've got the whole

gang here." He looked up when his wife walked in.

Samantha had a trayful of warm muffins, which she slid into the display case before walking over to put her arm around Beau's shoulders. "I hear there was quite the excitement yesterday afternoon."

Jen brought plates of quiche, a basket of muffins, and Cliff's usual chocolate croissants, hanging around to hear what Beau had to say as she refilled their coffees.

"So," the sheriff began. "Preliminary hearing and indictments were this morning. The feds really came through with impressive evidence that ties Vince Hutchins to similar con games in California, Nevada, and Arizona before he arrived here in New Mexico. Jax Rivera apparently was in on the Arizona scam, in which Vince told their potential *investors* that they had definitively located the Lost Dutchman Mine in the Superstition Mountains."

"Any unsolved historical legend is fair game for them, it sounds like," said Cliff between mouthfuls of chocolate.

"Exactly. People will always be drawn to the unknown, especially if there's any kind of infamous tale to go with it," Francine added.

Beau sat a little straighter, his audience captivated. "Anyway, long and short of it is that there are plenty of charges, in enough different jurisdictions, that the case will go to the federal level. The FBI has the lead on this. In a way, I'm fine with knowing that the cost of the trials and the burden of gathering all the evidence doesn't fall to Taos County. We're small potatoes in the whole scheme of things."

"What about the money? They were doing elaborate presentations here in town, luring people to give them lots of money in exchange for a share. What's happened to all that?" Emily wanted to know. She'd barely eaten a few bites of her quiche.

"Interesting question. It's going to take a while to unravel it all. Agent Johnson—that's the woman who found your rare book, Em—she told me they seized ledgers from the offices of Treasure Tours here in town, but they'll require deciphering and tracking. And the fact that the victims are spread out over several states … it's a mess." Beau took the coffee mug Jen offered, sending a smile her way.

"Meanwhile, it looks like Jax Rivera is cooperating. He's the one who first gave the FBI some photos of these ledgers. Seems he was increasingly sure he'd never receive his cut because Hutchins was constantly putting him off, not sharing information."

Emily remembered the way Jax had gone out of his way to hide the valuable documents in a place Vince was unlikely to look. "Will he still go to prison?"

Beau grinned. "That's a loaded question for a lawman. We never count on anything being a certainty. But if I had to guess, based on what I saw, yes. The evidence points to both men. Jax will probably get a lighter sentence, maybe none at all, depending on what kind of deal he cuts with the prosecutors."

The group fell silent for several minutes, contemplating what Beau had said. The sheriff stood, following Samantha back into the kitchen. By the time Emily, Francine, and Cliff had polished off their breakfasts, Beau had walked through the room, talking into the mic on his shoulder radio.

"A sheriff's work is never done," Jen joked as they all watched him get into his cruiser and drive away, lights and siren going.

"Well," said Francine, setting down her empty mug,

"it's probably time to hit the road, Cliff." They had decided she would follow him, making certain he had recovered from his ordeal and wouldn't have any trouble making the drive.

"Hey, if you ever decide you want to get a birds eye view of the location where the map shows the real gold mine …" Emily's eyes twinkled behind the lenses of her glasses. "I have a friend in Albuquerque whose husband runs a helicopter service. Give him a latitude and longitude, and I bet he could take you up there."

"Drake's an excellent pilot," Sam assured them, overhearing as she walked out of the kitchen, carrying an elaborately decorated cake. "And Charlie is quite the investigator, in her own right."

Francine laughed, a little nervously. "We may have had all the adventure we need for a while." She glanced at Cliff, who was licking the last of the chocolate off his fingers. "But I won't rule it out."

The group stood outside the bakery, five minutes later. A familiar figure came toward them, a woman walking from the direction of the plaza.

"Bettina!" Emily stepped forward to give her friend a hug.

Bettina remembered Francine from their visit, and she took one look at Cliff. "I see that you did find your missing colleague. I'm happy that the universe brought you together again."

"You know," Emily mused, her voice taking on the animated tone it often did when discussing local history, "in a way, this whole ordeal reminds me of the turbulent history this state has seen over the centuries."

Francine chuckled. "Leave it to you to find a historical parallel, Em."

"I can't help but think about what my grandparents would say if they'd been here to see this," Emily said, her voice soft with emotion. "They always believed in the power of integrity, even when it seemed like the world was falling apart around them."

Bettina nodded, her smile reflecting the memories she and Valerie had made together.

Francine pulled Emily into a hug. "Thank you for your help in finding my absentminded colleague who can't seem to figure out a cell phone." Her eyes were moist when she stepped back. "Your grandparents would be so proud, Em."

Emily smiled, a surge of warmth in her chest. "Thanks, Francine. I was glad to help. I just hope that by preserving our history, we can help build a better future for Taos."

She watched as the two academics climbed into their respective cars, waving fondly to both of them.

As she bade Bettina goodbye at the bakery door and walked the two blocks back toward the Morton Library, Emily's thoughts drifted to the events of the past few weeks. The autumn sun felt warm on her back and she breathed in the fresh air, faintly scented with the piñon smoke from local fireplaces. She paused at the library's entrance, the familiar adobe structure standing as a testament to the Plankhurst family legacy, and ran her hand along the sun-warmed wall, loving the renewed sense of connection to the generations that had come before her.

When she stepped into the library, the familiar scent of vintage books and leather enveloped her, and Emily felt a sense of peace settle over her. A plaintive sound came from the back of the room, not to be excluded. *Mrroww.*

Author Notes

The night before I wrote the scene introducing Bettina, a dear friend appeared to me in a dream, and the character instantly came alive for me. Gioia Tama is one of those friends who has continued to influence me, and although she passed away more than ten years ago, I miss her still. Born in Argentina, raised in Ecuador, she spent most of her adult life in New Mexico where she blended into the small town life in the northern mountains. We met because our husbands both played flamenco and classical guitar, so while the boys shared music, Gioia and I shared ideas. She taught me much about what it was like to be a *curandera* in a tiny community, about how she used the native plants in amazing ways, and how to embrace life on all levels. We talked endlessly about various philosophies, about history, and about life and death. She loved to imagine. She would have wanted to believe in the conquistadors' gold, and she would have adored Moonbeam because she believed there is magic in this world.

When she passed, I knew, instinctively, that she had chosen the moment to go. I felt sad, and yet not sad, if you know what I mean. Gioia was the sort of person who inspired everyone she met, and I have a feeling she would have believed that every word of this book is true.

My eternal thanks go out to those friends who've inspired me over the years and, on the practical side, to my editor and beta readers who catch everything from basic typos to lapses in logic that manage to get in. Thank you, Stephanie Dewey, Marcia Koopmann, Dawn Hasiotis, Susan Gross, Sandra Anderson, Eve Osborne, Isobel Tamney, and Paula Webb! My stories are always better for your input.

And—perhaps most importantly—a huge thanks goes out to all my readers. You are what makes all the hard work worthwhile. Thanks for sharing my stories with your friends and family. You make my day!

Thank you for taking the time to read *Haunted Gold*. If you enjoyed it, please consider telling your friends or posting a short review. Word of mouth is an author's best friend and is much appreciated.

Thank you,

Connie Shelton

* * *

What's next for Emily, Moonbeam, and the library ghosts?

Emily is doing some early Christmas shopping and comes across a painting she believes is by Nicolai Fechin, her grandfather's favorite artist. Em thinks perhaps Grandpa, now in Alzheimer care, might have a spark of recognition for the painting. But while she's considering it, an art conservator comes into the library. Miles Grantham specializes in forgeries and is in town to verify the authenticity of several "newly discovered" pieces. What Emily and Miles learn is that nothing is as simple as it appears.

Get a free book when you sign up for Connie Shelton's free mystery newsletter at connieshelton.com
Each month you'll receive advance information about new books, along with a chance at prizes, discounts and other mystery news!

Contact by email: connie@connieshelton.com
Follow Connie Shelton on Twitter, Pinterest, Instagram, and Facebook

Books by Connie Shelton

The Charlie Parker Series
Deadly Gamble
Vacations Can Be Murder
Partnerships Can Be Murder
Small Towns Can Be Murder
Memories Can Be Murder
Honeymoons Can Be Murder
Reunions Can Be Murder
Competition Can Be Murder
Balloons Can Be Murder
Obsessions Can Be Murder
Gossip Can Be Murder
Stardom Can Be Murder
Phantoms Can Be Murder
Buried Secrets Can Be Murder
Legends Can Be Murder
Weddings Can Be Murder
Alibis Can Be Murder
Escapes Can Be Murder
Old Bones Can Be Murder
Sweethearts Can Be Murder
Money Can Be Murder
Road Trips Can Be Murder
Cruises Can Be Murder
Holidays Can Be Murder - a Christmas novella

The Ghost in the Library Series
Haunted Gold
Haunted Palette (coming soon)

The Samantha Sweet Series
Sweet Masterpiece
Sweet's Sweets
Sweet Holidays
Sweet Hearts
Bitter Sweet
Sweets Galore
Sweets Begorra
Sweet Payback
Sweet Somethings
Sweets Forgotten
Spooky Sweet
Sticky Sweet
Sweet Magic
Deadly Sweet Dreams
The Ghost of Christmas Sweet
Tricky Sweet
Haunted Sweets
Secret Sweets
Spellbound Sweets – a Halloween novella
Thankful Sweets – A Thanksgiving novella
The Woodcarver's Secret – prequel to the series

The Heist Ladies Series
Diamonds Aren't Forever
The Trophy Wife Exchange
Movie Mogul Mama
Homeless in Heaven
Show Me the Money

Children's Books
Daisy and Maisie and the Great Lizard Hunt
Daisy and Maisie and the Lost Kitten

www.ingramcontent.com/pod-product-compliance
Lightning Source LLC
Chambersburg PA
CBHW020604110726
47899CB00002B/371